For my parents,
Who showed me that blood does not make a family,
And who loved me unconditionally, even though I wasn't their own.

BECAUSE I LOVE YOU

TORI RIGBY

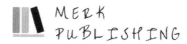

MERK
PUBLISHING

2nd Edition

© 2018 **Tori Rigby**

http://www.trigbybooks.com

ISBN: 9781720167891

CHAPTER 1

The lights in Brad's Mini Mart flickered as I swiped the pregnancy test from the shelf, tucked it under my arm, and sped out of the aisle.

A woman smiled at me as I passed. I shrank back and shoved the box higher in my armpit. Could she see what I was holding? I stood like a statue as she turned into a new aisle, and when she didn't look back at me, I let out a breath. I needed to get out of this store.

My pulse hammered in my ears as I neared the counter. Every glance in my direction catapulted my stomach to my knees. I bounced on the balls of my feet, waiting for my turn to pay and dash. *Come on.* Any minute now, I was going to vomit all over the old lady in front of me who was taking her time counting each individual penny.

I tapped my foot, glancing again and again at the storefront. The last thing I needed was for Heather or Carter to come in, wondering if I'd died, and spot the bright pink box. Especially since Carter was the whole reason I was taking the test in the first place.

I nearly pushed the old woman out of the way when the cashier handed her a receipt.

"Can you put that in a paper bag?" I asked, dropping the pregnancy test on the counter.

The girl stared at me like I was counting my pennies too. Then she turned and yelled across the store, "Neil! I need paper bags!"

My skin crawled, and I fought the urge to plug my ears.

"God, Lacie. I'm just down the damn aisle," a familiar voice said.

Oh, no. My heart leapt into my throat. Neil Donaghue—town bad boy, the older brother of my worst enemy, and my ex-boyfriend—approached the register. Had I known he worked here, I never would've asked to stop.

"You know what? Never mind." I threw a twenty on the counter, grabbed the test, and ripped the package open as I raced from the store. *Should've just done that in the first place.* I tucked the two plastic tests into my purse—along with the directions—and tossed the rest in the trash.

Carter's red BMW idled near the front door. I plopped in the back-seat, praying I didn't vomit all over his leather interior.

"God. You took so long that I thought we were gonna turn into pumpkins," Heather said. "Did you even buy anything?"

Carter peeled out of the parking lot. "Give her a break. She looks like she's going to puke."

"No, seriously," Heather continued. "I could use one of those antacids. I drank too much pop at the theater. Think I'm gonna be sprouting some nasty farts here soon."

Carter's nose scrunched. "You never cease to amaze me."

"They didn't have what I was looking for," I said, answering Heather's initial question. "Sorry."

"You going to be able to go to the party?" Carter asked.

I knew enough about pregnancy to know you didn't drink if you were. Although I wasn't sure yet, I didn't want to chance it. Which meant I would stand out like a cardinal in a flock of crows when I didn't repeatedly fill my cup. And if anyone questioned why, I'd break.

"No. Just take me home," I said.

"Aw, man." Heather turned in her seat, pouting. "Now who's gonna talk me down from sneaking upstairs with Brady Montgomery? Have you seen that guy? He's h-to-the-double-t *hot.*"

"There's so much wrong with that statement that I don't know where to start," Carter replied.

Usually, I'd crack a smile. This type of conversation was pretty typical, especially when Heather was tipsy. It wasn't really pop she'd been drinking at the movie theater. Pre-gaming was her solemn ritual. But a smile was impossible. I tapped my shaking hands on my knees to keep Carter and Heather from noticing.

When Carter pulled into my driveway, I refrained from jumping out of the vehicle so I didn't look like someone poked me with a cattle prod. Gripping my purse, I told them to have fun and not to do anything I wouldn't—which got a few snickers from Heather, who said I should know better—then hopped out of the car.

She leaned out the window and screamed, "Bye, feel better!"

And with a squeal of his tires, Carter peeled down the driveway and out of sight.

I stared at my home, willing myself to go inside. My feet felt like they were sinking, as if my driveway had turned into quicksand. If I looked at my house the right way, a face stared back at me, the front door a gaping O. The same expression I expected my mom to make when—if—I told her I was pregnant. A face that said, "Oh my God how could you do such a thing? I thought you were better than that!"

My stomach couldn't take it any longer. I ran to the bushes along the right side of my house and puked until my guts turned inside out. Then I pulled a Kleenex from my purse and wiped my mouth before punching the security code into the garage door's keypad.

"Annie home!" Micah, my three-year-old cousin, yelled as soon as I stepped into the kitchen. Tiny arms wrapped around my legs, and I nearly toppled as my cousin bounced without unleashing me. My aunt and uncle were on leave from their missionary work in England and had been staying with us the past week. I'd hoped to sneak upstairs after a quick hello, but my mother was still seated at the kitchen table, grading papers. Which meant my aunt and uncle were still at the church after the Saturday night service. Uncle Doug was the weekend's guest speaker—another reason they were home.

And since they were apparently still chatting with attendees—or schmoozing people to empty their wallets to fund their missionary work—in ten seconds, baby duty would be handed over to me.

Great.

"Yes, Andie's home," Mom said weakly from beneath her curtain of dark hair. Man, she sounded tired. "Give her a second to breathe, buddy. She'll play with you in a minute."

Micah somersaulted into the living room before jumping on the sofa like a baby kangaroo.

"What happened to the football party?" she asked without looking up from her work.

I dropped my purse on the counter and slipped off my lavender ballet flats, scrambling for a reason that would keep her from shoving a thermometer down my throat. "Just didn't feel like going."

She glanced at me, and I kept my face as impassive as possible, though my heartbeat thudded in my ears. My act of indifference seemed to work. Mom started scribbling again.

"Okay, well, can you help me with Micah, then?" she asked. "I need to get these graded by tomorrow. Doug and Kathy should be back in an hour."

I sighed. After Dad died two years ago, Mom had taken a teaching job at the University of Denver. Most nights, she had a lot of work, but tonight, her stack of papers might as well have been the Leaning Tower of Pisa. It was going to be a while before I could take the pregnancy test.

I marched across the living room's tan, plush carpet. Micah's gaze stayed glued to the television as he held out his arms—still bouncing —and I rested him on my hip. He's what my mom called "an unexpected gift from God." My aunt had never planned to have kids, then, three years ago, she got married and—whoops. Would Mom think the same thing if I popped out a grandchild at sixteen?

I re-entered the kitchen and pulled Chinese leftovers from the fridge. As the microwave beeped and Micah bounced in my arms, singing along with the Dora theme song, I silently prayed that Mom would stay away from my purse, that I'd make it through the next hour without puking.

And that my missed period was just a fluke.

But it was ten o'clock before I got a moment alone. After Aunt Kathy and Uncle Doug returned and put Micah to bed, Mom insisted I sit and tell her about my day. And, with Mom, a simple "it was good" never sufficed. She always wanted details. Details, details, details. That was definitely one trait I didn't inherit from her. I would've hated to be a student in one of her English classes. She regularly marked off points for "not enough fluff."

After locking my door—which was against the rules; God forbid I wanted privacy—I pulled the two tests out of my purse with shaking hands. I entered my attached bathroom, read the directions, and then tried not to break into a fit of hysteria as I peed on "the stick." That's what Heather would've called it. Then I placed the test on the counter and plucked my cell phone from my pocket.

Three minutes. How was I going to be able to wait three minutes? Sitting on the toilet lid, I watched the seconds count down on my timer.

Two minutes. My legs jiggled, and my pulse raced.

One minute. I bit my lip, hard. Sweat ran down my face.

A second before my alarm went off, I hit the end button, stood on wobbly legs, and with a deep breath, I grabbed the directions off the counter. *Two lines, pregnant. One line, not pregnant.*

"Okay, I can do this."

I shook my hands out at my sides, like I did before every cheerleading competition and half-time show, and closed my eyes. As I let all the air out of my lungs, I snatched the test off the counter and opened my eyes.

Two lines.

The room spun.

My back hit the wall with a thud, and I slid to the floor.

The edges of my vision darkened.

Climbing onto my knees, I threw open the toilet seat and left my dinner in the bowl.

I glanced at the stick again. Maybe I'd read it wrong.

Still two lines. I bit my finger to keep from screaming.

I was pregnant. *Pregnant*. With Carter's baby.

I rocked back and forth, my face in my hands, and hyperventilated into my palms. Any dreams I had of becoming a doctor were gone. My year as co-captain of the cheerleading squad was over. My clothes would stop fitting. My boobs would swell to the size of over-filled water balloons. And I would be the laughingstock of River Springs, Colorado.

Heather's going to kill me. She'd admitted to me the night after Carter and I slept together that she had a crush on him, but I didn't have the courage to tell her what happened. Not only had the three of us been best friends since kindergarten, but we'd made a pact at the beginning of freshman year that we'd never date each other and ruin our three musketeer status. She'd told me she was only letting me know because she had to tell someone. That she'd never act on her feelings.

Oh, God, what did I do?

Another wave of nausea heaved through my body. Amazing that I had anything left in me. After another round of vomiting, I tucked the pregnancy tests deep in my book bag and made a mental note to throw them in someone else's trash on the way to school on Monday. I unlocked my bedroom door, climbed onto my bed, and then burrowed under the blankets.

Would Mom lose her job at the university if she had to pick up another to make ends meet? We lived in a tiny, conservative, church town. Would anyone hire me for an after school job, knowing I was pregnant? And my school was a private prep school. Would they kick me out?

Burying my face in my pillow, I tucked my comforter under my chin as tears burned my eyes.

My life is over.

I didn't stop crying until I fell asleep.

CHAPTER 2

"Up, Annie! Up!" Micah jumped on my bed, and my exhausted stomach roiled with seasickness. Or was it morning sickness?

"Micah, stop. I'm not feeling good today."

"I tell An' Soosie. You no get donuts."

Ugh. Just the thought of eating donuts after church was enough to make me almost spout puke like the girl from *The Exorcist*.

Micah ran from the room, his little legs no match for his speed. He fell in the hall with a laugh. I rolled out of bed and shut the door before racing to the bathroom to gag into the toilet. After last night, I wasn't surprised nothing came out.

A patter of footsteps approached, and a cold hand touched my forehead. "You don't have a fever," Mom said. "I really don't want you to miss church when your uncle's speaking. We'll pick up some ginger ale for you on the way."

Again, my stomach tried to jump out of my body. I'd have to be in a freaking coma to get out of church.

"Get dressed, and come downstairs when you're ready." *But don't take too long,* I attached to the end of her sentence. Mom hated dilly-dallying.

When my bedroom door closed, I flushed the toilet and brushed my teeth. My skin was paler than yesterday, if that was even possible. My blonde hair stuck out of my ponytail every which direction, and my blue eyes were framed with glowing, red circles. All I needed were dry lips and skin falling off my cheek. I'd make the perfect zombie. What I wouldn't give for Mom's olive skin right now.

After attempting to put on makeup, I dressed in a knee-length jean skirt and a long-sleeved, pink sweater. I slipped on white ballet flats and drifted downstairs where Mom attached a tie to Micah's shirt. He looked up at me with a big grin, his cinnamon hair standing like someone had attached a feather to the back of his head. He'd gotten his dad's looks, for sure. Aunt Kathy had spent every day this week trying to convince Uncle Doug to use hair gel to keep from looking like he just woke up.

"And we're all here! Time for church!" she said, as if going to church was more fun than Disney World.

I wouldn't know. Disney World was on my bucket list, along with ice skating at Crystal Lake and jogging through Central Park.

The three of us piled into Mom's yellow Jeep, Micah snapped tight in his car seat in the back and me riding shotgun. My stomach twisted into infant-sized knots. Did I have any business going to church? Already, I could picture the congregation's glares focusing on me, calling me "Sinner!" in their minds, and throwing mental stones at me, like I was some whore in Biblical times.

I swallowed and tried to still my bouncing knees. I was never going to survive.

Mom pulled into the parking lot of Brad's Mini Mart, and a wave of panic shot down my spine—hot, like a bead of wax dripping from a lit candle. Would someone remember me from last night?

She handed me a five-dollar bill. "Run in and grab a can of ginger ale. Try to hurry, please."

Hurrying would not be a problem.

I stepped out of the car and marched inside, avoiding eye contact with as many people as I could. The cooler was at the back of the store. With drink in hand, I fought the urge to sprint to the register and drop the money on the counter like I had last night. Mom would notice when I didn't bring back change, though.

The can made a loud *thunk* on the counter.

"Back so soon?" Neil asked.

I looked up. *Ah, crap.* My cheeks burned. His dark hair was in that perfect I-made-it-look-like-I-just-woke-up way that still made my insides flutter. Then an image of his lips on another girl's flashed across my mind. *Don't be stupid, Andie.* I amped up the attitude. "Am I not allowed to come in two days in a row?"

He smirked then leaned back on his heels and crossed his arms over his chest. "There's no rule that says you can't. Though, if you're back for your change from yesterday, sorry. Can't help you."

I glared at him. "Would you just ring me up?"

A playful—annoying—grin still on his face, he scanned the barcode and hit a button on his register. "That's a dollar-twenty-five."

I handed him the five and sighed when he moved at a pace slower than a snail on Ritalin. *Figures.* Finally, he placed the money in my hand. I didn't wait for his sayonara spiel and raced out of the store.

When we reached the church a little while later, Mom took Micah to the playroom while I found my seat in the sanctuary. Third row on the left. Very center. Dad had picked this spot when I was in elementary school. Even after he died, we hadn't changed seats. Today, I was extra thankful for being so close to the front of the room—there were fewer looks to catch as others sat. One or two people managed to single me out with their wandering gazes—like Aunt Kathy, who sat in the front row—and, each time, they offered a warm smile. I was in the clear. For now.

Mom sat next to me minutes later. She leaned back with a sigh.

"Oh, it feels good to relax," she said, wiping her dark hair off her brow. "So glad I don't have to worry about you too much. Your cousin can be a handful. I don't know how Kathy does it."

I fought the urge to gulp as the room around me closed in. I'd never been claustrophobic, but living on the moon sounded fantastic. Anything to get as far away from my mother as possible.

"Oh, I got a program for you." Mom handed me a folded piece of blue paper with *River Springs Christian Church* scrawled across the top. Underneath the text was a picture of the building. I opened the program and glossed over the events going on at the church over the next several weeks: Women's Bible study, Men's basketball league, Fall retreat for the junior high kids.

Then I looked at the sermon notes—and the program fell from my hands. Today's talk was about sexual impurity.

Mom picked it up. "I guess I shouldn't have pushed you to come. Doug would've understood. Do you want me to take you home?"

Man, I must look bad for her to offer. If I said yes, though, she'd call a doctor first thing tomorrow morning. "I'm fine. Just a stomach bug, like you said."

She asked anyway. "Do I need to make an appointment with the doctor?"

Probably. But not that kind. "No, I'm sure I'll feel better tomorrow."

Mom looked at me sideways, but I must've given her enough proof that I wasn't dying. She turned to face the pulpit as Uncle Doug silenced the congregation.

After his welcome and opening prayer, the music began. I closed my eyes, leaning forward as the melodies started. But, for the first time in my life, the music wasn't soothing. *God loves me anyway? Yeah, right.* My father had dedicated his life to traveling the world as a Christian speaker, and what did he get in return? An early death sentence. My pregnancy was definitely punishment for breaking some stupid, no-sex-before-marriage rule. My fingertips dug into the pew in front of me.

The sanctuary rang with praises for what felt like hours, and I ground my teeth to keep from screaming. Finally, as my hands began to cramp, the final notes played. My shoulders relaxed, and the moment my uncle said, "Be seated," I fell onto my bench.

"Ah, it's good to be home and even better to be standing up here," he continued. "Though, I have to say, I'm not sure I love how Pastor Chris scheduled this topic when he knew I'd be speaking." The congregation laughed, but I held my breath. "We live in a time, friends, where pornography is easily accessible, guidance counselors have boxes upon boxes of condoms in their office, and about one-third of sixteen-year-olds have sex. Sexual impurity is the greatest epidemic today."

I fingered the locket hanging from my neck. My parents had given it to me when I was days old. After Dad's car accident, I'd bought a longer chain so I could start wearing it again. I hadn't taken it off since. Listening to Uncle Doug's sermon, knowing how angry my family would be when they found out, the metal burned a hole in my chest. Or maybe that was just my heart, exploding. I couldn't take much more of this.

"The Bible says, 'But let marriage be held in honor above all, and let the marriage bed be undefiled, for God will judge the sexually immoral and adulterous.'"

I jumped from my seat, catching my uncle's gaze. He paused and watched as I stepped over feet, scrambling to get out of the pew. His voice followed me down the aisle.

"Therefore, it is with importance, friends, that I urge you to keep the wedding bed pure."

Oh, God.

"And, parents, encourage your children not to have sex."

Yeah, because that works like a charm.

I caught Carter's confused stare as I pushed open the double doors leading to the hall. My stomach fell to my knees, and, covering my mouth to keep the vomit at bay, I ran for the bathroom as soon as I was out of his line of sight.

"I can't believe your mom let me pick you up from *church*," Heather said as she drove me home. I was pretty shocked, too, when Mom came into the bathroom, telling me she'd called Heather. "So, do you have, like, the flu or something? I only ask in case I need to scrub down my car when I get home."

Heather was the biggest germaphobe I knew. The last time I'd told her I had a cold, she wore a mask while we did homework on my bedroom floor. She must not have had time to pick up one before getting me this morning. Not that it mattered. I wasn't sick.

"No, it's not the flu," I said.

"Is it mono? Please tell me you don't have mono."

"I don't have mono."

"Pneumonia?"

"Heather, I'm not sick."

She glanced at me from the driver's seat, eyes wide. I gripped the side of the car as she jerked out of and back into her lane.

"You mean you *lied* to get out of church? That's a first," she said.

"I didn't lie. I'm not feeling well, but I'm not sick."

"That doesn't make sense."

I sighed. Should I tell Heather now? I'd planned on telling Mom first—if ever—but the thought of telling Mom I even had sex was terrifying. Maybe having someone already in my corner would be good, someone I could talk to if Mom kicked me out of the house. Heather would be the most logical person. I mean, I had other friends and all, but not like her.

"Pull over," I said. Last thing I needed was to die in the process of revealing my secret.

Heather scrunched her face. "You're not going to puke, are you?"

I glared at her.

"All right. Don't get your panties in a bunch." She pulled into the parking lot of McDonald's.

I turned in my seat; the gnawing pain in my gut was back with a vengeance. Maybe I was going to puke, after all. This being-sick-all-the-time thing was really getting old, really fast.

I took a deep breath. "I have to tell you something, but you have to promise me you won't tell a single soul. Especially not Carter."

Her eyebrows rose. "Okay . . . ?"

Here it goes. It's now or never. Spit it out. Just say the words.

"I'm pregnant."

Heather's mouth gaped so big that our whole town of River Springs could've moved inside and made our own country.

"How?" she asked.

"Well, you see, when a boy and a girl—"

Heather rolled her eyes. "I know the mechanics. I just always pictured this conversation a little different. Like me saying it to you."

I tried to laugh, but, instead, my bottom lip quivered. *Not again.* "Oh, God, Heather. W-What do I d-do?"

"Well, have you told your mom?"

I shook my head.

"Okay, good. Don't tell her yet."

"What? Why would I not tell her? Don't you think this is kind of a hard secret to keep?"

"I said 'yet.' Jeez, Drama Queen. First, you've taken a test, right?"

I nodded.

"Okay, well, sometimes those things are faulty. See, there are things they don't tell you in sex ed. We need to have a doctor check in case there's something wrong with you."

I flinched. "What do you mean 'wrong with me?'"

"Like, ovarian cysts or whatever. I don't know. It's happened before. Some chick thinks she's pregnant, tells the world, and, turns out, she isn't. So, we go see the doctor, and *if* you're pregnant, we'll figure out how to tell your mom." She left McDonald's without even asking if I was okay with the plan.

A couple minutes down the road, Heather chuckled. "I still can't believe *you* had sex."

I rolled my eyes. There was no point in responding. I still couldn't believe it either. It just happened. Carter admitted to having more feelings for me than he let on; we both were buzzed and practically naked in a hot tub; he kissed me; there was an empty room upstairs at the party...

I closed my eyes as the memory flooded my mind. I'd slept with my best friend, and this was what I got in return.

Heather pulled her car into my driveway. "Tomorrow after school? Planned Parenthood does tests, and they're confidential, so your Mom won't know you were there."

With a nod, I tugged on the car door's handle. But Heather had hit the lock button.

"Hey," she said, "you don't get to leave until you tell me who the baby daddy is. I'd tell you."

My heart lurched. *Will Heather forgive me if I tell her the truth?*

I did something to Heather I hadn't done in years. "You don't know him. I met him over the summer when I visited my aunt and uncle in England." The words felt like acid on my lips. I wanted to take them back, but if I did, she might hate me forever. Heather wasn't the kind to ever let go of a grudge. And, I couldn't risk that.

Heather laughed. "Wow. You'd told me your week in London was life changing. I'm totally coming with you next summer." She hit the unlock button, and I flung the door open.

Before I got out of the car, I turned to her. "Please, don't say anything to anyone."

Heather crossed an X on her chest. She said the promise we'd made to each other in second grade after Beth Donaghue pulled down my pants in front of the whole class. It was corny, but we'd lived by it 'til this day: "Cross my heart and hope to die, best friends forever, you and I."

I sprinted up my driveway, needing to get away from her as fast as possible. I really was a terrible friend, and guilt kept me tossing and turning all night.

Exhausted and hollow, I climbed out of bed before my alarm and dragged myself into the shower.

Pausing in front of the mirror, I stared at my stomach. Still flat. I bit my lip as I pictured what my belly would look like when it grew to the size of a watermelon. I would look like I was standing in front of a funhouse mirror. After making sure the dark circles around my eyes were covered and my hair was styled normally—down and curled—I went to the kitchen and dug out a box of cereal.

"How are you feeling?" Mom asked when she entered the room.

"Good." I drenched my breakfast with more milk than it needed and sat at the table.

She felt my forehead. "Looks like you needed all that rest. I don't remember you ever sleeping that long." She stepped away to let me eat and gathered her papers into her oversized briefcase.

"Yeah, I guess." Truth was: I hadn't been sleeping. Not all day, at least. And not most of the night, either. Still, I wasn't going to tell her what I'd really been doing: reading pregnancy websites on my cell phone.

"Well, promise me you'll take it easy this week. No late nights with Carter and Heather."

"Fine. Oh, but I did tell Heather I'd help her with her French after school today." Almost forgot the cover story.

"Two weeks into the year, and she's already falling behind?" The judgment in her voice was so easy to hear. She'd never liked Heather.

"It's a tough class."

Mom sighed. "All right. But be home for dinner. You missed last night's, and Doug and Kathy are flying back to England tomorrow."

I nodded, finishing my cereal, and then dumped the leftover milk down the sink. Then I slipped on my white cheerleading sneakers and watched morning cartoons with a very drowsy Micah until Heather's car horn beeped in the driveway.

As soon as I sat in the front seat, Heather handed me a wad of cash.

"What's this?" I asked, closing the car door.

Backing down the driveway, she replied, "Money."

I rolled my eyes. "Yes, I can see that it's money. But what is it for?"

"The doctor. We're still going, right?"

"Yeah."

"Well, did you think it'd be free? I know your mom checks your debit card statements."

Mom *could* be a little overbearing.

"Heather, I don't need your money."

Heather waved. "Pay me back later. There were some really cute shoes at Willard's I want to wear to Homecoming."

I frowned. Would I even get to go to Homecoming? It was still four weeks away. How fat would I be in a month? "Fine. I'll buy your shoes."

Heather smiled. "Hey, do you care if I ask Carter to go with me? As friends, of course. Oh, and only if you get a date. Which you will. You always do."

My heart sank to my knees. Did I care? Heck yes! But if I told her that, she'd want me to give her a reason why. And I really didn't feel like spitting out, "I'm carrying his baby." I'd have to let them go and make up some excuse for not being able to attend. Maybe I'd wake up with morning sickness again, and it wouldn't be hard to pretend I was ill.

"Yeah, that's fine," I replied.

Heather patted my knee. "Maybe you can ask Mr. England to pay you a visit."

Ugh. She'd named my imaginary baby daddy. "Maybe."

She pulled into the parking lot of River Springs Prep. Heather linked arms with me as we walked into the school, wearing matching uniforms.

"We'll figure this out," she said. "I'm not leaving your side."

A lump formed in my throat. Would she say the same thing when I told her the truth about Carter?

CHAPTER 3

The halls of River Springs Preparatory School were covered in maroon and gold. Streamers hung from the ceiling, lockers were enclosed in wrapping paper, and everywhere students were dressed in some variation of school colors. Even Heather and I added to the ambiance in our cheerleading uniforms. We played our rival in football on Friday, which meant it was time for Spirit Week. Last year, it'd been one of the best weeks of my life. This time, it would be the opposite.

Heather paused in front of my locker so I could exchange my backpack for the first half of the day's books. I loaded my arms with textbooks then followed her down the hall. As we neared her locker, Carter approached us from the other direction, dressed in jeans and his football jersey. I fought every urge to run and duck for cover and instead forced a grin.

"Feeling better?" he asked, stopping with us at Heather's locker.

"Yeah," I replied. "Just some twenty-four-hour stomach bug thing."

He narrowed his eyes. "Wasn't it more like forty-eight hours? You had me take you home on Saturday, remember?"

Oops. "Oh. Yeah. Guess it was."

"Regardless"—Heather closed her locker—"Andie's feeling back to her perky self. Which means she can shake her little pom poms and shout like a crazed lunatic all day. Because apparently that's what cheerleaders do."

Carter walked with us as we made our way to first period. *"You're* a cheerleader."

"Only because Andie made me."

"I didn't *make* you," I chimed in. "You could've joined marching band."

Heather made a *pssh* sound. "And pass up the chance to look *this* hot in a skirt? Puh-lease."

Carter shook his head with a chuckle and dropped us off at our first class of the day—AP English. We were the only two juniors in the entire class. Well, us and Gwen, another one of our fellow cheerleaders. Where I excelled at science, Heather's best subject was English. And as my love of reading knew no bounds, it'd been easy to keep up. Would I have to switch classes when—*if*—she realized who I'd slept with? My stomach did a backflip.

Heather and I grabbed our seats in the middle of the room. I shook my head when she sent me raunchy texts about Tower-of-London-sized penises and English fetishes. She was trying to lighten the mood, but when I read, *Did Mr. England have a whale boner*? I tossed my phone in my purse. We'd hear enough about sex when we visited the clinic after school.

Ten seconds after the second bell, Mr. Bingham began his lecture. "Over the weekend, you should've finished reading *Of Mice and Men*. Now, who can tell me one of the main themes of the story?"

I raised my hand. The book had been an easy read for me. "Loneliness?"

"Yes, that's part of it. But let's look a little deeper."

The room went back to silence. I racked my brain, searching for a better response, unwilling to admit that I hadn't uncovered the larger theme. I loved books, and after the science classes, English was my favorite subject.

"All the characters, at one point in time, not only suffered from loneliness but isolation."

I turned in my seat at the sound of Neil's voice. He leaned back in his chair with his eyes closed and his hands behind his head. *Typical.*

He continued, "And because of that isolation, they sought out those who also suffered and demoralized them as a way to attempt to make themselves feel better. Therefore, one can assume that oppression is not only caused by the strong and powerful but also by those who are oppressed. And so, the vicious cycle of loneliness and isolation continues to turn."

Mr. Bingham raised an eyebrow. "Well, look at that. Mr. Donaghue did his homework."

"Nah, I just read Spark Notes." He opened his eyes long enough to give me a wink then resumed his I-don't-give-a-crap position.

I fought the urge to chuck my pen at his head. I'd broken up with him two years ago after only a month of dating, and he still only responded in class when I got the answers wrong. *Jerk.*

"Of course you did," Mr. Bingham said. "Well, *Spark Notes* is correct. Oppression is one of the major themes in *Of Mice and Men*. So, here's tonight's homework: What are some of the ways we, today, persecute those around us? And how might we reverse it? Take the last twenty minutes of class to start working. I expect ten pages, typed, double-spaced."

After writing all those pages, the rest of the morning was uneventful. Only lunch and afternoon classes remained between Planned Parenthood and me, and one of them was Advanced Chemistry, my favorite subject and a double period that would keep my thoughts preoccupied for over an hour. I'd take possibly-explosive experiments over thinking about pregnancy any day. For the hundredth time, I shouted a silent prayer that I just had an ovarian problem.

Heather joined me minutes later at our usual lunch table in the quad outside—in true, late fashion—and the majority of our cheerleading squad followed. Only Beth Donaghue, Neil's sister and my archenemy, and her mini-me, Gwen, were missing.

"So, pep rally on Friday," Monica White, my co-captain, began. She was one of those girls who was so nice that you could curse her out and she'd apologize to you. Never would I have pegged her to lead a cheerleading squad, but she was not only a great dancer and gymnast, she looked the part. All the guys at River Springs Prep had her at the top of their wish lists.

She continued, "I was thinking it'd be really cool to do this, like, double pyramid, basket toss thing. And then Andie could flip forward while Beth goes backward. It'd be *so* fun. What do you think?"

"We haven't practiced that yet," April, one of the other cheerleaders, said. Where Beth and I were the two main flyers, April was a base. At five foot eleven, she was a girl with a pretty face who could take down a linebacker. She was a fierce and powerful gymnast, but if any of us tried to hold her in the air, she'd come crashing down.

"So? Beth's already on board. Really, it's up to you, Andie. I promise we won't drop you. And we'll practice it on Wednesday, so it won't be, like, totally foreign."

I shrugged, unwrapping my turkey sandwich. Could I still cheer while I was pregnant? The doctor would probably say no. But I'd never had a problem with last minute changes before, so a negative response was out of the question. They'd know something was up, and I didn't feel like creating a cover story. "I'm in."

Monica clapped her hands together. "Oh, I'm so excited! I think it's going to be amazing."

I bit into my sandwich, my stomach growling. But instead of my taste buds jumping up and down, my stomach decided it did not want turkey. As soon as the scent of lunch meat hit my nose, my gut punched the reject button. Jumping out of my chair, I dropped the sandwich on the table and ran for the nearest trashcan, my hand clasped over my mouth. I reached the rubbish just in time to avoid vomit shooting between my fingers.

As my body emptied its contents, I squeezed my eyelids closed. The gazes of my schoolmates burned into me. Someone touched my arm.

"Hey, you okay?" Carter asked.

Wiping my mouth with the back of my hand, I turned and pushed him away. First, the answer to that question was an obvious "no." But, second, I didn't want *him* asking if I was fine. I didn't want him anywhere near me. This was his fault. He was the one who told me he loved me. He was the one who kissed me. And he was the one who sobered up the next morning and told me we should just be friends, for Heather's sake.

Heather grabbed my arm. "I got this."

She led me to the bathroom before any tears fell and I made a bigger scene than I already had. Heather tucked me in a stall and instructed me to "get it all out" while she ran to her car for a toothbrush. I knelt with my arms wrapped around my waist and heaved until my throat was on fire. Grabbing a huge wad of toilet paper, I wiped my lips and flushed.

Heather leaned against the sink when I exited the stall, twirling a toothbrush in her fingers. She stared at me, her head slightly tipped and an eyebrow raised.

"Sorry." I took the toothbrush and toothpaste from her hands and avoided meeting her stare in the mirror as I brushed my teeth.

"Don't apologize to me. I'm not the one you pushed in front of the whole school. You know he's going to ask me what the hell that was about."

"You promised you wouldn't say anything to him."

Heather raised her hands in exasperation. "What do you think he's going to do, Andie? Slap a big W on your chest and paint whore across your locker? This is *Carter*, your best friend. I know you're freaking out, but don't take it out on him."

I rinsed my mouth and spit into the sink, my insides still in a knot. "I didn't mean it, I swear. I just . . ." I shook my head, unable to tell her the truth. I wanted to. God, I wanted to. But the words stuck in my throat.

Heather sighed. "Fine. I won't spill the beans. But you know he's going to be pissed if he finds out from someone else."

"I know."

She handed me a long strip of paper towel, and I asked, "Do you always keep a toothbrush in your car?"

Heather looked at me like I should've known better. "Well, yeah.

Having an older brother in college comes with its perks, if you know what I mean." She wiggled her eyebrows.

How was *I* the one who'd ended up pregnant?

I shook my head on our way back to lunch, and only little snickers flew at me from a few of Beth's friends—and one person asked if I'd boarded the bulimia train. Though comments like that usually bothered me, I preferred they thought I stuffed my fist down my throat to stay skinny.

When the final period ended, I traipsed to my locker, wandering the halls to delay today's after-school activity. I took my time cramming my homework into my backpack and fiddling around with the makeup kit I kept at school.

"Are you going to tell me what happened at lunch?" Carter's voice startled me.

I forced myself to gently close my locker door. "I'm sorry. It wasn't about you."

He shoved his hands in his pockets. "Then what's going on? Did something happen at home? Heather said you were fine, but she was obviously lying."

I shook my head. "It's nothing like that. Look, I have to go, but I'll call you later."

I peeked over my shoulder as I hurried to leave. Carter's hands rose in the air, and he spun around, marching down the hall to the football team's locker room. I bit my lip and pushed open the doors leading to the parking lot.

CHAPTER 4

"You have the money?" Heather asked for the millionth time as we pulled into Planned Parenthood.

"*Yes.*"

"God, don't get pissy. Just making sure." She parked near the front door.

Stepping out of the car, I glanced around. Buildings across the street had bars over the windows, and two doors down, some guy leaned against a wall, smoking pot. I could smell it from where I stood. Holding my breath—both out of fear we were going to get mugged and because the stink of weed was making me sick—I followed Heather inside.

Pregnant women sat around the blue-carpeted room. A few were older, but the majority looked to be in their twenties. Scanning the room to make sure I didn't know anyone, I followed Heather to the front desk where a graying woman with long, red fingernails typed away at a keyboard.

Heather snapped after a few minutes of being ignored. "Um, *hello?*"

The woman held up a clipboard without making eye contact. In a flat voice, she said, "Fill this out. Sign in. We'll call your name when we're ready. Bring the clipboard back when you're done." She went back to typing, as if she were getting points for the most gibberish words in five minutes.

"Bitch," Heather mumbled under her breath as we walked away. She handed me the paperwork and scrawled my name across the sign-in sheet. The two of us found a spot near a barred window at the far side of the yellow-walled room.

"God, we're going to be here for hours," Heather said. "There were, like, thirty names on that list."

I clenched my fists. The last thing I needed was to miss supper. Mom had made it very clear I was supposed to be home by then. She'd search for me if I didn't show up.

"Maybe it's a running total of all the people who visited today," I replied.

"Maybe. You want a magazine? I think they have something other than pregnancy crap." She chucked an *Abortion or Adoption: Which One is Right for You?* pamphlet over her shoulder.

I bit my lip. Part of me still hung on to the hope that my test had been a false positive—nothing but an ovary problem. Heather said it happened. But, what if it *was* positive? I tried to picture what Carter would do when I told him the truth: "It'll be okay. I'll take care of you," he'd say and pull a ring from his pocket.

Who was I kidding? His parents would do everything in their power to keep their perfect son away from me.

Carter was expected to graduate at the top of our class, get into an Ivy League school on a football scholarship, and become a famous lawyer like his mother. As soon as they found out the baby was his, they'd pay for me to have an abortion before shipping me off to Australia so I could never bother their son again. But abortion was out of the question; I couldn't go through with it. Just the thought made my skin crawl. Would I be able to put a baby up for adoption, though? I pictured doctors snatching my baby from my arms and shivered. If I *was* pregnant, I was definitely keeping it.

Though, I'd rather just wake up from this stupid nightmare.

After two hours of restless waiting, my name was called. My cheeks burned as I followed the nurse to the back of the facility.

People watched me, probably thinking I was some screwed up kid who slept around and had it coming.

"How tall are you?" the nurse asked.

"Five-two."

"Step on the scale, please."

I slipped off my shoes, handed Heather my purse, and then stepped on the large, metal platform. One hundred and ten pounds. At least I hadn't started gaining weight, yet. After I slid my feet back into my sneakers, Heather and I followed the nurse down a balloon-wallpapered hallway. Inside a small room, I climbed onto an exam table while Heather plopped into a wooden chair against the wall. The nurse took my vitals then left us alone.

"I just thought of something," Heather said. "What if they check your vagina?"

"What?" My jaw dropped. They wouldn't do that, would they? I mean, I guess if I *was* pregnant, I'd have to start seeing an obstetrician. But right here, right now? My legs clenched together.

"I swear I will run like Forrest Gump if I hear the words 'drop your pants.'"

I rolled my eyes. What was she going to do if I had a baby? Move to a different country?

A knock at the door made me jump. In walked a woman, maybe in her mid-forties, with a cute dark brown pixie haircut. She held a clipboard to her chest and extended a hand to me.

"Hi, Miss Hamilton. I'm Dr. Jankowski. The paperwork here says you came in for a pregnancy test?"

I nodded. The lump in my throat was softball-sized.

The doctor sat on a swivel stool. "All right. We'll do that in a minute. But let's first go over a few basic questions, okay?"

Again, I nodded and gripped the edge of the examination table.

"You're sixteen. Any history of medical issues?" she asked.

I shook my head.

"And up until recently, your periods have been regular?" When I nodded again, she continued, "Have you taken a home pregnancy test?"

I nodded.

"When was your last period?"

"Um"—I touched my forehead with shaking fingers—"maybe eight weeks ago? I can't remember."

Dr. Jankowski jotted a note. "How many partners have you had?"

"One." *Crap, my voice shook.*

"No STDs that you know of?"

I hoped not. But I'd been Carter's first too. Or so he'd said. I shook my head. He wouldn't lie to me.

Dr. Jankowski wrote a few more notes on her clipboard then looked at me. "Okay, well, why don't we take the test now? We'll start with a urine test, and if the results are iffy, we'll move on to a blood test." She stood and pulled a sealed plastic bag with a cup inside from a cupboard. "There's a bathroom across the hall. After you seal the cup, hand it to a nurse, and she'll take it to be processed. I'm going to go check on another patient, but I'll be back."

Nodding, I took the bag from her and waited until she left the room before climbing down to take my official test.

Heather was typing away on her phone when I returned. "Carter wanted to know where you were. Your mom told him you were at my place, and I guess he stopped by to talk to you."

"What did you tell him?"

"That we were at the doctor."

Every cell in my body froze. "What?"

"Don't worry. I didn't tell him what for. Just that we were going to be a while still."

Climbing onto the table again, I lay back and covered my face with my arms. The room spun. Now he would definitely know something was wrong, and the more questions he asked, the quicker I would break. *Thanks a lot, Heather.*

Dr. Jankowski waltzed into the room, her gaze skimming over a piece of paper in her hands. "Okay, let's see what came back."

When her lips pursed, I knew I had my answer. I turned my head so when she looked up, she wouldn't see the tears in my eyes. Somehow, I managed to keep them at bay until we were on our way home.

In the car, I stared at the trees lining the expressway with my forehead pressed against the window. After Dr. Jankowski had announced I was about eight weeks pregnant, she handed me a bunch of pamphlets about abortion, adoption, what to eat, what to avoid, what pills to take, blah, blah, blah. At some point in time, I'd stopped listening.

Heather turned down the music. "You haven't said a word in, like, an hour. Do you want to talk?"

"Not really."

I pretended to fall asleep. But my thoughts danced with too many questions. How do I tell Carter? How do I tell Mom? Cheerleading was out; the doctor had said so. Would anyone notice if I disappeared for months? My jaw stiffened as I fought the urge to smack my head against the glass. Maybe if I knocked myself unconscious, I'd wake up in seven and a half months and not be pregnant anymore.

I stared at Heather out of the corner of my eye. Tapping her fingertips on the steering wheel, she looked like she was about to crap herself. She was trying to leave me alone, but I knew it was killing her to stay silent. She had an opinion about everything.

Guilt boiled in my gut. I couldn't lie to her anymore. And if I told Carter and my mom that he was the father before her . . . well, that'd just make things a thousand times worse. She had to know the truth.

I straightened. "Okay, maybe there *is* something I need to tell you."

Heather relaxed. "Oh, thank God. Seriously, I thought I was going to have to start talking to myself over here. So, I was thinking that maybe telling Carter would be a good practice run for your mom."

"Heather—"

"And then, between Carter and me, we could give you alternate scenarios with different responses—"

"Heather, shut up."

She clamped her mouth closed and raised an eyebrow.

Yes, I know. You hate being cut off. "Look, I need to tell you something, and I know you're going to hate me, but please try not to."

"O . . . kay?"

Taking a deep breath, I dug my fingernails into my thighs. I spoke the words quickly, forcing them out of my mouth before I lost my courage. "I've been lying to you, and I know we don't do that, and I'm sorry. But I couldn't tell you the truth because it sucks so much more."

Heather narrowed her eyes.

"'Mr. England' isn't the baby's father. Carter is."

At first, I wasn't sure she'd heard me. But then Heather's gaze hardened, and her knuckles whitened. The car accelerated. "You two *slept together?*"

My fingernails dug deeper into my legs. "I know. I'm sorry. We were drunk. It just sort of happened."

"Was this before or after I told you I liked him?"

"Before. I swear I wouldn't have done it if I'd known."

Heather glared at the road, her nostrils flaring. She screamed. "God, Andie! Carter, really? You did it with my best friend?"

"Hey, he's my best friend, too."

"Not anymore, he isn't! Now he's your freaking baby daddy! What do you think's going to happen when he finds out, huh? It'll be you two against the world, and I'll be tossed to the fucking curb!"

"No. We wouldn't do that."

"You know what? Stop talking. I don't want to hear it." Her face was so red that it glowed. "I get now why you were so adamant he didn't find out, but I swear to God, if you don't tell him soon, I will."

Tucking my knees up to my chin, I stared out the window again. Heather blasted the music the rest of the ride home, and when we pulled into my driveway, I tried to say goodbye, but Heather didn't even acknowledge my existence. As soon as I shut my car door, she backed out of the driveway without a word.

Backpack slung over my shoulder, I gripped my purse to my chest, watching as she peeled around the bend. I sniffled and took a deep breath, knowing Mom was home and would grill me as soon as I walked in the door—my red eyes had stared back at me in the window's reflection the whole ride home.

But I wasn't ready to tell her the truth.

CHAPTER 5

After punching in the garage's security code, I entered the house and was again greeted by an excited Micah. He squeezed my legs, and I tousled his red hair before he went running to the living room where Aunt Kathy and Uncle Doug were playing what looked like a game of Scrabble. Mom loaded mashed potatoes into a bowl.

"Hey, honey," she said. "Go wash up. Dinner's almost ready." Then she turned and squinted at me. "Everything okay?"

"Heather and I had a fight. But I'm fine." I marched through the kitchen and up the stairs. The pregnancy pamphlets were tucked deep in my backpack, but the last thing I wanted was to leave the bag in a place accessible to Mom's wandering hands. I'd caught her going through my things on a few occasions.

Locking my door, I tossed my book bag on my bed and grabbed a roll of tape off my desk. Then I fished out the pamphlets and taped them to the back of a dresser. If Mom moved any furniture soon, I'd be shocked. And if she was nosy enough to check behind here . . . well, let's just say I'd be signing up for anger management.

I jogged downstairs. Aunt Kathy tucked Micah into his booster seat when I entered the dining room. I grabbed a chair across from my cousin, waiting for Mom to begin the evening prayer. As soon as Aunt

Kathy sat, Mom started, "Thank you, Father, for all the blessings we share. Our family, our home, this food. Give us wisdom in our daily decisions, and remind us of your love and mercy. In your Son's name, Amen."

"Amen!" Micah shouted and dug into his food like the little kid in *A Christmas Story*. If I was in a better mood, I might've shouted, "Show me how the piggies eat!" But all that ran through my head was some variation of *Tell her* or *Don't tell her*. Like a scene from a cartoon where your inner evil sat on one shoulder while your conscience planted itself on the other.

"Micah, use your fork please," Aunt Kathy scolded.

He grabbed his mini-utensil like a caveman and stabbed a bite of chicken.

"So, how was your day, Andie?" Uncle Doug asked.

Awful. "It was fine."

"Andrea, you know we want to hear more than 'it was fine,'" Mom said. "Did you decide yet if you're going to run for homecoming court?"

I shrugged. *Definitely not. No one wants a pregnant chick wearing a crown.* "I'm not sure yet. They never crown a junior."

"That doesn't mean you don't go for your dreams," Uncle Doug said. "I went for mine, and look what God gave me—a beautiful wife, a spirited son, and a great job serving the homeless in London."

Ugh. Why did my family always have to follow everything with something gag-worthy? Homecoming queen wasn't a dream, anyway. Graduating with honors and becoming a doctor—now, that was a different story. But, apparently, God had turned a blind eye to me.

"So, what happened with Heather?" Mom asked.

I swirled the mashed potatoes on my plate. "It was a misunderstanding. I'm sure everything'll go back to normal tomorrow." *Doubt it.*

"Yes, this isn't the first time you girls have had a fight. Remember when you were about eight years old, and you refused to talk to her because she bought the Barbie you liked after you told her you wanted it for your birthday?"

I nodded. She'd taken it to school and showed it off like she was the coolest kid to roam the earth, which is what I'd been planning to do a week later. But Carter wasn't a Barbie, and we weren't eight. This wasn't going to blow over in a week.

"Friends fight, and they move on," she continued. "I'm sure you girls will figure it out."

Sticking a bite of mashed potatoes in my mouth, I avoided eye contact. My mom was one of those people who could see into a person's soul if she caught your stare. She didn't need to know I was lying about Heather and me having a simple argument.

For ten minutes, Mom and Aunt Kathy reminisced about my childhood, telling stories of when I first learned to ski and the time I told them I was going to grow up and become a firefighter with Carter. The more stories they told, the harder it was to keep myself under control. And the last thing I wanted was to blurt out over dinner that I was pregnant.

"May I please be excused?" I asked.

Mom tilted her head. "You've barely eaten."

"I'm still feeling kind of queasy"—which wasn't a lie—"and I have a lot of homework to finish before I can go to bed." Also not a lie.

"Come on, Susan. Let the girl go. I'm sure you remember what it was like, being a teenager and listening to your parents prattle on about you." Uncle Doug flashed me a warm smile.

I forced myself to return it.

"Oh, all right," Mom said. "I'll put your food in the fridge in case you get hungry later."

Nodding, I stood and left my plate on the kitchen counter before walking—not running—up the stairs. Again, I took a risk locking my door, but if Mom paid a visit, a few seconds to hide the pamphlets would save me from an even worse punishment. Grabbing the booklets, I hopped onto my bed and, with shaking hands, flipped through the ones about prenatal care, what to avoid, and how my body would change over the next few months.

I held my breath as I looked at the pictures of baby bellies, dreading the day I glanced in the mirror and saw my own abdomen distended. The symptoms were listed by trimester, and I slammed the brochure closed. A shiver rolled down my spine. Was that really what was to come?

I can't do this. An abortion would just be easier, right?

Jumping off the bed, I returned the brochures to their hiding spot. Leaning against the dresser, I put a hand on my aching chest. I closed my eyes, breathing deeply and forcing the panic into the pit of my stomach. If I could calm myself before every dancing, gymnastics, and cheerleading competition, I could do it now.

When I opened my eyes, my insides still tossed, like I'd stepped onto a ship in the middle of turbulent waters without my sea legs, but the tears were gone.

I can do this. Heather's plan was good: tell Carter, then, together, we would figure out a way to tell my mom. I'd already decided if I was pregnant, I'd keep my baby; the fear of what was to come wouldn't get in the way.

Clenching my jaw, I grabbed my textbooks. Once I talked to Carter, everything would be okay. He was a reliable friend and ally, not some jerk like Neil Donaghue who made out with a girl behind the reference section of the library when he was dating another. Not that I still held a grudge against the only other guy I'd ever had a crush on.

I sighed, opening the pages. Everything would be fine. I was sure of it.

Mom checked on me a few hours later, but, by then, I'd buried myself in homework, so her visit didn't last long. Fingering the locket around my neck, I read ahead in my English textbook, anxious for when I'd hear the clicks of bedroom doors closing. Around 10:30, my family finally went to bed, and at 11:00, I dialed Carter.

He picked up on the third ring. "I was beginning to think you were going to blow me off."

"I know. Sorry. Overbearing mother." I used that defense all the time, but no one questioned it. The excuse wasn't far from the truth.

"So, are we going to talk about what happened at school?" he asked.

I bit my lip. Telling him the truth over the phone was a pretty crappy thing to do. Somehow, I needed to see him tonight. "Can you come over?"

"Right now?" Though he lived maybe five minutes away—walking distance—his parents were pretty strict about curfew.

"Yes."

There was silence on his end, and at first, I thought he'd hung up, but then his voice came through. "Okay, yeah, they're sleeping. Give me ten minutes." He hung up without saying goodbye.

Tucking my phone into the pocket of my sweatpants, I opened my bedroom door and snuck, barefoot, down the hall. I stopped at Mom's doorway then the guest room's, listening for the sounds of soft snores. When they met my ears, I tiptoed the rest of the way downstairs and eased the sliding door open. After shutting it behind me, I crossed the yard to the swing set. The air had that cool-yet-muggy feel of early fall, and the scent of a wood fireplace met my nose. Soft chirps of crickets filled my ears. Lightning bugs brightened the sky with tiny balls of fire. Damp grass tickled my feet.

I sat in a yellow swing and pushed myself gently back and forth, grasping the metal chains. Carter came around the left side of the house, his sandy hair falling into his face. My heartbeat raced. This was it—the moment everything changed. Would the baby have blonde hair like his, like mine? Would it get Mom's Egyptian features or Dad's Irish ones? Carter and Heather always joked I was adopted, but supposedly a baby could inherit genes from its grandmother or grandfather.

I swallowed hard, took a deep breath, and tried to calm my racing heart. First things first: tell Carter.

Carter sat in the swing next to me. "We haven't done this in a long time."

I forced a smile. "Not since our ninth grade homecoming dance."

He chuckled. "Your shoes got all muddy, and you ended up wearing those bright green, Kermit slippers."

"You remember that?"

Carter's dark brown gaze flickered over my face. "Of course. You had your hair curled over your right shoulder"—his fingertips grazed the side of my neck—"and you wore that blue Cinderella-dress-thing."

I jumped up and wrapped my arms around my waist. He was flirting again, just like he had in the hot tub. I needed to get the truth out before he sucked me in. "Did you mean it when you said you loved me?"

With a sigh, he stood and put a hand on each of my upper arms. "Is that what this is about? Andie, you know I meant it. But I thought we'd decided, for Heather's sake—"

"I'm pregnant."

Color drained from Carter's cheeks, and his hands dropped from my arms. He took a step backward. "What?"

"It's yours." My voice shook.

Carter ran his hands through his hair and down his face. He sat back in his swing. "How? I thought . . . I mean . . . we were safe, right?"

"I know. I didn't want to believe it either, but Heather took me to Planned Parenthood to have a test."

His gaze snapped to me. "Heather knows?"

"Of course she knows."

He jumped out of his seat and put his hands on his head. "I thought we agreed we weren't going to tell her what we did."

"What was I supposed to do? Not tell my best friend I was pregnant?"

"You could've at least kept my name out of it!"

I glared at him. "I wasn't going to lie to Heather. How do you think she'd feel if she found out the truth from someone else?"

"She didn't have to find out. You made an appointment to get rid of it, right?"

My heart stopped. Was that really what he wanted—for me to get an *abortion?* I searched his face for any sign he might be joking and took in a quick breath when I found none.

I pressed a hand to my stomach. "I'm not going that route, Carter."

"Then what'd you go to Planned Parenthood for?"

"To have a test! I already told you that."

Carter paced in front of me, his hands clenching and unclenching at his sides. He stopped and looked at me, and his shoulders fell. "Andie, you know I can't do this. My parents . . . ."

He didn't have to finish the sentence. His parents had a strict ten-year plan for him to follow. I was there the day his mother found a pack of cigarettes in his gym bag and threatened to pull him from River Springs Prep so he could "go hang out with all the deadbeats in the world of public school." A baby would get him kicked out of the house, for sure.

I placed a hand on his chest and looked at him through bleary eyes. "We'll figure it out. Just give me a couple days to tell my mom, and then we'll come up with a way to tell your parents. I'm sure if we have a plan—"

Carter removed my hand, letting my fingertips linger in his palm. For the first time in years, he was on the verge of tears. He dropped my hand, kissed my forehead, and stepped back. "I'm sorry, Andie. I wasn't lying when I said I loved you, but I can't be a father. Not yet. If you do this, you'll have to do it without me." He turned and jogged around the side of the house without another glance in my direction.

I stared after him, coldness rolling through me. My knees buckled, and I crashed to the ground. Shivering, I dug my fingers into the grass. *This can't be happening, this can't be happening, this can't be happening.* My shoulders rolled forward as a sob broke free.

Another followed. Another. I gripped the back of my neck and rocked as heat radiated from my knees, all the way up my spine. He'd abandoned me. My best friend had actually walked away. With shoulders curled over my chest, my sobs turned into gasps, and I clenched my teeth, desperate to ensure my family remained asleep. I whipped my cell phone out of my pocket.

I hate you, Carter Lambert! I hate you! I texted him, meaning it with all that was left of my heart.

CHAPTER 6

For two days, I managed to skip school. Both mornings, I woke up puking my guts out, so I was able to convince Mom to let me stay home. But the third day, she threatened to take me to the doctor. It was time to go to school, regardless of how miserable I felt. After applying coats of concealer to my almost-swollen-shut eyes, I dressed in my cheerleading uniform—it was still Spirit Week, after all—and moseyed downstairs.

"How are you feeling?" Mom asked when I entered the kitchen.

"Better."

"You look better."

Thanks?

She kissed me on my cheek and grabbed her briefcase before adjusting her belt around her ever-shrinking waistline. "I've got an early meeting, so I need to go. Make sure you call your aunt and uncle and say goodbye. They left before you were up, but their flight hasn't taken off yet. Oh, and come home right after school."

I nodded as she walked out the door. Where else was I going to go? Neither Heather nor Carter had texted me in two days.

I dug my phone out of my purse, dialed my aunt, and then, after pouring a bowl of cereal before deciding I wasn't hungry, sat at the kitchen counter and stared at the rooster magnets on the fridge. When it was obvious Heather wasn't going to pick me up, I swung my book bag over my shoulder, grabbed my purse, and made my way down the street. It'd been a long time since I'd ridden the private bus that shipped students to and from my high school. One of these days, I had to convince Mom to let me get my driver's license.

When the bus stopped at the corner, I climbed in and shuffled down the aisle. Almost everyone was a freshman, but there were a couple juniors I recognized from the halls. I sat next to one of them, a Native American girl I'd seen maybe once or twice, not planning to make conversation. That lasted only five minutes.

"You're Andie Hamilton, right?" she asked. Her bright pink glasses slid down her nose, and her sleek, black hair fell over her shoulder.

"Um, yeah. Why?"

She flicked her thumb across her phone then turned the device in her hand so I could see what was on her screen—a text that read, *Dude, did you hear Andie's preggers?*

The world slowed. If she'd gotten that text, how many other people had? Heat burned through my body, and I clenched my jaw to keep from throwing up all over my schoolmate.

"Who sent that?" I asked, my voice shaking.

"Someone from homeroom. But, apparently, they heard it from Beth Donaghue."

Of course. Neil saw me buy the test. And if he told his sister, that meant the whole school knew. I gripped my book bag and stared out the window.

How long did I really think I would be able to keep it a secret? *Newsflash: Teen daughter of deceased Christian speaker, Kyle Hamilton, pregnant! Read all about it!* That was how our city worked. Everyone's dirty laundry aired out in Town Square for all to see. But still—three days? That's all it took?

Fighting tears, I turned to her. "You won't delete that from your phone, will you?"

She tapped her phone a few times. "There. Gone."

"Seriously?"

"Seriously."

Wow. Not many people would be that kind. I flashed her the most genuine smile I could muster. "Thank you. I'm sorry—what's your name again?"

"Jill. Jill Anderson." She held out a hand, and I took it.

"Do we have any classes together?"

"Yeah. History. And Chemistry. And French."

I grimaced. Was I really that self-absorbed? "Sorry."

She shrugged. "No one remembers me. I'm used to it."

The bus pulled into the parking lot, and my stomach sank. I really didn't want to go in there. I fought the urge to cling to the seat.

I turned to Jill. "Did you maybe want to sit with me at lunch today?"

If I was going to make it through the day, I would need someone to help me.

She smiled. "Sure."

I tried to return the gesture, but only one corner of my mouth twitched. For someone so kind, I was amazed more people didn't notice her. Myself included.

Stepping off the bus, everything seemed normal. No one looked at me weirdly. In fact, they didn't really look at me at all. But as I entered the school, more and more people turned their backs to me, giggling amongst each other. I winced, my neck and ears on fire, and forced myself to keep moving. If people thought I didn't care that they were laughing at me, maybe they'd leave me alone.

Then I reached my locker, and I forgot how to breathe.

Mary's not a virgin anymore! Whore! was written with bright red lipstick on the door. Underneath, a picture had been taped to the metal—my cheerleading portrait with a pregnant belly drawn on in permanent marker.

My book bag fell to the floor as I leaned against the locker next to mine, my knees weakening.

Snickers floated down the hall, and I turned my head. My skin flushed from head to toe. Beth leered, twirling the lipstick in her fingers as she stood next to Gwen and April—and Heather. Grabbing my backpack, I ran from the school and around the side of the building.

I paced, my hand on my stomach as I tried to catch my breath. It was bad enough that Beth had been the one to write the message on my locker, but why did Heather have to be involved? She'd smiled that devilish grin she usually reserved for *Beth*. Did Heather really hate me *that* much for sleeping with Carter?

"Hey, Hamilton. You all right?" a guy asked not far from where I stood.

I snapped my head in the direction of his voice. *You've got to be kidding me.* Neil Donaghue flicked his cigarette to the ground. Because that's how my luck went.

I stormed at him. "You! You . . . assbutt! What did you say to your sister?"

Neil's hands went up like I was holding him at gunpoint. "Whoa there, crazy woman. I didn't tell my sister anything. She doesn't even live with me anymore. And assbutt? Really?"

I pushed him. "I know you saw me buy that test. Did you tell her I was pregnant? Did you?"

He raised an eyebrow. "You're pregnant?"

I rolled my eyes. "Oh, like you didn't know! It's all over school, especially now that your sister wrote it on my locker. What did I ever do to her?"

"Well, you did take the co-captain spot."

"Ugh!" I stormed away before I could smack him and crossed the parking lot, heading home. So what if it was a twenty-minute walk? Anything was better than sitting in classrooms full of jerks. Maybe I could transfer to some other school—or finish high school at home. It wasn't like I had to worry about college anymore, not if I wanted to raise a baby on my own.

I'd gone three blocks when the anger subsided enough for humiliation and despair to set in. I'd known it for days, but the fact that I couldn't go to NYU, that I wasn't going to become a doctor, finally hit me. Not to mention, I had become the laughingstock of River Springs Prep. It wouldn't be long before the news got back to my mom.

And now Carter *and* Heather had betrayed me. I was alone. Helpless and utterly alone.

Stopping in someone's front yard, I screamed, stomping my feet on the ground. I punched my stomach again and again. *Why did you have to ruin my life?* I fell on the grass, bringing my knees up to my chin, and wrapped my arms around my legs. It wasn't the baby's fault that my life was completely screwed up.

It was mine.

I wept into my knees, scrunching my eyes until they hurt, and balled my hands into fists. A loud motor echoed down the street. Next thing I knew, the driver stopped in front of me. I looked up as a rusty, brown truck parallel parked, and then Neil climbed out and walked toward me.

"Oh, God." I dropped my head back to my knees.

"Get up, Hamilton."

Lifting my head, I glared at him and the hand he extended to me.

He flexed his fingers. "Get up."

"Why would I ever get into that truck with you?"

"Hey, there's no stranger danger here. Plus, I'm thinking you probably don't want to go home right now, but you don't want to go back to school. Otherwise, you wouldn't be sitting on some poor old lady's front yard, flashing your bright purple underwear."

My cheeks burned, and my legs dropped until they were flat against the grass. I'd forgotten I was wearing my cheerleading skirt—and that I didn't have on spanks beneath it. Unless I had a game to go to, granny panties remained in my dresser at all times.

"So, what? You're here to help me play hooky?" I asked.

"Exactly." The corners of Neil's baby-blue eyes crinkled as a mischievous grin spread across his face.

I remembered now what had drawn me to him in the first place. He *was* incredibly attractive. Tall, dark, and handsome. He wasn't as muscular as Carter, but neither is Ian Somerhalder, and he's freakin' sexy. But bad boys have a bad reputation for a reason, and Neil's was pretty dirty. Getting into a car with *him* was something I had told myself I'd never do.

Until now.

I hated to admit he was right, but going back to school was out of the question. I also didn't want to go home. Thursdays were Mom's shortest days, and I'd already spent two wallowing in my room. With a sigh, I took Neil's hand, and he pulled me to my feet.

He led me to his truck without a word. Inside, Owen Danielson, Neil's best friend and fellow pothead, snored in the passenger's seat. Neil pushed him over. Owen sprung awake, flinging his arms like Kermit.

"Change of plans. I'm dropping you off at your house," Neil said.

"Why?" Then Owen spotted me standing behind Neil. "Oh." Owen wiggled his eyebrows. "Well, in that case, I won't coc—"

"Move, shithead."

Owen laughed and slid to the middle. With a grimace, I hopped into the passenger's seat, scrunching my nose at the intense tobacco smell.

"Hello," he said, his voice laced with a cartoonish, hey-baby tone.

I rolled my eyes and squeezed my book bag to my chest.

"See, not so bad," Neil said, climbing into the truck.

"Not so bad? It reeks in here," I replied.

"You'll get used to it, Princess." He winked.

My hand twitched as Owen laughed. Did Neil have to be so arrogant?

Neil got back on the road, and I fought the urge to plug my ears as the boys screeched along with the heavy metal music blaring from the speakers. Finally, Neil dropped Owen at a swanky house in the outskirts of River Springs. I wasted no time smacking the off button on Neil's radio.

"Hey, in this truck, driver picks the music," Neil said.

"Not when there's a pregnant girl in the passenger's seat with bleeding ear drums."

He smirked and merged the truck onto the expressway, taking us toward downtown Denver. He turned the radio back on but decreased the volume and switched it from screamo to classic rock.

"Where are we going?" I asked.

"You wanted to play hooky; I'm going to show you how."

"You do this often." It wasn't a question. His relaxation with skipping school made it clear.

He shrugged. "School's a time waster. As long as you get the grades, no one cares where you are."

"Aren't you always in detention?"

The corner of his mouth twitched. "I'm flattered you watch me."

I made a disgusted sound in the back of my throat and, with a roll of my eyes, turned to look out the window. *Why* had I thought this would be a good idea?

"Look," he said, "you say the word, and I'll take you home. But today, I'm skipping school for you 'cause you looked like you needed a break. So, climb off your high horse, and let me show you a good time."

I glared at him. "I am not on a high horse."

"Oh yeah? Then let's play a game. You manage to keep your eyes from rolling in that pretty head of yours for twenty minutes, and I'll buy you lunch."

On instinct—and not five seconds later—I rolled them. It wasn't until he laughed that I realized I'd done it. My cheeks warmed. Twice today I'd been called out for being stuck up. And, twice, they'd been right. When had I gotten this bad?

"I'll get off my high horse," I mumbled.

Neil cupped a hand behind his ear and pretended to strain to hear me. "What was that?"

"Oh, just drive."

He smiled, his blue eyes sparkling over his lopsided grin. My chest fluttered. *Idiot.* He was Beth Donaghue's older brother, my ex-boyfriend, *and* the guy with a black book thicker than a dictionary. While I was using him today to keep from going home, even being his friend was a bad idea. After today, I'd stay as far away from him as possible.

Fifteen minutes later, we entered the city. After a few turns, Neil pulled his truck into the Denver Zoo.

"Seriously? *This* is where you're taking me?" I asked.

He maneuvered his truck into a parking spot and then sat back in his seat. "Do you have a better idea? The zoo kills hours, cursing out caged animals is loads of fun, and they have a shit ton of fried food."

I fought the urge to roll my eyes. "Fine. Let's go."

Pulling the door open, I jumped out and slammed it behind me.

"Hey! Don't hurt Matilda!" Neil said.

I raised an eyebrow. "You named it?"

"Don't you name your cars?"

"I don't have a car. But I wouldn't name it, anyway. It's a *car*."

Neil grasped his chest and made a sound like he'd been wounded. "Cars do have feelings, you know."

Shaking my head, I approached the ticket counter and pulled my wallet out of my purse.

Neil shoved me gently. "You're not paying."

"What? I can pay for my own ticket."

He grinned at the woman in the booth. "Two tickets, please."

I crossed my arms. Who knew Neil Donaghue was a gentleman? Though, come to think of it, wasn't this how he tried to get into girls' pants? Flattery and chivalry?

He handed me a ticket, and I followed him through the gate. I had to hold my breath as we passed food carts and restrooms. The mixture of fried food and sewage was nauseating. It wasn't until we passed the Information Desk and grabbed a map that the smell started to dwindle and my stomach stopped churning.

"Looks like there's some sea lion thing at 2:30," Neil said. "That'll kill some time, but it's four hours from now. What's your favorite animal? We can go there first." He was like a little kid, his eyes wide with excitement as he surveyed the map.

"The polar bears, I guess."

"Sweet. They're to the left. We'll go that way."

He took off without waiting for me to agree. Forcing my eyeballs to stay put, I followed closely, not wanting to look like a loner.

Neil got distracted by the felines on our way to the Northern Shores section and spent a good ten minutes shouting your-momma jokes in a ridiculous effort to get them to wake up. If I wasn't so worried about getting in trouble, I might've laughed at him. When it was obvious the felines "had no shame," as Neil said, we made our way past the arctic foxes and river otters to where the polar bears lived. Two cubs played, chasing each other in a game of tag.

Neil leaned over to me. "What do you call a polar bear wearing earmuffs?"

I caught his stare. The way he looked at me reminded me of a five-year-old on Christmas morning. "What?"

"Anything you want. They can't hear you."

I shook my head to hide my traitorous smile.

"There's also one about a bear with white fur and lederhosen," Neil started.

"Let me guess—a polka bear?"

Neil squinted at me, crossed his arms, and then turned back to the polar bears. "Well, I guess that one's kinda lame."

Smiling again, I watched the two cubs chase each other around the platform and into the water. They were having an absolute blast.

If only I could remember what it felt like to have no cares in the world.

CHAPTER 7

For the next few hours, we wandered the park, staring at camels and elephants and giraffes. Neil continued to crack jokes until I finally couldn't help but laugh at every one, and when we stopped for lunch, he refused to let me pay for my own meal. I had to admit, as much as I didn't want to, I was having a great day.

"Here, I got you a pop," Neil said as he sat across the table from me.

"I can't have caffeine." I frowned. A good day could only last so long.

"Oh. Well, take mine. It's Sprite."

"You don't have to give me your drink. I'll be fine."

"Andie, just take the damn thing."

I snatched it out of his hand.

Neil slid my pop to his side of the table. "See, now that wasn't so bad."

Glaring at him, I stuffed a fry into my mouth, stifling our conversation. For ten minutes, we ate in silence—then my appetite disappeared. Here I was, pretending everything was normal when it wasn't. Not even close. I had no right to be parading around a zoo, laughing on a sort-of-date with Neil. This was a bad idea. A very, very bad idea.

My bottom lip quivered against my will. *Crap.* I'd read in the pamphlet that, starting soon, some women struggled to control their emotions. But right here, right now, was the worst possible moment for a mood swing to go Tarzan-ing. I chugged my drink, attempting to keep the tears at bay.

Neil saw right through me. "Hey, I'm sorry. I shouldn't have cursed at you." He handed me a napkin.

Taking it, I wiped away a traitorous tear. "It's not you. In fact, today's been surprisingly great. Which is the problem."

"How is having fun the problem?"

"I have no right to be. Not me."

"Because you're pregnant?"

I looked away, casting my gaze to the floor.

Neil shook his head. "So, you made a mistake. That doesn't mean your life is over or that you can't enjoy it."

I glared at him. "I'm going to have a *baby*, Neil. My life *is* over."

"You don't have to keep it."

"I can't get an abortion!" A few heads turned in our direction, and I slunk in my chair. I hadn't meant to shout.

He ran a hand through his dark hair and spoke softly. "I didn't figure. I'm talking about adoption. Why do you have to be the one who raises it?"

"I created it. I should have to deal with it. I'm not going to pawn it off on someone because I made a mistake. Besides, who are you to suggest what I should do? You don't really know me."

The muscles in Neil's jaw twitched. He took a deep breath before speaking, his expression hard. "Some kids would be better off if they were raised by parents who didn't consider them a burden."

I stared at him, trying to understand where that had come from. His words were packed full of emotions; I'd hit a nerve. Neil sat back in his chair, his face complete stone.

"I'm sorry." Didn't know why I felt like I needed to apologize, but I did.

He broke from his statuesque position, but his demeanor remained icy. "I don't need your sympathy, Hamilton. I'm going to take a leak. I'll meet you at the exit."

Jumping out of his seat, Neil stormed away, stopping just long enough to toss his entire tray into a trashcan.

No longer caring about my food, I stood, dumping what remained of my lunch in the garbage. I made my way out of the cafeteria, stopping only to brace myself in the doorway when a wave of sobs threatened me. Closing my eyes, I took a deep breath and willed the tears to stop. I'd been able to control my emotions yesterday. I would do it again today.

Calm. Down. Now. I took two more deep breaths.

"Are you okay?" an elderly man asked from behind me.

I opened my eyes. The tears were gone. Turning to him, I said, "Yes, thanks," then stormed through the park, determined to get home and away from Neil Donaghue. For good.

I didn't get far, however. As I neared the exit of the park, Neil was braced against the wall next to the men's room, one arm behind his back. His other hand held a cigarette to his lips.

Stopping a few feet away from him, I crossed my arms. "Put that out."

He blew out a puff of smoke. "What's the magic word?"

I glared at him. With a smirk, he dropped the cigarette on the asphalt and smashed the tip with his toes.

"You shouldn't smoke," I said.

"Around a pregnant chick? I know. Which is why I was doing it here rather than in the truck with you."

"No, because it's bad for you."

"So is holding a computer in your lap. Makes your balls shrivel up. You going to tell me I can't do that, too?"

I made a disgusted sound and stomped toward the exit. Neil, with his long legs, stayed right on my heels, laughing.

"Do you have a funny bone?" he asked.

"Shut up."

"Oh, come on. I know you were laughing earlier, before I got all pissy. Which I apologize for. So, let me make it up to you." He grabbed my wrist before I could walk through the gate.

I turned, ready to smack him, when a stuffed polar bear met my face. Was that what he'd been holding behind his back?

"Did you buy this for me?" I asked.

"Well, I *am* handing it to you."

I took it from him. "Why?"

Sticking his hands in his pockets, he shrugged. "I told you. I was an ass earlier. And after this morning, I thought you could use something to make you smile. You're pretty when you smile."

Neil stiffened and pursed his lips, scratching the back of his neck and playing it off like he meant to say that.

I took a moment to study him. I'd known Neil since elementary school and then went out with him for a month. Flirtation, I expected. Compliments? Not so much.

My cheeks warmed, and I squeezed the polar bear. "Well, thank you. And, I guess, I should apologize to you for being a bitch." I mumbled the last word.

Neil tipped his head back and laughed. "Oh, man, Hamilton. We've got to work on your language. Sure you don't want to stay for the seal show?"

I pressed my lips together. If I went home, I'd have to explain to Mom why I didn't stay for the whole day. But I also didn't want to end up walking in through the door late. Either way, I was going to have to come up with a lie. The longer I waited, the better. Might as well stay to see the show.

"Fine," I said.

He grinned, his beautiful, blue eyes creasing in the corners, and my heartbeat tripped. Turning my gaze away from him, I headed toward the primate section and shook my head. *Remember, Andie: You aren't the first girl he's brought to the zoo.*

Neil was still laughing at the animal handler's accident when we reached his truck. After demonstrating how gentle and friendly seals were, the female had turned on her handler, barking at him and chasing him around the stage. The handler's face was wide with terror and humiliation, and when he fell in the water, the entire crowd burst out laughing, me included. But no one found it funnier than Neil. When the seal began her attack, Neil pulled out his cell phone and started recording, talking about how many views he was going to get when he posted the video on YouTube.

"The poor guy was humiliated," I said, climbing into the passenger's seat.

"I know. That's the best part." Neil started the truck, and it sputtered to life.

I shook my head as he pulled out of the parking lot, but a smile lingered on my face.

We drove in silence through the city, Neil's classic rock station filling the vehicle. He tapped his fingers to the beat on his steering wheel. Then "Carry On Wayward Son" came on, and he spun the volume dial with excitement. I fought the urge to plug my ears. At least it wasn't screamo, like earlier.

"Man, I love this song." He sang along like he'd written it. His voice was really good. Like, professional singer—maybe even Broadway—good.

"I didn't know you could sing," I said.

"Hey, I have many talents. Music, poetry, rolling the perfect joint."

I scrunched my nose. "Do you really smoke pot?"

He smiled. "Nah, but everyone thinks I do, so don't blow my secret."

"Why do you let people think that kind of stuff about you?"

"This isn't my normal self, babe. I'm holding back for you." He winked.

God, I hated when he did that. "Can you be serious for one minute?"

"Nope."

"Ugh!" I smacked my hand on the side of the door and stared out

49

the window. For a few minutes, I sat like that, then Neil turned down the volume.

"Look, Andie, if you knew the real me, you'd get why I let people say that shit. It's better they think I'm a cheater and a pothead than know the truth. Two things I'm not, by the way."

"Except for when you made out with Abby Young in the library two years ago."

"Oh, yeah. Forgot I did that. That was a pretty shitty thing to do to you. I'm sorry."

I looked at him, but his focus stayed on the road, his fingers no longer tapping to the beat.

"Well, if it helps, I had a really good time with you today. So, the real you can't be all that bad," I said. Obviously, he had a temper—and his snark made me want to smack him—but he was also playful and kind. And as far as his apology: I hadn't expected that. He really needed to let people see this side of him more often.

Neil's gaze flicked to me then back to the road. He pressed his lips together, and something deep inside me hoped he'd open up, even a little bit. The day *had* been really good, and maybe he could be the friend I needed, even given our history. But he turned up the radio and continued to stare straight ahead.

My heart sank. *Guess today was just chump charity, after all.*

Ten minutes later, he pulled into my driveway. I stuffed the polar bear into my book bag and slung my purse over my shoulder before pushing open the truck's door. "Thanks for today."

"Wait." Neil rubbed the back of his neck.

I pulled my legs back into the truck and shut the door.

"Give me your phone." He held his hand out to me.

I raised an eyebrow. "Why?"

"So I can give you my number."

Timidly, I pulled my cell out of my purse and handed it to him. He punched a few buttons then passed it back.

"Call me any time," he said. "Day or night. I don't live far, and half the time I'm at Owen's—which is even closer—so whatever you need."

After a day of jokes and sarcasm, his sincerity was unnerving—as was his penetrating stare. A lump caught in my throat. "Thanks."

He flashed me a soft smile. "Later, Hamilton."

I climbed out of the truck and waved goodbye as he backed out of the driveway.

CHAPTER 8

Mom jerked awake at the dining table as soon as I stepped into the kitchen. I squinted at the stack of ungraded papers she must've used as a pillow. Had she really fallen asleep with her head on the table?

"Hey, honey." Mom pinched the bridge of her nose. "How was your day?"

"Fine," I replied. My grip strengthened on my backpack, and I took a step toward the hall, biting my lip.

"Your school called me today. They said you didn't show up this morning."

Crap. With a sigh, I dropped my bags on the floor and sat across from her. Could I come out and say, *I'm pregnant, and people at school called me a whore, so I skipped. Please don't make me go back?*

One look into Mom's loving gaze told me no.

"It was stupid. A couple friends were going to the zoo and asked if I wanted to come along, and I said yes. I'm sorry."

Mom stared into my eyes, and I forced myself to look away. If I didn't, she'd know I wasn't telling her the whole truth.

"Was there drinking involved?" she asked.

I shook my head and looked her in the eye. "No."

"Drugs?"

"No."

"Sex?"

"*No.*"

She stared at me then sighed. "Well, you know I'm going to have to ground you. One week. You go to school and come straight home. Understand?"

I flinched when she reached across the table to take my hand.

"You're a good girl, Andrea. And this is an honest house. Next time you want to go somewhere instead of school, call me first, and we'll talk. Letting my daughter miss a day or two of school is much better than finding out she's sneaking around because she's afraid to tell me what she's up to. Promise you'll call me next time?"

I nodded and my throat tightened, like someone was strangling me. Mom patted my hand when my eyes filled with tears. I couldn't tell her. She'd be devastated. And after these last two years of struggling to parent me by herself, to find out her daughter was pregnant . . . I'd break her heart, and I didn't think I'd ever recover.

"There's no reason to get upset, honey. I know you're sorry. Now, go upstairs and do the work you missed today. I set a list for you on your desk," Mom said.

She didn't need to tell me again. After jumping out of my chair, I grabbed my bags off the floor and then ran to my bedroom, locking the door the moment I was inside. I leaned against a wall, a hand on my stomach as the room blurred. I counted to five, breathing slowly through my nose. The sob waned.

A small gold box was sitting on my bed, no bigger than a paperback book. Biting my lip, I opened it. Inside was a new cheer bow with a note from Mom that read: *For Friday's game. Your dad would be so proud of how far you've come. Love, Mom*

Clutching the box, I collapsed on the edge of my mattress, my bedroom ten degrees colder. *Oh, God.* My vision blurred as a giant weight slammed into my chest and threatened to take me down.

I'm sorry. I'm so sorry, I repeated again and again, fighting tears. How would I ever tell her about the baby? She'd never be proud of me again, and Dad—could he see me right now? Did he already know what I'd done?

My phone buzzed in my purse. I plucked it out of the bag's front pocket. A text from Heather. *Carter sez u told him it was his. He said u lied.*

Why would I lie about that? I sent back.

Dunno. U 1st told me it was sum dude in London. So which is it? Btw, word round skool is u dropped ur pants a couple times this summer. Sounds like it could've been ne 1. Guess ur not the friend I thought u were.

The phone fell from my hand. This couldn't be happening. How could Heather, my best friend since kindergarten, believe that crap? I pressed the back of my hand to my forehead as the room spun.

Maybe if I never got fat, maybe if I never left school, I could say the whole rumor was started by Beth.

I can't be pregnant, I thought, raking my hands through my hair. *I don't want to be a mom. I want my friends back. I don't want Dad to stop being proud of me. I want my life back!*

My breaths were shaky as I reached for my phone to dial Neil. He picked up on the third ring. "Hello?"

"Hey, it's Andie." *Don't cry, don't cry, don't cry.*

"Couldn't wait a whole day to talk to me, huh?"

"God, would you stop with the sarcasm? That's not why I called." My voice broke. *Crap.*

He mumbled something to someone on his end, and I heard a door close. "You okay?"

"I need you to do me a favor." *Great, I sound like Minnie Mouse.*

"What's up?"

I covered my mouth, unable to say the words. *Dang it.*

"Hey, it's all right," Neil said. "Just tell me what you want me to do."

I blew out a long breath. "Can you take me to a clinic tomorrow?"

"An abortion clinic?" When I didn't answer—because he couldn't see me nodding—Neil continued, "Are you sure that's what you want to do? Is the baby's dad even okay with that?"

Oh, I'm sure he'd be just fine with the decision. Anger boiled inside me. "Will you take me or not?"

"Jeez. Yes, of course I'll take you. I told you whatever you needed, didn't I?"

I bit my tongue, hard, trying not to turn into a weeping disaster. Was it what I *wanted* to do? No. But it was what I had to do if I wanted my life to go back to normal.

"I'll be there at 8:30 tomorrow, okay?" he said. "Hang in there. Call me if you change your mind."

"Thanks," I whispered as my phone beeped in my ear, alerting me that the call had dropped.

For the next ten minutes, I kept myself preoccupied, hiding the cheer ribbon from view, picking up piles of clutter, withdrawing textbooks from my book bag before stuffing them back in—fighting the football-sized lump in my throat. Finally, I climbed under my sheets, not caring that the sun hadn't set yet or that my homework was still untouched, and let myself cry.

I slept for twelve hours, waking at 7:00 a.m. when my cell alarm filled the room. In a daze, I showered and pulled my light blonde hair into a bun. There was no point in styling today. I didn't even bother with makeup. As much as I hated to admit it, I was going to be a blubbering mess on the ride home. The last thing I needed was to look like the new member of *KISS*.

After throwing a hoodie over yoga pants, I found the website for the clinic and made sure I didn't need a reservation. *No appointment necessary for medical abortions,* the site said. Fine by me. *Parent's signature required for minors.* The heck with that. I was sure I could convince Neil to sign it. He *was* a rebel, after all. And he'd said whatever I needed, right?

I grabbed my purse and wandered downstairs. The house was empty. I contemplated calling Neil and asking him to get me but changed my mind. It didn't matter when we got there. It was still going to be one of the worst days of my life.

Numb, I shuffled outside to sit on the front stoop, and at 8:29, Neil's truck pulled up to the house.

"You sure you want to do this?" he asked when I climbed into the passenger's seat.

I nodded, and he backed out of the driveway and remained silent until we pulled into the parking lot a half hour later. Unlike when Heather took me to Planned Parenthood, this clinic was on the good side of Denver. Instead of barred windows and run-down houses, the streets were filled with shopping centers and restaurants.

Neil hopped out of the truck as soon as he shut down the engine, but I sat there, staring at the front door, willing myself to go inside. This was the right choice. Carter wasn't going to help me, Heather had more-or-less disowned me, and I couldn't break my mom's heart. I had to do this.

Neil opened my door. "You coming?"

I nodded, prying my nails from the truck's seat, and hopped out. I grabbed his arm before we went any farther. Man, it was strong. "Wait, I almost forgot." From my purse, I dug out a pen and the Certificate of Notice I printed off the clinic's website. "I need you to sign this."

Last thing I needed was to fill out paperwork and have a nurse notice the signatures were too similar.

He raised an eyebrow. "Not that I mind breaking the law, but you know we could both get in serious trouble for this, right?"

"Please?"

He sighed, snatched the pen from my hand, and forged my mother's signature. With a quiet "thank you," I led him into the building, and he grabbed a seat near the back of the waiting room. I gave the secretary my name, I.D., and the certificate. With a smile, she handed me a clipboard and instructed me to fill it out while I waited for the nurse to call my name.

"You think her boobs are real?" Neil asked when I sat down, showing me the open magazine he held.

It's like being with Heather all over again. "No."

He flipped a couple pages. "How 'bout hers?"

"No."

"Hers?"

"Neil."

"Sorry. Can't help it if I like real boobs."

Shaking my head, I started on the necessary paperwork. I expected the medical history and confidentiality information, but when I got to the detailed descriptions of my options, my pulse raced. Have it sucked out like a vacuum cleaner. Take one pill here, take another at home, and boom—miscarriage.

My stomach sloshed, and I let out a deep breath. *You can do this, Andie. You* have *to do this.* I checked the box for the one with the pills.

When the nurse called my name, I stood on noodley legs and wobbled through the waiting room. Neil grabbed my arm, placing my hand inside his elbow.

"You looked like the scarecrow from *The Wizard of Oz,*" he whispered.

In my head, I punched his arm—the one I clung to like a baby monkey to its mother.

"Are you the father?" the nurse asked him when we reached the doorway.

"Why? Can I go back with her if I'm not?"

"No. You'll have to wait—"

"He's the father," I shouted, blushing.

"Uh, yeah. What she said," Neil replied.

The nurse's expression showed that she knew better, but she responded with, "Come on back."

Gripping Neil's arm, I followed in a daze and found myself seated on a table. Had Neil helped me up here?

"Andrea?" The nurse's voice was loud. I must've zoned out.

"Yes?"

"Your vitals are good, so I need to make sure you're here for the medicine." *She took my vitals?* "Otherwise, I'm going to need to make you an appointment."

I nodded. "I am."

She handed me a clipboard. "I need you to sign below and initial the boxes, stating that you've read the information about the procedure, consent to the procedure, and fully understand that you're terminating a pregnancy."

Maybe it was the way she worded it—"terminating," like I was destroying something. Every part of me constricted. I grabbed the pen, but my hands trembled. The boxes on the paper moved. My lungs burned, and my fingers weakened. When had my world turned so upside down that I was ready to kill an innocent baby because of *my* mistake? The clipboard fell out of my hand. Dropping the pen, I gripped the edge of the bed and wheezed, my sides throbbing like Goliath stepped on my ribs.

"I'll give you two a minute," the nurse said, leaving the clipboard and pen on the counter.

As soon as she left the room, I leapt off the exam table and wrapped my arms around my waist. Words spewed out between gasps as I paced. "I can't do it, but I have to. I can't. I have to."

Neil tried to interrupt me. "Andie—"

"I have to do it. I have to. Oh, God, *I can't*." My knees weakened as a howl rolled out of me, and I hit the floor. If I had to, then why did it feel like my life was ending? Like I was signing away a piece of my soul?

"Shit." Neil jumped out of his chair and crouched next to me. He put his hands on my shoulders as hyperventilating took over. "Hey, breathe. You've got to breathe."

I shook my head, bawling as black spotted my vision. I grasped his forearms when the room spun.

Eyes tight, Neil drew me into his arms. "You're all right. Let it out."

I gripped the back of his jacket in my fists, and, for minutes, we stayed like that—Neil rubbing my back, me soaking his shoulder. Why had I thought I'd be able to go through with this? I never should've come.

Soon, my breathing eased, and my sobs turned into soft cries and sniffling. Still, Neil held me tight. I closed my eyes, letting myself relax. Exhaustion filled every muscle. If we didn't leave soon, I'd fall asleep, right here on the floor.

"Take me home," I spoke into his chest.

"Well, that's mighty forward of you."

I pushed him away with a glare.

He smirked. "That's better."

I rolled my eyes, and he hoisted me to my feet, holding my hands until he made sure I could stand. Then, with an arm around my shoulders, he led me from the room, stopping only to let the nurse know I'd changed my mind. Neil heaved me into the truck before hopping into the driver's seat. He peeled out of the parking lot like a man on a mission.

I rested my head on the cold glass of the truck's window. My cheeks were still hot from crying like a blubbering fool. Ugh, this was such a mistake. Picturing the scene from Neil's point of view, my skin crawled. I hated to cry when I was alone, and even more so in front of other people. Especially when they were someone like Neil.

Five minutes down the road, I found the courage to thank him for what he did at the clinic. "I should never have asked you to do any of this."

"Yes, you've been a terrible inconvenience." His voice was playful.

I scowled at him. "Are you capable of anything other than sarcasm?"

"No, not really."

"Well, humor me, because I'm trying to offer you a sincere apology."

His gaze flicked to me. "We're seriously going to turn this into a chick flick moment?"

I crossed my arms without breaking my stare.

"Oh, for God's sake. *You're welcome.*"

"That's it? 'You're welcome?'"

Neil shrugged. "What else do you want me to say?"

"Maybe 'don't ever call me again?'"

He shook his head.

"So, what? Bad boy Neil Donaghue has a heart? He actually comforts women without expecting them to jump into bed?"

Neil yanked the truck off the side of the road, slamming on the brakes.

He jerked his head in my direction and curled his lips. "How is it, given everything, you still think the worst of me? I came after you when the whole school laughed in your face. I committed a possible felony because you needed my help. I drove you to a fucking abortion clinic and pretended to be the damn father so you didn't have to be alone. And you think I did all this because I want to *get in your pants?*"

I mumbled, "Well, you do have a reputation."

His face reddened, and he turned away, hands balled into fists. Neil grabbed the wheel, every muscle in his toned forearms taut, and wrenched the truck onto the expressway without a word.

My stomach churned. He was right. I was jumping to conclusions and being judgmental when I had absolutely no right to be. *What is wrong with me?*

"I'm sorry," I said. "I just don't know why you would do all this for me."

His fingers loosened and then tightened around the steering wheel, but he didn't respond.

I watched him for a few minutes, hoping he'd say something. But, when he didn't, I put my feet on the seat, tucked myself into a ball, and leaned against the window again.

CHAPTER 9

For the next fifteen minutes, I waited for some angry or sarcastic comment, but every time I looked at Neil, the muscles in his jaw remained rigid. He never once looked in my direction. Like he forgot I existed. But when we reached River Springs, he missed the turn that would've taken me home.

"Where are we going?" I asked.

He didn't respond. Instead, he drove through town until we reached the outskirts. The part of River Springs no one ventured into unless they wanted to get lost in the forest. I pursed my lips. *Why would he take me out here?* Then he pulled into a hidden driveway, and there, in front of me, was a house that took my breath away.

In its time, the place had to have been beautiful. A Victorian home with wood siding that looked like it had, at one time, been painted jade green. Now, the paint was chipping off, shutters were missing, and one of the upstairs windows was boarded over with plywood.

"Where are we?" I asked.

"Get out." Neil shut off the engine, jumped out of the truck, and then slammed his door closed.

I followed, my insides twisting in knots. The front porch steps creaked under my weight. When Neil pushed open the front door, the hinges screeched like a dying cat. I cringed. Inside, the rooms were in much better shape, for the most part. Smells of fresh paint and cleaner filled my nose, and the furniture appeared to be in good condition. The place still held the ambiance of a well-to-do Victorian family, the kind of place you once went for tea and finger sandwiches while discussing business affairs.

"You live here, don't you?" I asked.

Neil dropped his keys on an antique chest in the foyer. "Try to keep it down. You don't want to meet my mother." His gaze flicked everywhere but toward me. "Hungry?"

"Sure."

I followed Neil through an outdated dining room and into the kitchen. From off-white, yellowing cabinets, he pulled a loaf of bread, some peanut butter, and a bag of potato chips. A rickety stove sat beneath a cracked window, and a rusting refrigerator was tucked in the far corner. Sympathy warmed my chest.

"My parents bought this house before I was born," Neil said. "It was their intent to fix this place up and flip it, like those families you see on TV. They started with the inside and worked their way from top to bottom. Completed the upstairs then finished the living room, family room, and foyer."

His hand movements were jerky as he slathered his bread with peanut butter. I knew what was coming next; his dad had died when we were in elementary school. My fingers twitched, aching to touch Neil's arm, to tell him he didn't need to share this with me. But he continued before I had the chance.

"Then on my eighth birthday, my dad came to pick me up from a sleepover at Owen's, and on our way home, our car was struck by a semi." Neil's gaze caught mine for the first time since I lashed out at him on the side of the road. There weren't tears in his eyes, but the spark that had filled them the last two days was gone.

Someone stuck a hot, jagged piece of iron in my chest and twisted as my own memories flooded my mind. I'd been sitting on the couch in our living room when the police officer walked through the front door and gathered my mom and me together. As Mom screamed and collapsed to the floor, I stared at the dark television, dazed, like it was a dream, like I'd wake up the next morning and hear my dad call me "sweet pea."

But Dad never read his newspaper at the kitchen table again, or brought me a present from one of his speaking tours, or chauffeured me to another dance class. The ache I felt in my bones every time I saw Mom sitting alone in the stands at football games . . . there was no comparison.

"Neil . . . ." I placed my hand over his.

Dropping the knife he'd been using for the peanut butter, he stepped back. "I'm not done. In case you can't tell, this place was never touched again. Mom started drinking and never stopped. I became a parent to a younger sister who still blames me for her dad's death. And the only thing that keeps us from complete poverty is my asshole uncle who, because of some promise he made my dad, pays for our tuition and bills while holding it over our heads. The rest of it— the clothes, the groceries—it's all from the monthly check we get from my Dad's life insurance or the money I make on the weekends, working for my uncle.

"So, next time you want to accuse me of being a low-life asshole with nothing better to do than use women like toilet paper, remember this: I built that reputation so people don't get close enough to see *this*."

My heart pounded in my ears as Neil's nostrils flared and he seemed to forget how to breathe. I understood why he'd want to hide this from people, why he'd pretend to be something he wasn't. I hated the pity stares and comments from people who knew about my dad's death, and I didn't have poverty looming over my head. If I were in Neil's shoes, I wouldn't want people to know the truth either.

I swallowed a lump in my throat. "I'm sorry. I didn't know."

"Precisely."

"Look, about what I said—"

He sighed. "Forget it."

"No, let me finish." I held up a hand, fighting the burn in my throat. "I lost my dad, too, two years ago."

Neil's shoulders drooped. "I know."

"And you've been nothing but kind to me these last couple days. Why, I don't know, but I still shouldn't have lashed out at you, even without knowing about your family. I'm sorry."

We stared at each other for a few seconds, like two cowboys in a standoff. It was so quiet; I could almost hear the wind rustling the trees outside. My curiosity got the best of me. "I have to ask: Why are you sharing all this with me?"

Neil squinted. "I never told you why I asked you out all those years ago, did I?"

I shrugged. "I figured you just thought I was pretty."

A corner of his lip twitched in a smile. "You are, but that wasn't it." He scratched the back of his neck. "I was in third grade. It was right after my dad died. Some of the older kids called me 'orphan boy.' Lame, I know. But I hid behind the climber thing and cried. You brought me a flower and said, 'Those boys are jerks. They just wish they were you.' I've never forgotten the way that made me feel."

The room silenced. My heart flopped like a fish out of water. I couldn't remember what I had for lunch two days ago, let alone something from third grade. I rubbed my chest, unsure if I should be honored by the reason he'd liked me—not the fact that I was a cheerleader—or bothered that such a small act of kindness had such a profound effect.

The words left my mouth before I could stop them. "Then, why Abby Young? Why did you kiss her?"

He looked away and ran a hand down his face. "Because—ah, hell. Because I liked you, okay?"

My eyebrows scrunched. "*That* was your reason?"

He sighed and met my gaze again. "Look, Andie, I'm sorry. I really am. I just . . . You were the first girl I actually cared about, and I was afraid that if you knew that my life was seriously fucked up, you'd—I don't know—look at me differently. It was easier knowing you hated me because I was an ass than because I was some poor kid from a broken home."

Oh, wow. The ache that ran to my toes left me breathless. My throat burned. *This* was the real Neil. Right here. Not knowing what else to do, I crossed through the kitchen and into his arms.

He gave me a gentle squeeze. "Okay. Not quite sure what that was for."

"You hugged me earlier when I needed it. You looked like you could use one."

"Nah, I'm not much of the teddy bear type. Though, I don't mind the boobs pressing against me part. Maybe I'll reconsider the hugging thing."

And we were back. I stepped away and smacked his arm as he laughed. But, for the first time in two days, I didn't mind the snark so much. In fact, I even remembered what it was like, falling for him the first time. The way he'd purposely trip over his own feet to keep me from being embarrassed about tripping over mine.

I shuddered and shook the thought from my mind.

"What do you say to grabbing McDonald's for lunch?" I asked. "I'm really craving a cheeseburger. My treat. I figure I should, you know, make up for how I acted today."

He tapped his chin. "Free food, huh? A guy can't say no to that."

With a smile, I helped him put away the bread and peanut butter before following him out the door and back to his truck.

When we pulled into the driveway a few hours later, the door to the garage was wide open, and Mom's car sat inside. I glanced at the clock. 3:00 p.m. She should still be teaching a class.

"What's wrong?" Neil asked when I didn't climb out of his truck.

"My mom's car is here."

"So?"

"So, she shouldn't be home yet."

"Maybe she got off work early."

I tapped my fingers on my knees. "Maybe." Though Mom never would've canceled her afternoon class if it weren't an emergency. Something was wrong.

"Do you want me to come in with you?" Neil asked.

"No!" I shouted. Then when I realized how my quick response might be interpreted, I said, "I mean, I'll be fine. It's probably just some misunderstanding." Or the school had phoned Mom to tell her I'd skipped. Again.

"Okay, well, call me if you need anything. Otherwise, I guess I'll see you Monday."

Nodding, I pushed open the truck door. I caught his eye before jumping out. "Thanks again, for everything."

He nodded, his lips turning up in a soft smile. I climbed out of the truck and raced for the garage before Mom peeked her head outside.

The house was quiet. No Mom sitting at the kitchen table.

"Mom?" I called out. Someone shuffled upstairs. A door opened.

"I'll be right down. Have a seat in the living room." Her voice was shaky.

Oh, crap. Something was definitely wrong. Something had happened, and I was in big trouble.

I set my purse on the table and wiped my clammy palms on my pants before finding a spot on the couch. I picked at my fingernails. My right leg bounced. *What's taking her so long?*

Finally, I heard the door open again, and footsteps echo as she made her way downstairs, through the hall, and into the kitchen. I turned in my seat. Mom's eyes were swollen and red. I swallowed.

She sat on the love seat across from me and wiped her nose with a wadded tissue. "Did you skip school again today?"

Earlier, when I thought I was going to abort the baby, I hadn't cared about being grounded for missing another day and keeping it a secret. But, now, I regretted my decision. I could've at least called her and told her I wasn't feeling well. Then she wouldn't have known I was going behind her back again. As if that was better than lying.

I nodded, unable to talk.

Her gaze didn't falter. "Can you tell me why you skipped school?"

I cleared my throat. "I was with a friend."

"Who?"

Oh, crap. Who do I say? Mom knew everyone in this town. "Carter."

She stared at me; she knew I was lying. "Did yesterday and today have anything to do with the rumor spreading around your school?"

My lungs constricted. I clenched the fabric of my yoga pants into a ball. "Who told you?"

"Your guidance counselor called me today." Her voice shook again. "She was concerned about your prolonged absences. The days you missed when you told me you were sick and the two days you skipped. She wanted to know if there was anything the school could do to help with your situation."

My bottom lip quivered. This was it. I should just come out and say it.

But I couldn't open my mouth; I couldn't move.

She knew. *She knew.* I could see it on her face—the pain, the disappointment, the fear. I did this to her. Her life was going to crumble, and it was all my fault.

"Is it true?" she asked. "Tell me right now—are you pregnant?"

I looked away. My resolve broke, and I dropped my face into my hands. "I'm sorry. I'm so sorry."

Mom let out a tearful moan. "For crying out loud, Andrea! How did this happen?"

"I don't know," I squeaked out between cries.

"You don't know? Were you raped?"

"No! It wasn't like that. But I didn't mean to. I swear, I didn't mean to."

"How could you not mean to? You knew very well what you were doing when you took your clothes off! I thought you were better than this!"

I wrapped my arms around my waist. This was the first time she'd ever yelled at me. Sure, she'd raised her voice or scolded me. But never like this. I shrank away, each of her words like a lash from a whip.

Out of the corner of my eye, I saw her pinch the bridge of her nose, tears rolling down her reddened face. She wiped her nose with her tissue and leaned forward in her seat. This time, when she spoke, her voice was gentle. "Andie, I need you to tell me what happened. How long have you known about the baby?"

"A week," I replied with a sniffle. "Mom, I'm sorry. I really am."

She sighed. "I know. And I appreciate your apology, but this is going to take me a while to get used to. I never wanted this for my little girl."

A whimper escaped my lips. Why did telling the truth have to hurt so much?

Mom continued, "But you can't go back and change it, so all we can do is pray for forgiveness and figure out what to do from here."

For the first time since the yelling began, I turned my body toward her. Tears rolled down Mom's cheeks, but her gaze was filled with nothing but love. Since when had she become so understanding?

I climbed off the couch and dropped to the floor next to her legs, resting my head in her lap. Mom stroked my hair. How there were any tears left to fall was beyond me, but, for minutes, we sat like that until my crying subsided.

"Andrea, you know I have to ask. Who's the baby's father? Is it someone I know?"

Though I didn't want to tell her, I knew I had to. I sat up so I could see her. "Carter. We'd had too much to drink. It wasn't supposed to happen."

Mom flinched at the mention of alcohol but didn't pry. "Have you told Carter the baby's his?"

I nodded. "He flat-out refused to have anything to do with it. He abandoned me, and so did Heather." Another wave of tears stung my throat. I wanted to scream. Not because I was angry at my ex-best friends, but because I couldn't figure out how to turn off the darn faucet in my brain.

Mom patted my hand. "Well, we'll have to have a talk with the Lamberts because Carter has to own up to this as much as you do."

A chill ran down my spine. She knew very well how much his parents controlled his life. "No, Mom, you can't. His parents—"

"It's the price he has to pay for impregnating my daughter. He's as much a part of this as you are."

I pursed my lips. Carter might not hate me yet, but after my mom called his, he would for sure. There was no stopping her. No matter how much I pleaded for Carter's sake, Mom wouldn't back down. And part of me was glad. Though I hated to admit it, I didn't want to do this alone.

"How far along are you?" Mom asked.

"About nine weeks, I think."

She nodded, and for what felt like hours she simply sat there, her face paling. Acid roasted my throat, and heat began to climb the back of my neck. She wasn't going to tell me to get an abortion too, was she?

Mom sighed, and a moment of panic flashed across her face. Then she looked at me, her gaze full of the tender love that felt like a dagger to my chest. "I'll call an OB on Monday and get you her first available appointment. In the meantime, I want you to relax this weekend. I'll get you some prenatal vitamins, and maybe tomorrow we can go shopping for clothes that'll fit you a little more comfortably and hide the weight gain as you start to show."

She touched my cheek, and a lump formed in my chest like when I swallowed soda too fast. I'd expected her to be mad, sure. Heartbroken, even. But gentle and understanding? Not so much.

"Why aren't you punishing me?" I asked.

"Well, you're obviously grounded until further notice. But I think being pregnant at sixteen is punishment enough without me screaming at you." She tucked a loose strand of hair behind my year. "And right now, I think you need your mommy more than ever. Am I right?"

She was. And, just like that, I fell into another sobbing mess.

CHAPTER 10

On Saturday, true to her word, Mom took me shopping for more forgiving pants and tops with empire waists. She would continue to let out my school uniform until buying a new one was our only choice —that is, if I even wanted to return. The idea of homeschool sounded amazing, but I didn't want to give up yet. If there was a chance I could still go to River Springs Prep, I had to take it. Monday would be the deciding factor.

The delicious scent of scrambled eggs hit me when I entered the kitchen Sunday morning, but the moment I caught Mom dressed in her church clothes, my stomach rolled. Half the congregation had to know about my pregnancy by now. I could already picture people's stares and hear their comments. Maybe I could convince Mom to let me stay home.

"Do I have to go to church?" I asked.

"Yes, Andrea." She brushed eggs from the skillet onto plates.

I sat at the table with a grimace and fidgeted with the sleeve of my pajama top.

"Besides," she continued, "I need to speak with Evelyn, and I want you to be there."

"You're going to confront Carter's mom *at church?*" I shouted.

"Well, I don't think this is a conversation that should take place over the phone, do you? She's too busy at her law office during the week for me to drop by unannounced. Church is the easiest place to catch her."

I'm gonna puke.

"We'll pull them into a classroom after the service," she said, setting a plate in front of me. All I could do was move the eggs around with my fork.

I looked at her through teary eyes. "Please, don't make me do this at church." *Or at all.* When she'd said she'd talk to the Lamberts, I didn't know I was going to be involved.

"I'm sorry, honey, but part of being an adult is doing a lot of things you're uncomfortable with. Now eat, and go get dressed."

Standing at the kitchen counter, Mom pressed a shaking hand to her forehead before scarfing down her breakfast—and then pressing her fingertips to her lips like she was afraid the food would come back up. I squinted at her. Was she really that nervous to talk to Carter's mom?

After Mom dropped her plate in the sink and left, I stared at my own plate for minutes then stormed away without touching a bite of food.

When we entered the church a little while later, I didn't hear too many comments. A lot of sad and judgmental stares, yes, but everyone's conversations were in hushed whispers. Probably a good thing. I couldn't afford to have another breakdown.

I stayed close to Mom as we entered the sanctuary. Carter and his mother sat near the back. His dad, a coach for the Denver Broncos, must've had an away game this week, otherwise Evelyn would've dragged him along. I groaned when Mom stopped to say hello.

"Evelyn, how are you?" Mom's voice was chipper. Too happy. But if Carter's mom noticed her friendliness was half-faked, she didn't show it.

"Fantastic. Did you hear Tom got a new contract with the 49ers?"

Jeez, it's like an episode of Suburgatory. I caught Carter's eye. He looked away instantly. Crossing my arms, I turned to stare at the front row. If I didn't look at the Lamberts, they wouldn't see there was something wrong.

"No! That's so exciting," Mom replied to Evelyn. "Wait for us after church, would you? I have to grab my seat, but I'd love to hear more about it."

I rolled my eyes, still turned toward the front of the sanctuary. Mom was one heck of a manipulator; I had to give her that.

"Oh, of course," Evelyn said. "It'll be nice to catch up before we move to San Francisco."

My head snapped around. Carter's eyebrows gathered together. Was he even going to tell me they were *moving?* I opened my mouth to yell at him, but Mom grabbed my hand.

"Yes, absolutely. We'll see you after the service." Mom waved at Evelyn while pushing me down the aisle.

My nails bit into my palms. Mom's conversation with Carter's parents was supposed to convince him to change his mind about being there for me—for his baby. No matter how hard we tried, no matter how guilty Mom made them feel, nothing was going to work. Especially if they were moving. I knew Evelyn too well. She'd pay whatever money she had to keep Carter out of legal trouble, but I'd never see him again.

Mom tugged me down the pew and into my seat. "Andrea Marie, *do not* make a scene in front of everyone. Now, please, try to calm down. The service will be over in an hour, and then I'll handle it."

She said "an hour" like it was nothing, but my jiggling legs were proof that it'd be the longest one of my life. Even the music didn't have its usual calming effect. Instead, I sat with balled fists, waiting for the chance to unleash my anger on my former best friend.

When the pastor said the last benediction and people filed out of their pews, I wasted no time running up the aisle and grabbing Carter's arm. I pulled him down the hall and into an empty classroom.

"You're *moving?*" I yelled at him.

"Yeah, so?"

My mouth fell open. *He's joking, right?* "So, don't you think that's something you might've wanted to tell me? Considering I'm—"

"Ah, here you are." Mrs. Lambert burst into the room. "Is everything all right, Andie? You worried me when you grabbed Carter and ran off like that."

"No, everything's not all right." Mom appeared out of nowhere and closed the door behind her. "Evelyn, we need to talk." She brushed her dark hair out of her face and sat in one of the classroom's chairs.

Carter stepped back, glaring at me, and crossed his arms.

Mrs. Lambert sat across from Mom and put a hand over my mother's, her gaze full of concern. "Oh, darling, is this about Andie's problem?"

My jaw dropped. *Excuse me?*

His mom continued, "You know we will do everything we can to make sure she's looked after. Even from California, if you need legal advice, I will fly back as often as I can to make sure the father is pulling his share of the weight."

Mom raised an eyebrow. "You do know the father is your son?"

Evelyn sat back in her chair. "I beg your pardon?"

Mom looked at me as if she needed to double check I'd told her the truth. When I didn't say anything, she returned her attention to Carter's mom. "Andie said they were at a party—"

Mrs. Lambert shot out of her chair and spun around, sticking her finger in Carter's face. "You tell me right now. Is this true?"

Carter dropped his arms and rolled his eyes. "No, Mom."

My heart fell to the floor. I gripped the back of the chair in front of me, my legs weakening.

"Son, you look me in the eye when you answer my questions." His mom's voice was so stern that chills ran down *my* spine. "Now, tell me the truth. *Did you sleep with Andrea Hamilton?*"

Carter turned his head, his posture rigid. His glower met hers, and he replied with a steady voice, "No."

"You *liar!*" I screamed. "Tell her the truth, Carter. You at least owe me that much."

"I am telling the truth." Again, his stare never left his mother's, but he slipped a shaking hand into his pocket.

"I've heard enough." Mrs. Lambert spun around to glare at my mother. "I am truly sorry for Andie's misfortune, but I'm not going to allow her to take my son down with her. Let's go, Carter." She grabbed his arm and pushed him toward the door. He yanked it open. The two of them disappeared into the hall, getting swallowed up in the crowd.

I stared after him, unblinking. Mom hugged me, and I shook in her arms. "He's lying, Mommy. He's lying." Tears caught in my throat.

Mom stroked the ends of my hair. "I know, honey. We'll figure something out. I promise."

Unable to hold it in any longer, I cried.

Sunday night's sleep was restless, and I awoke the next morning with dark circles around my eyes. *Great. I look like a freaking raccoon.* Determined to prove to Carter that he meant nothing to me anymore, that all he was doing was hurting himself by denying his soon-to-be child, I applied makeup liberally and took my time styling my hair. Again, what I wouldn't give to look like my mother. At least she constantly had color in her face.

When I went downstairs, though, Mom wasn't dressed for work. Instead, she was on the phone in her pajamas. I caught the tail end of the conversation.

"Yes, thank you. We'll be there at ten o'clock sharp. You too." Mom hung up and jumped when she saw me standing there. "Sorry, honey, but you're not going to school today."

"What? Why?"

"Because my OB/GYN was able to squeeze you in this morning, and you're overdue for a first appointment. Go change into something more comfortable, and we'll grab breakfast on the way."

I sighed. So much for proving to Carter that he couldn't hurt me.

A short while later, after stopping at one of the local diners for food—and discovering that the baby didn't like onions at all—Mom and I reached the doctor's office at 9:30. She filled out basic paperwork on my behalf, asking me questions when she didn't know an answer. Like what symptoms I was experiencing. I hated telling her about *that* kind of stuff, but then I remembered that she'd done this before. Birthing babies. So, I tried to relax.

Until I was taken back to one of the rooms and told to strip naked and throw on a gown that felt like a see-through curtain.

After having blood drawn and undergoing a series of awkward tests that were sure to give me nightmares for weeks, Dr. Brandt prepared for my final test. The one I wished I could flee from like the Roadrunner.

"All right. Let's see if we can hear the heartbeat," she said. "Do you want me to get your mom for this?"

I shook my head emphatically, my palms sweating. Dr. Brandt had already explained my first ultrasound was going to be done differently. As in something being stuck *up there*. I did *not* want my mother to be here for that. Why couldn't Dr. Brandt just throw sticky slime on my belly and be done with it?

"Okay, that's fine. We'll tell her all about it afterward." She smiled, and I ached to grab the pillow from under my head and cover my face. But then she started the test, and a very quiet, almost inaudible *whoosh-whoosh* came out of her machine.

My breath caught in my throat.

"There it is." Dr. Brandt's smile grew.

Blood rushed into my cheeks. Emotion flooded me—amazement, fear, shame, sadness . . . maybe even love. I bit my tongue, hard.

"Well, everything looks good," she said when the exam was finished. "I do want to see you once a month, though. Your young age and small size are enough for me to want to monitor you closely. But after today, I'd say we're heading in a good direction. I'll let you get dressed. If you have any questions, please don't hesitate to call the office, okay?"

I nodded, and Dr. Brandt left the room. Bringing my knees up to my chin, I wrapped my arms around my legs and smiled. A small flutter of hope tickled my chest. Maybe it was a good thing I'd walked away from the clinic, after all.

CHAPTER 11

On our way home, Mom took me for ice cream, just like she had for years after every bad day of school. At some point, I'd started to think mother-daughter dates were uncool and worried about getting fat, so we quit going. But today, when I asked her to stop, it was like I'd handed her the keys to Heaven. She glowed. Mother and daughter reunited at the ice cream parlor.

At 8:00 p.m., after hours of homework and cheesy TV shows to keep my brain preoccupied, Mom joined me in the living room and looked at me like she was afraid I'd turn into a pumpkin.

"What?" I asked.

Mom fidgeted with her nails. "Well, honey, I've been thinking. There's nothing we can do about Carter without getting lawyers involved, and we can't really afford to do that right now. Evelyn refuses to let Carter even take a paternity test."

I nodded, swallowing deeply. I'd known since the beginning that Carter would never budge. One of the hardest things I had to do was give up hope that he'd change his mind. But I had to come to terms with it. Especially after hearing the heartbeat today. With help or on my own, I didn't care. Either way, I would keep my baby.

Mom continued, "So, I was thinking that maybe it'd be a good idea to meet with a few couples. We could talk with someone from family services—"

My body went cold. "Wait, what? You want me to speak with an adoption agency?"

"Honey, you can't do this on your own. I've been a single parent for the last two years; I know how hard it is."

I jumped up. "No! I'm keeping it, Mom. It's my baby!"

"Andrea—"

"No. Don't tell me to put it up for adoption. This is my decision to make."

She spoke softly. "Think about the baby. There are plenty of couples out there who can't have children of their own and are better equipped to be parents."

I narrowed my eyes. "You don't think I'm capable of being a mother?"

"That's *not* what I said. But you have to think about your future. Do you really think you can take on raising a baby while finishing high school and planning for college and a career?"

"I don't have to go to college. I can get a job after high school."

She shook her head. "Oh, Andrea . . . ."

"No one will love my baby as much as me! I'm its mother."

Mom raised a hand. "Now, that's not true. From the moment a baby is placed in your arms, it doesn't matter if you gave birth to it or not. You still love it like it's your own."

I put a hand on my hip. "How would you know? I am your own."

Mom sat back, paling. Her lips pressed into a tight line, and she stared at me with a look I knew too well—she was hiding something.

My pulse raced. The room filled with suffocating tension. I sucked in a quick breath. "I *am* yours, right?"

Mom's eyes glassed over. "I'm sorry, sweetie. I was going to tell you when you were older—"

"*Oh my God!*" I screamed, clenching my hands into fists. "When I was older? Are you serious? What's wrong with you?"

Mom stood and reached out for me, but I backed away, sweeping an arm in front of me.

"Don't touch me. How could you keep something like that from me? I had a right to know I'm *adopted*."

"Andie, your dad and I tried for six years, and when it didn't happen for us—"

"No, I don't want to hear it." I shook my head, my cheeks on fire. "You never should've kept that from me. *Never.*" Marching out of the room, I grabbed my cell phone out of my purse and ran for the front door.

"Where are you going?" Mom called, chasing after me.

"Outside. Is that okay? Or do I need to be older before I can walk around the block, too?" I stared her down, too angry to care about the tear falling from her eye.

I knew I didn't look like either of my parents. How had I not put the pieces together? God, I was such a fool, always telling Carter and Heather to shut up when they called me the milkman's kid. They were right all along. I was just an orphan. Abandoned for someone else to deal with. Unwanted.

Without waiting for a response, I yanked the front door open and then slammed it behind me. But as soon as the cool fall air hit my face, I decided I wasn't just going around the block.

I was getting as far away from this place as I could.

And I walked until my feet ached. When I left, I was too upset to think about shoes, then too sad to turn around and go back. So I kept going, hands clenched and nostrils flaring, hating the parents who'd abandoned me and the parents who'd lied to me.

I found myself in the middle of town, past Donaldson Park, in the more populated area, full of restaurants and shops. I passed the Mini Mart, and my heart panged. Days had passed since I spoke to Neil. Was he worried about me when I didn't show up at school today?

I yelped as a throbbing wave of pain shot up my leg. Stopping, I lifted my foot. My soles were raw and bloodied. *Just great*. My trek through River Springs was over.

I limped to a bench, screaming through closed lips with every step I took. I pulled my cell phone out of my pajama pocket.

Neil answered on the third ring. Lots of noise carried from his side, like he was at some sort of party. "Hey, can I call you later? I'm kind of in the middle of something."

Owen shouted in the background.

After walking for an hour without shedding a tear, Neil's flippant hello was all it took. I unraveled. He'd said I could call him for anything, and after he opened up and showed me a piece of his life he'd shown barely anyone else, I thought, just maybe, he'd be there for me like he said he would.

Guess not.

"Whoa, what's wrong?" he asked.

"Never mind. I'm sorry I bothered you."

I was about to end the call when he shouted, "No, no! Don't hang up. I'm sorry. Talk to me. What's going on?"

After another sob, I squeaked out, "I ran away."

"Wait, what? Where are you?"

"By the Mini Mart." I sniffled.

"Okay, I'm coming to get you. Stay there."

I nodded, as if he could hear me, then hung up. Ten minutes later, he parked his truck next to the sidewalk. Neil jumped out and ran to me.

He brushed my hair out of my face and held my cheeks in his palms. "Are you all right?"

I shook my head and tried to speak. I wasn't crying anymore, and I didn't want to jinx it.

"Are you hurt?" he asked.

Nodding, I turned over a foot.

"Why aren't you wearing shoes? Wait, don't tell me. An elf asked to borrow them but ran off without giving them back?"

I laughed. "That doesn't even make sense."

"Got you to smile, though, didn't it?" He grinned, the corners of his eyes creasing.

Without thinking, I leaned forward and kissed him. Fireworks exploded on my lips, and an almost-silent whimper escaped me. Then Neil gently pushed me away, and reality smacked me across the face. *Oh crap. Idiot, idiot, idiot.* I covered my mouth, my chest constricting.

"I'm so sorry. I don't know what I was thinking. I shouldn't have done that—kissed you, I mean," I rambled.

Neil smirked. "I think you're loopy. Come on." He snuck one arm behind my shoulders, the other under my knees, and lifted me off the bench.

I wrapped an arm around the back of his neck and clung to him as he carried me to the truck.

"I'm going to take you home, okay?" he said when he climbed into the driver's seat.

I gripped the door handle, prepared to jump out if I needed to. "No, please. Take me to your house, or Owen's, or anywhere. I don't want to go home."

Neil pressed his lips into a thin line, and then he turned in his seat, gripping the steering wheel, and stared through the windshield. His knuckles whitened. Why did he not want me to go somewhere with him?

He started the truck with a sigh. "All right. Owen's isn't happening. It's a madhouse over there. But let me make sure Mom's asleep before I bring you inside mine." With a frown, he drove away from the Mini Mart.

CHAPTER 12

I leaned against the car door, staring through the window at the starry sky. Neil drove through the rest of downtown River Springs and into the forest-covered mountains where his house sat tucked away. Soft music played from the radio, and as we pulled into his hidden drive, I turned to look at him. He was still staring straight ahead, his posture rigid. He'd said his mom had a problem with alcohol the last time we were here. Was that why he'd hesitated?

When we reached the house, he shut down the engine and paused before glancing at me out of the corner of his eye. "I'll be right back."

He pushed the truck's door open and half-jogged inside.

I waited in the dark truck for a good ten minutes. The trees surrounding Neil's house blocked out almost all the starlight. My feet burned, and I adjusted my position a few times to try to get the throbbing to stop. No luck. My heart raced. What was taking him so long?

The front porch light flicked on, and I sat up straighter in my seat. Neil rushed out of the house, and I relaxed—until he opened my truck door. A flaming red handprint glowed on his cheek.

I touched his face. "Oh my God. Did your—?"

"I'm fine." He slipped an arm behind my back and the other under my knees, just like he had when he picked me up the first time.

"Neil—"

"*I'm fine.*" He pulled me out of the truck and then kicked the door closed. With my arm around his neck, he carried me into the house, through the foyer, and up the stairs. Like the rest of the rejuvenated rooms, the second story was in good shape, its Victorian design kept intact. Neil took me to a room at the end of the hall and pushed the door open with his back.

A queen-sized bed, made of dark wood, rested under a window on the far side of the room. A navy blue comforter covered the mattress. Straight across from where we'd entered, a keyboard was positioned next to a guitar, and on the wall opposite his bed hung a poster of John Lennon. I knew Neil could sing—I'd heard him in the truck the day he took me to the zoo—but I never would've guessed music was his passion.

My pulse quickened as I glimpsed another piece of the real Neil. The guy who would run out into the night for a pregnant girl he once dated. The guy who took care of his mother, even though she hit him. The guy who put on a façade so people wouldn't see the pain he went through every day. I leaned into him, my chest fluttering. Unwillingly, I was falling for him all over again. *Crap.*

Neil sat me on the bed, and I winced when my raw heels touched the fabric. "Sorry," he said. "Make yourself at home. But, you know, don't claim a drawer or anything."

I rolled my eyes, then he left the room, and a light switched on farther down the hall.

A dark dresser that matched his bed was pressed against the right wall of the room. There wasn't much on the dresser except for a trophy and a picture—a young boy with dark hair, on a boat, a fishing rod in his hand. An older man sat next to him, almost identical to the boy. My throat cramped. Neil couldn't have been older than six or seven in the picture. Was this the last one taken of his dad before he died?

Neil returned seconds later with arms full of medical supplies and dropped them on the bed.

"I'm guessing you know what you're doing?" I asked.

"Unfortunately. Can't tell you how many times I've had to patch up Mom. I'd make one hell of a plastic surgeon by now." He sat on the other end of the bed, near my feet, and crossed one leg under the other.

I frowned. He'd been taking care of people his whole life. And I was adding myself to the list. "I'm sorry."

"Why? Plastic surgeons make really good money."

"You know that's not what I meant."

A corner of his mouth rose as he pushed up my pant legs. He lifted my more-injured foot onto his knee, and his fingertips lingered on my ankle. My skin tingled under his touch. He swallowed, not meeting my gaze, then bent back my big toe. I yelped.

"Sorry," he said. "I'm going to have to clean your foot. You going to be okay?"

When I nodded, he drenched a cotton ball with rubbing alcohol. "You might want to grab a pillow."

I raised an eyebrow.

"It sometimes helps if you have something to squeeze." He shrugged, holding the cotton ball in his right hand, and grabbed a towel with his left. "Okay, this is going to hurt. I'm gonna count down from three. Ready?" When I nodded, he started his count. "Three, two—"

I clutched the pillow to my face to muffle my shriek as Neil not so gently scrubbed the bottom of my foot. I bit down hard, stifling another shout as burning pain rolled down my leg with each stroke, then finally soft fabric pressed against my sole as Neil delicately held the towel to my foot. Warmth radiated from his palm through the cloth, easing the burn the rubbing alcohol had left behind. I took the moment to breathe.

After wrapping my foot in gauze, Neil rested his fingertips on my other ankle. His light touch sent a chill up my spine, even though the foot he'd cleaned still felt like it had stepped on hot coals.

Beneath the pillow—thank God—my cheeks warmed as he lifted my other foot to wipe down any spots I'd rubbed raw from my bare-foot, miles-long trek. Again, intense heat spread from the sole of my foot into my hip, and I ground my teeth to keep from shouting in pain. He repeated the action with the towel then the gauze, and then stood and gathered the medical supplies.

"Next time, remember shoes," Neil commented before the sound of his footsteps left the room.

Uncovering my face, I leaned against the headboard and clutched the pillow to my torso as my stomach churned. This was so humiliating. I never should've called him.

Neil returned minutes later, carrying a glass of water and a medicine bottle in his hands. "You can take Tylenol, right?"

I nodded, and he plopped a couple pills onto my hand. Taking the cup, I swallowed the painkillers and finished off the liquid. Man, I was thirsty.

"You want more water?" he asked.

I shook my head. Neil set the cup and the medicine on his nightstand before sitting on the floor, his back against the table. With hands clasped in his lap and legs straight out in front of him, he leaned his head back and closed his eyes.

I wasted no time apologizing. "I'm sorry. Again. You shouldn't keep having to come save me."

"Just call me Sir Donaghue. Knight of the round table, slayer of dragons, saver of damsels in distress."

"Neil."

He smiled. "You're welcome."

I played with the hem of my shirt. Now was as good a time as any to bring up what happened—what I'd done—when he showed up to rescue me. "About the kiss—"

"Right. Well, on a scale of one to ten, I'd give it a seven."

"Neil!"

He smirked. "What about it?"

I bit my lip. "It was a mistake."

He opened his eyes and looked right into mine. "Was it?"

My breath quickened. His gaze was intense. No, I hadn't meant to kiss him. He said I was loopy, and I was. Right?

I turned away from him. "You play guitar?"

He didn't answer right away, and I silently begged him to respond. "Yeah. My dad taught me."

Looking at him, I expected to see pain on his face. But he'd closed his eyes and leaned his head against the nightstand again. I mimicked his position on the bed. Except I kept my eyes open, glancing around the room at all the pieces of Neil. The music falling off the stand behind the keyboard. A towel haphazardly tossed into a corner of the room. A dent in the wall that I guessed had been made with his fist. Was I one of the few people who'd been in here, who'd seen this side of him?

Not ready to let the conversation close up, I spoke in a quiet voice. "I always wanted to learn to play an instrument. Just never got around to it, you know?"

"I can teach you, if you want."

A soft smile crept onto my face. I would like that. A lot. But maybe later. I had too much on my mind. I wanted to forget that I was adopted, that I was pregnant, and relax.

"I'm pretty good, you know," he added. "You'd be learning from the best."

A corner of my mouth twitched. "Naturally, you'd think so."

Neil opened his eyes and smirked at me. "Hey, one day I'm going to get a business degree from Harvard and open my own studio. Just you watch."

Wow. Talk about ambition. "Fine then," I played along. "Prove how good you are. Play for me."

"Right now?"

"No, I asked because I wanted to hear myself talk. Yes, right now."

Sitting up straight, he laughed. "Wow. A witty comeback from you. That's a first. Guess I'm gonna have to."

After pushing himself off the floor, he grabbed his guitar and pulled the chair out from under his keyboard. He sat then stuck a pick in his mouth and thumbed one string after another while twisting the nobby-things at the top.

"It's not going to be in tune, but whatever. What do you want to hear?" he asked.

"I don't know. Anything."

Neil tuned the guitar strings for another few seconds, pulled the pick from his mouth, and then began to strum with his right hand. The fingers on his left moved like lightning as he played random notes, then he moved into chords. He looked up at me with a smirk and started to sing, "This is a song that I made up. You said anything. So I made it up."

I laughed. "Play something I'd know."

Neil's smirk softened. His gaze fell to the strings. A familiar melody rang out from the guitar, and, at first, I couldn't place it. Then Neil started to sing, and by the end of the first line, I knew what I was listening to: "Hallelujah."

I leaned my head back and shut my eyes. Neil's voice was one of the best I'd heard in a long time. A deep, smooth tenor. I knew he was good when he sang in the truck, but he was goofing around. Now, goosebumps rose on my skin, and, soon, I was squeezing the pillow like it was a tube of toothpaste on its last drop. Neil's emotion rang through with every note he played. He sang each lyric like the song belonged to him. He hadn't picked the tune randomly.

Would my baby be able to play like this? Maybe when I was older and had a bad day, would my son or daughter say, "Mom, I love you; let me play you a song because I know how much it calms you."

When Neil played the last note, I kept my eyes closed and grasped the pillow a bit tighter, my hands clammy.

"That bad, huh? Must've lost my touch," Neil said.

I shook my head. "No, that was beautiful." My voice broke on the last word, but I held in the tears. Pregnancy hormones really, really sucked.

The guitar made a *clink*, then I tipped sideways as Neil sat next to me on the bed. He slid his arm around my shoulders and pulled me close. Normally, I'd tell myself this was a bad, bad idea, but, right now, the closeness was comforting, and even Neil's normal musk of soap and cigarettes—a smell that, at first, had annoyed me—was soothing.

"I heard the heartbeat today." I couldn't avoid telling him about my day any longer.

He stroked my arm with his thumb. "So it *is* human."

I snapped my head up, scowling at him.

"I'm kidding." He smiled softly. "I bet that was intense."

Sitting as close as we were, every speck of color in his irises glistened. Not only was the blue speckled with silver, but around the edges, the shade deepened to the color of the night sky. Tingles ran down my legs, and I slid out of his hold. Warmth flooded my cheeks, and I tucked my hair behind my ears.

"Yeah," I replied to his comment, avoiding eye contact. At least I didn't feel like crying anymore.

"Is that why I found you barefoot and in pajamas in front of the Mini Mart?"

My cheeks burned hotter. I was wearing pajamas, wasn't I? And no bra. I squeezed the pillow to my chest. *Idiot.* "No, that's not why."

"Well, look, I was going to wait until you were ready to tell me. But I have to ask: What's going on?"

I bit my bottom lip, replaying tonight's revelation in my mind. Heat flushed in my gut again, and when I spoke, my words were coated with anger. "I'm adopted."

Neil slightly tipped his head. "So?"

"So, my mom waited until tonight to tell me."

"Oh. Well, she does have really poor timing."

I glared at him. "That's all you have to say?"

Neil scrunched his eyebrows. "What do you want me to say?"

"I don't know. Like, maybe, 'I'm sorry,' or, 'yeah, your mom sucks.'" I chucked the pillow to the floor.

"Okay. I'm sorry."

I rolled my eyes. "Yeah, well, now I know you don't mean it."

Neil leaned against the headboard and ran both hands down his face. "You know, sometimes you can be so aggravating."

"*Me?* What about you? You're always spouting off some joke right and left when, sometimes, I just want to hear some honesty or sincerity from you."

He turned to me. "Okay, fine. You want honesty? Here's some: So what if you're adopted? The only parent I have left doesn't give a shit about me. Your mom loves you, and you have at least one other biological parent who loved you enough to give you a chance at life. Be thankful for what you have, because some of us don't have the luxury."

My mouth fell open. Sure, I'd asked for honesty, but did he have to be so blunt about it? The worst part was he was right. Although I felt abandoned and lied to, I still felt loved. And here I was complaining to *him*, of all people. God, I was such a fool. A selfish, egocentric fool.

I turned away as my eyes watered.

Neil swore. "See, this is why I pick humor."

I shook my head. "No, you're right. I'm being a whiny bitch."

"Hey, look at that. Andie said a bad word."

I couldn't help but smile the moment I caught sight of the lopsided grin on his face. Sometimes, maybe humor was the way to go.

"I should probably let Mom know I'm okay, shouldn't I?" I asked.

"Probably."

"Will you take me home?"

"Anytime, Princess."

When he smirked, I rolled my eyes and jumped off the bed. Five minutes later, we pulled out of his driveway. The clock in the truck read 2:00 a.m. Man, I was going to have a lot of groveling and explaining to do.

CHAPTER 13

The lights were still on in the house when we pulled up. At least there weren't cop cars in the driveway. Not that I'd be shocked if someone had called them.

Neil grabbed my hand. "I can come in with you."

I shook my head, watching the front window for any sign Mom saw us. I'd made Neil turn off his headlights, but I couldn't be too sure. Knowing her, she'd checked the front yard for signs of me every five minutes.

"No, I don't want you to get dragged into this," I said. "She's going to be mad enough that you didn't bring me home when you found me."

"Well, just as long as she doesn't keep me from seeing you again."

His expression was bright and unwavering. Hopeful. My stomach knotted. "Neil—"

He squeezed my hand. "We'll talk later. Have a good night."

I nodded, frowning. When he let go of my hand, I climbed out of the truck. Each step felt like walking on porcupine needles. It was a good distraction from the gnawing pain in my chest.

In my condition, was I wrong to want to get close to someone? Carter's mom said she wouldn't let her son go down with me. If I didn't squash the feelings cropping up for Neil, would I take him down too?

I couldn't call him again. He deserved so much more. My eyes burned. *Never thought I'd say that.*

The front door was unlocked when I pushed the handle. I stepped inside and breathed in the burnt vanilla scent of Mom's reed diffusers. Footsteps pounded above me as soon as I closed the door.

"Andie?" Mom peeked her head over the railing of the landing overlooking the foyer. Seeing me, she burst into tears and sprinted down the stairs, enveloping me in her arms.

"I'm sorry," I said, hugging her. The sweet smell of her ocean-breeze shampoo filled my nose, and my throat tightened. I never should've left the house.

Mom stepped back and brushed hair from my face. "Please tell me nothing happened."

"Nothing happened. I walked to the Mini Mart and called a friend to pick me up."

She nodded, wiping a tear from her cheek. "Normally, I'd be angry you didn't come right home, but I'm just glad you're okay." Mom put an arm around my shoulders. "What do you say we talk about this more tomorrow?"

I nodded. Now that I was here, exhaustion was setting in. I would've passed out in the middle of a conversation anyway. Between all the walking and the crying, I didn't have energy left to even be mad at her.

I leaned into her as she led me upstairs and didn't even notice the pain in my feet. I passed out as soon as my head hit the pillow. And I didn't wake up again until after suppertime, hungry as a bear after hibernating. I stuffed my face and apologized to Mom, promising that I wasn't naïve when it came to the baby and would start searching for a part-time job. Then I sat on the couch and watched sitcoms with her until I fell asleep. Next thing I knew, the clock above the TV read 4:00 a.m.

Mom wouldn't be awake for at least another hour, so I winced my way to the bathroom—I could feel my feet again—and took my time in the shower. I washed off all the grime of the last two days then wrapped a towel around my waist and finished my beauty routine before returning to my room. There, I pulled out my uniform, determined to return to school. I'd missed a week and a half already, and I couldn't take another moment of being holed up in the house.

Pulling my shirt on first, I groaned when it barely fit across my boobs. Had they really grown that much? My breathing hitched. Would my skirt fit?

Turning sideways in front of the floor-length mirror, I lifted the bottom of my shirt and placed a hand on my abs. They weren't as flat as I remembered, but maybe I was being paranoid. There was only one way to tell for sure: I grabbed my skirt and stepped into it.

Holding my breath, I zipped up the side and let out a sigh of relief. It was a little snug, but it wasn't popping at the seams. Maybe that was a good sign for how the day was going to go. My classmates had to be used to the idea of me being pregnant by now. Right?

I stuck my face in a book until Mom's bedroom door opened. *Finally.* Picking up my blow dryer, I styled my hair in long, loose curls, like I would any other day. Then I took my time with my makeup until I was positive I could prove to my classmates that I still belonged at River Springs Prep.

I joined Mom in the kitchen ten minutes before I had to leave.

"Honey, please don't tell me you're going to school," she said. *Not too often you hear that from a parent.* "What about homeschool?"

"I don't want to give up on River Springs if I can help it."

Mom stared at me. I shot her a stop-pestering-me look and crossed my arms.

"All right." She broke. "But if it gets to be too much, you'll finish out this year at home and go back next fall." She handed me a peanut butter and jelly sandwich and a banana.

I ate my breakfast like some genie made the food go *poof* off my plate, stuffed my purse with granola bars, and then raced down the street to catch the bus. As soon as I climbed in, I searched for Jill. Since I'd missed the last three days of school, I hadn't yet followed through on my promise to eat lunch with her. I sighed, thankful she was sitting alone and that she didn't glare at me. I slid into the seat next to her.

"I'm sorry I didn't eat with you on Thursday," I said.

Jill shrugged. "I know you left early. It wasn't like you could be two places at once." Her brown eyes widened, playful. "*Can* you be two places at once?"

"I wish. It'd be nice to get my education without really being here."

"If I could ace my tests from the Eiffel Tower, I'd never come home."

I smiled. "Paris would be pretty cool."

We talked the rest of the ride, not about school or babies but about our interests, what we had in common. Jill was super smart—almost rocket-scientist smart—and totally nerdy. For at least five minutes, she went on about *Star Trek* until I admitted I'd never watched the show. Which, of course, got me a gaping mouth and a promise to be nerdi-fied. Not that I'd mind. It'd be nice to talk about something other than shoes, clothes, and the latest gossip on who was hooking up with whom.

By the time we reached school, I felt like I could take on the world. If only I'd known Jill Anderson sooner. She seemed like the kind of person who was real twenty-four/seven. Not to mention, she was super nice. And I needed that.

Jill and I parted as soon as we entered the building. I dodged snickers and snide smiles the whole way to my locker. Only one person tossed me a, "'Sup, Virgin Mary?" to which I shoved my book bag higher on my shoulder and mentally flipped him off. No one was going to ruin my day.

When I reached my locker, Neil leaned against its door, eyebrows furrowed. As soon as he saw me, he sighed before straightening up and stepping out of the way.

"I'm guessing I shouldn't say good morning?" I turned the lock.

"No, probably not. I was hoping you wouldn't come back."

My knees weakened. Had I misinterpreted everything Monday

night? Forcing my voice to stay steady, I replied, "Wow. Nice to know you've got my back."

Neil moved in closer so he could whisper, "You know that's not what I meant."

With my books in my arms, I slammed my locker door closed. "I'm tired of hiding. All I want to do is go to class and pretend, for once, that my shot at med school hasn't gone down the toilet." I stormed away from him without waiting for a response.

Of course, he matched my stride. Sometimes, it really sucked to have short legs.

"Hey, I'm just trying to look out for you," he said. "You know how people are here. Besides rich and obnoxious."

"I'm perfectly capable of ignoring them."

"Andie—"

I stopped and glared at him. "I'm staying."

He raised his hands. "Fine. But promise me you'll text if anything gets out of hand."

With a roll of my eyes, I marched down the hall to English. Although I appreciated his concern, I *could* take care of myself. It was time I stopped calling Neil to rescue me.

I glanced over my shoulder and found him still following me. "I can walk myself to class, you know."

"Do you see me holding a leash? I'm in your class, Princess. It's usually where I take my morning nap, remember?"

Oh. Right. I forgot Neil was a senior—and that he had a knack for the subject, much to my initial chagrin.

We entered the classroom and parted ways, Neil to the back where he could sleep and me to a desk toward the front of the room. Three minutes later, the rest of our classmates filed in.

Heather's perfume hit me first. I glanced up from my notebook to find her staring wide-eyed at me. She hadn't expected me to come back either. Then her gaze turned wicked, and I could practically read her thoughts: *How dare you think you can come back and pretend like nothing happened? Backstabbers get what they deserve!*

I slunk down in my seat, Heather's features blurring behind my teary gaze. Heat ran up the back of my neck, and I breathed slowly, trying to keep myself under control. As if she wanted to make the scene as awkward as possible, Heather mumbled, "Whore," as she sauntered past me, her heels clicking on the floor. I gripped my pen tighter, fighting the urge to jump out of my seat and flee.

My cell phone buzzed in my purse. With shaking hands, I drew it from the bag and tapped on the message Neil had sent me: *You got this. Don't let that bitch ruin your mojo.*

I took a deep breath and swallowed my tears as the final bell rang. He was right. I was stronger than this. Screw Heather.

Mr. Bingham shuffled to the front of the room. "Your test on *Of Mice and Men* is tomorrow. Make sure to ask any questions you have on the material today, or you're out of luck."

"How many essay questions are there going to be?" someone asked.

"Two. There are always two questions. Anyone else?"

The room was quiet for a full thirty seconds. Then, as Mr. Bingham turned to write on the whiteboard, someone shouted, "I have a question!"

I turned in my chair as a cold wave chilled me from head to toe. The person speaking was Gwen, Beth's mini-me.

"You said one of the main themes of the book is oppression, right? Well, what if people oppress others, not because they want to look powerful but because they're afraid?"

"I suppose. What would the characters have been afraid of?" Mr. Bingham asked.

Gwen shrugged. "Maybe they were afraid their soul would go to Hell for associating with the wrong kind of people." She stared right at me, a smug look on her face.

"Your soul's already damned, Freeman. Too many blowjobs. I would know," Neil said.

The class burst out in laughter.

Gwen spun in her seat, her cheeks red. "I did not—"

"Mr. Donaghue, I will not tolerate that kind of language in my classroom. You can see me after class for your detention slip," Mr.

Bingham interrupted. "Quiet down, everyone. As for your question, Miss Freeman, if that's what you gathered from the novel, then that's your prerogative. I'll expect to read more about it on your exam. Now, let's move on to . . ."

I tuned out the rest of Mr. Bingham's speech. Instead, I focused on putting Gwen's and Heather's comments out of my head. *I can handle this.* Eventually, they'd get tired, or people would simply stop caring. Either way, things would get better. And I was strong. They couldn't hurt me unless I let them.

CHAPTER 14

The rest of the morning went by without much of a problem. I'd still gotten jeers in the halls, and people were obviously whispering about me in my classes. But no one else had tried anything like Gwen or Heather. Twice, I'd caught Neil's worried stares when we passed each other in the hall, but all I had to do was smile, and he'd continue on his merry way.

After purchasing a salad and bottled water from the cafeteria, I met Jill in the quad outside. It was October, and the air was chilly, but the sun was shining. Time to soak up as many good days as I could before the snow hit.

"Don't tell me you're one of those vegan people," Jill said, biting into a turkey sandwich.

I covered my mouth and nose, remembering how I'd reacted the last time I'd tasted—and smelled—lunch meat. "No, but your sandwich *is* going to make me sick."

She looked at her food then back at me. She shrugged and tossed the meal into its plastic bag. "There. All gone. I do have chips, though. I can eat them, right?"

I smiled. Heather never would've put her sandwich away; she

BECAUSE I LOVE YOU

would've asked *me* to move farther away from *it*. "Yes, I can handle the chips."

Neil watched me from his usual table across the courtyard. I made a face at him that, I hoped, said, *I'm fine. Stop babying me.* He smirked and turned away to chat with Owen.

"Is he the baby's dad?" Jill asked.

My head snapped around. "Who—*Neil?* No. Definitely not."

She shrugged. "What? He'd have really good genes."

I raised an eyebrow. Was she the only girl in the entire school who didn't know about his reputation? "How are you not telling me to stay far, far away from him?"

"Please, the only guys who score a lot of game don't talk about the game, because they're smart enough to know that most girls won't do the touchdown dance if they're number thirty."

I burst out laughing. To have someone put sex in *those* terms was hilarious. "Seriously, Jill? You're going to make me pee."

"I have another one. Most girls won't ride the Millennium Falcon if they know they're number thirty."

My nose scrunched. "The what?"

Jill sighed and shook her head. "We seriously have some work to do in your nerd department."

At that moment, the cheerleading squad entered the courtyard. Beth, Gwen, Heather, and April glanced at me then whispered and giggled while Monica shushed them. My shoulders dropped as I flicked away my gaze.

"Here." Jill held out a Hershey bar. "Chocolate will make you feel better."

I forced a smile. "Thanks, but I'm okay." Could I have the chocolate, anyway?

She dropped the candy in front of me. "In case you change your mind."

I rolled my eyes and stuck the chocolate bar in my purse as she launched into talking about the latest fantasy movie coming out around Christmas. But the pain of Heather's continued dismissal lingered, and, soon, I had no appetite for my food.

Walking into the chem lab after lunch, I parted ways with Jill and grabbed my assigned seat in the middle of the classroom. Beth and Gwen filed in minutes later, eyeing me, smirks growing on their faces. My stomach flipped, and I took a deep breath. *Just get through the double period. There's a teacher. Nothing can happen to you.*

When the final bell rang, Dr. Fitzgerald turned off the lights. We were one of the few schools in Colorado privileged enough to have a high school chemistry teacher with a PhD—one of the many reasons I loved this class so much.

"All right," she said. "As I told you yesterday, today's video is on anabolic and catabolic reactions. There will be a test covering this, so make sure you're paying close attention."

I opened my notebook.

Dr. Fitzgerald pulled down the projector screen and pressed a button on her remote. The movie came to life, and I jotted the date on the top of my paper as the opening credits rolled. I relaxed, listening to the narrator give a brief overview of the video—then from the movie, a woman screamed at the top of her lungs. I shot my gaze to the screen.

We were in a birthing room where a woman continued to scream as if someone were ripping her apart. And you could see everything. *Everything.* I gripped the edge of my science table as cold sweat beaded on my forehead. Classmates stared. Beth sneered. Dr. Fitzgerald scrambled to her computer as laughter filled the room.

Then, the worst happened—someone had gone in and pasted a picture of my face over the woman's. The room spun.

"Push, Andie, push!" a voice yelled from the projector's speakers.

"It's a virgin baby!" another said.

Yet another shouted, "No, it's a demon!"

I was glued to my chair, my breathing labored. Sobs caught in my throat.

"Someone get Andie out of here!" Dr. Fitzgerald yelled. "And does anyone know how to work this thing?"

A hand touched my back. "Come on," Jill said. "I'll come back for your stuff." She slipped her hand into mine and yanked me from my chair, dragging me out of the classroom.

My feet felt like they were drenched in cement, weighing me to the floor. By the time we reached the hall, I shook like I'd awoken from centuries of being frozen in ice.

Someone shouting my name caught me off guard. Ears ringing, I didn't recognize the voice. I turned. Neil ran at me, his face pale.

"What happened?" he asked, putting his hands on my shoulders.

"I'd bet my whole bank account *your sister* is what happened," Jill replied, her voice seething with rage. "Someone switched Dr. Fitzgerald's video to some lady giving birth, vagina and all. *And* they taped voices over it. Did you know what people were planning to do? Is that why you were waiting out here?"

"I overheard something about chemistry, but that was it. Beth doesn't live at home. Damn it, she's shaking. Andie, talk to me."

"She's in shock, pea brain," Jill said.

Carter's voice filled the hall. "Andie? Hey, what happened to her?"

That was all it took to send me over the edge. My former best friend—my baby's dad—swooping in, trying to rescue me, when he'd been nothing but a cold, heartless dick.

I snapped, lunging at him when he got close and scratching his face with my nails. "You *asshole!* You left me to fend for myself, you worthless piece of shit. I'm going to kill you. *I'm going to kill you!*" Strong arms wrapped around me from behind, yanking me away from a wide-eyed Carter.

"Andie, calm down!" Neil yelled, but I kept screaming, fighting to get out of his arms so I could pummel my ex-best friend.

"Let me go!" I screamed.

"Lambert, get out of here," Neil said.

Carter took off, his hand pressed to his bloodied cheek.

By now, students were flooding the halls, anxious to see what was going down. A couple of the teachers moved toward us, as if thinking they needed to break up a fight. But Neil had already beaten them to the punch.

"Andie," he whispered in my ear, "it's over. Let me take you home. You're safe now."

If it wasn't for Neil holding me, I would've sunk to the ground. A loud, weeping moan rolled through me, and I curled over Neil's arms, clutching at my neck. With a groan, he straightened me and turned me around. My hands on his chest, I melted into him, wishing I could disappear. I buried my face in his shirt and bawled.

"Nothing to see here," he said. "Get lost, people."

Feet shuffled, and the hall filled with the rolling sound of a train on its track. A third hand touched the back of my head, and fingertips combed through my hair.

"I'm going to get her stuff," Jill said. "And I'm coming with you. Give me a minute."

Neil must've nodded because Jill's hand disappeared. His arms tightened around me, and his cheek rested on the top of my head. For minutes, we stood there, Neil silent while I cried until my abs ached and my lungs burned.

"Andie, you need to breathe," Neil said into my hair.

Listening to his steady heartbeat, I tried to mimic his breathing as his chest rose and fell under my palms. Soon, my throat relaxed and my stomach calmed. I pulled back from him with a sniffle.

"Sorry," I said, unable to look at him.

He wiped the tears from my cheeks. "Don't apologize. I take it Lambert's the dad."

I frowned. "Yeah."

"Was he any good?"

I glared at him, open-mouthed. *Did he really just ask me that?*

Neil smirked. "Welcome back."

I rolled my eyes as Jill appeared next to me, breathing heavily. "Okay, I think I got everything." She handed me my purse and book bag. "Sorry, I had to break into your locker. Well, I didn't really break in. But I thought you'd want your books, so I didn't think you'd mind—"

"Thank you," I replied. "And I probably shouldn't be surprised that you can crack a combination lock."

Jill blushed and shrugged. "It's easy, actually."

"Noted," Neil interjected. "Now, let's go before the bell rings and my sister finds us. I might wring her neck, and I really don't feel like going to prison." He turned and headed for the exit.

Jill and I had to jog to keep up.

"Um, don't you want to stop at your locker?" Jill asked Neil. "I mean, not that it's any of my business, but you should probably grab your books so you don't fall behind."

Neil smirked. "That's not a problem."

"Why? Did you steal the teachers' tests?"

He laughed and tapped his head. "I take pictures with my brain. No cheating necessary."

"So, that's why you sleep in class," I said.

"Yep. Gotta catch up on my beauty sleep. It isn't easy looking like me." He winked.

Jill shot me a look that read, *Is he always like this?* Though my heart still felt like someone had rung it dry, I couldn't help but smile as we left the building.

The house was empty when we got there. Jill dropped her stuff on the kitchen floor while Neil went for the fridge. *Guess he doesn't have a problem making himself at home.*

"Got anything to eat?" he asked, staring at the well-stocked insides.

"Didn't you just have lunch?" Jill asked.

"Nope. Evil sister took my last five bucks." He grabbed a bag of pepperoni and started munching.

"There's a pantry next to the fridge if you want chips or cookies or whatever," I said, dropping my book bag and purse next to Jill's as I wandered to the living room. I plopped on the couch and flicked on the TV. Anything to keep my mind off school.

Mom was right. I never should've gone back.

Jill joined me in the living room, followed seconds later by Neil who'd found a box of Oreos and a glass of milk. I should've offered to make him something healthier. He cozied into the recliner with an enthusiastic sigh.

The three of us sat, watching over-acted soap operas, for what felt like hours. Neil, of course, took every opportunity to comment on whose boobs were real and tried to take bets on how many of the actresses had nose jobs. Jill laughed at nearly everything that popped out of his mouth, which, naturally, fueled his narcissism. Soon, he moved into his ridiculous jokes, like the ones he'd used on me at the zoo. Jill hung on his every word until my throat burned and my jaw ached from clenching my teeth. They were flirting. Right in front of me.

Which shouldn't bother me. Neil and I were just friends.

Then why did my chest hurt so much, seeing the way his eyes crinkled as he laughed with her—the same way he used to laugh with me?

I jumped off the couch, startling them both. Neil watched me, an eyebrow raised.

"I'm going to . . . go." I turned and marched down the hall to the foyer before slipping my feet into tennis shoes.

"I'm confused. Isn't this your house?" Neil asked.

I jumped slightly, surprised he'd followed me. He'd looked pretty engrossed in little Miss Doe-eyes over there.

"No." *Crap.* I'd answered automatically, thinking he was going to ask me if something was wrong. "I mean, yes. It's my house. I just need some fresh air. You two make yourselves comfortable—but not too comfortable. Never mind." I yanked open the front door and practically ran to the street.

Neil grabbed my hand before I reached the sidewalk. *Stupid long legs.*

"Hey, did I do something wrong? I can regurgitate the food, if that's what you're mad about," he said.

"What? No." *Gross.* "I told you—I just need to walk."

"Andie, I've been watching you for a long time. I know when something's wrong. Wait, did that sound creepy?"

"Kind of."

"Well, I didn't mean I've been *watching* you, like some stalker. That'd be weird. I just meant, y'know, we grew up in the same schools, so I passed you in the halls all the time, and then we dated for a month, and—man, what happened to my words? I think my brain broke."

I fought the urge to smirk. It wasn't often someone caught Neil off guard. "So, what you're trying to say is, you've been stalking me since you were in fourth grade."

"Not stalking. Watching. At school. Sometimes."

I bit my lip. Should I tell him it hurt to see him flirting with Jill? Did I even have a right to develop a crush on someone, given I'd become a freaking baby oven?

Neil waved his hand in front of my eyes. "Earth to Andie. Come in. Breaker, breaker."

Blinking, I stepped back from him and kept my voice steady. "Seriously, I'm fine. Go inside and keep Jill company. I think she likes you."

Neil squinted at me but didn't follow when I turned and walked away.

Good. I would've hated for him to see the tears fall.

CHAPTER 15

I really should've remembered a jacket, I thought while sitting on a bench in Donaldson Park. To me, it always resembled a small Central Park. Not that I'd ever been to New York City, but I'd seen pictures. Concrete paths twisted through grassy hills, and in the very center kids played on a large playground where I'd spent many evenings with Carter and Heather up 'til seventh grade. Before we became "too cool."

I missed those days.

My feet had taken me here, as if programmed. My mind tripped over thoughts of Neil and the baby, and when I took a second to figure out where I was, the playground was the first landmark I spotted. Longing for the past somehow found a crack in my heart, and I'd sat down. Now, I watched children play, laughing with their parents, their friends. That would be my kid, some day.

"Andie?"

I leapt off the bench at the sound of Carter's voice. "Stay away from me!"

My heart couldn't take any more pain.

He held up his hands. "Look, I'm not here to start anything. I just wanted to say I'm sorry."

My cheeks burned. "You're *sorry?* You walked away from me, Carter. You told your mom the baby wasn't yours!"

His gaze was unwavering, yet I could see the pain radiating from his eyes. "I know. And I deserve all the hatred you have for me. But I couldn't move to California without seeing you, without saying goodbye."

I rocked on wobbly legs but crossed my arms and glared him down. "I don't care what you have to say. I'm glad you're moving 'cause I never want to see you again. Now leave."

Carter's jaw flexed as he swallowed, tears building in his eyes. He reached behind him and pulled an envelope from the back of his waistband. He laid it on the bench.

"It's not much, but . . . I hope it'll help." His voice shook.

I wrapped my arms tighter around my waist, my chest seconds from exploding. I refused to answer him, to do more than glare at the guy who'd pulled my hair on the playground, carried me to the car after my dad's funeral—and left me standing, alone, in my backyard when I needed him more than ever.

Carter swallowed, nodding. "Take care of yourself, Andie." He backpedaled, tossing me a quick wave before digging his hands into his pockets and turning away.

When his red BMW was no longer in sight, I grabbed onto the bench and fell back into my seat, unable to breathe. He was gone. He was really gone.

Yet, I was numb.

Eyeing the envelope like it was a bomb ready to explode, I slowly grabbed it and opened it, my fingers shaking. Inside was a $500 cashier's check. Every ounce of me wanted to rip it up and throw the pieces in the trash. Yes, he was sure going to be repenting to his parents when they realized what he'd done, but how far did he honestly think the money would go? I'd needed *him*!

I unclenched the check from my fist and stared at a signature I'd come to know so well. Heading home, I sighed, tucked the money into my pocket, and tore only the envelope to pieces instead. I was going to need every penny I could get.

Neil's truck hadn't yet moved, and Mom's car was in the garage. *Oh, crap.* I knew I'd lost track of time, but I didn't think I'd wandered *that* long.

Opening the door to the house, I expected a loud confrontation with my mother. But, instead, I heard laughter. With eyebrows raised, I took a few more steps and found Mom, Neil, and Jill drinking hot chocolate at the table.

Mom spotted me first. I was frozen with my mouth hung open.

"Andie, come join us," she said. "How was your walk?"

"Um, fine, I guess." I stepped farther into the room.

"Your mom threatened to call the cops when she found us sitting in your living room, but we convinced her we are your friends," Jill said.

Wonder how that *conversation went.* Mom really didn't like surprises.

"Yeah, Neil drove me home from school, and Jill came along," I explained. "Sorry I didn't ask if they could stay."

Mom waved. "Oh, it's no big deal. I know the Andersons and the Danielsons. They're both good families."

Danielson? Why did Neil give Owen's last name?

"Oh, wow, is it 5:00 already? I better get food started." Mom jumped out of her chair and raced to the fridge.

Jill stood and grabbed my hand. "Are you okay?" she asked in a hushed voice, pulling me toward the living room and away from my mom.

I nodded, catching Neil's glance. Butterflies shot to my knees. I turned back to Jill.

"How long has she been here?" I whispered, nodding toward Mom.

"Like, twenty minutes. We told her you'd gone for a quick walk around the block and kept her busy so she'd lose track of time."

Geniuses, both of them. Most people couldn't pull that over on Mom.

"Do you two want to stay for dinner?" Mom asked, peeking over her shoulder.

"Sure!" Jill said. "Need help?" She skipped into the kitchen.

I watched as she dazzled Mom into letting her make a salad and shook my head.

A hand touched my lower back. "We need to talk," Neil whispered, his lips close to my ear.

I shivered. Did he really have to do that? I was about to turn and tell him, *Maybe later*, but he grabbed my elbow and led me to the foyer.

"So, I talked to Jill about what you said." Neil slipped his hands into his pockets and stepped back, his stance effortless and casual.

My stomach hit my feet. I tried to smile. "That's great."

"Is it?"

I crossed my arms over my chest then dropped them to my sides, unsure of what to do with the stupid things. "Well, of course. I mean, you two have a lot in common. You're both really smart, you both have a good sense of humor—"

"And we're both into women." He flashed me a smug smile.

"Wait, what?"

"You heard me. Jill prefers her men, well, not men."

"Oh." My heart fluttered. But I shouldn't be happy. I should be sad. For Neil. "I'm sorry."

"No, you're not." His gaze was unwavering, staring not at me but *into* me.

A bead of sweat ran down the back of my neck. "Of course I am." My voice wavered. "I'm your friend. I want to see you happy."

Neil stepped toward me. "Right. You think I don't know why you left the house? I can read it in the way you stand, see it in your eyes: You're jealous."

I backed away from him. "No, I'm not."

He smirked and took another step toward me. "We should play that card game where you try to lie about what cards you have in your hand. I'd kick your ass."

My pulse was in my ears, my throat. So what if I was falling for him again? I had to do it—I had to push him away. I'd decided to keep my baby. This was my choice, and my choice alone. What Carter's mom didn't want for him, I didn't want for Neil. Now was the time to set him free. To stop whatever was happening between us. Even if his deep blue eyes haunted me for the rest of my life.

"Neil, stop. I can't—I won't—have this conversation with you. Now or ever. We're friends. *That's all*." I pushed past him to join Mom and Jill in the kitchen. I needed to get away from him before my nerves—and unwanted feelings—overtook my brain.

He grabbed my hand. "What if that's not enough for me?"

I spun around, yanking my hand out of his. "Well, it should be, or did you forget there's something *growing* inside me?"

"I don't care."

"It's not even yours!"

"*I don't care.* Blood isn't what makes a family."

I tugged on my hair. *This can't be happening.*

Mom shouted from the other room, "Andie, dinner's going to be ready soon. Would you set the table, please?"

"I'll be right there," I replied, my voice wavering. I returned my attention to Neil. "I can't allow myself to care about you. You deserve someone better than me. I'm not worth it."

Neil slipped his hand into mine. "Why don't you let me be the judge of that?"

My bottom lip quivered. "Neil, please. Don't make this harder than it already is."

I pulled my hand from his, my heart twisting as the usual humor in Neil's eyes disappeared. Turning away from him, I walked until I was about halfway down the hall then leaned against the wall as a single tear rolled down my cheek. Wiping it away furiously—Neil was watching—I took a deep breath and opened my eyes, rushing into the kitchen.

"Sorry. I got distracted." I opened the silverware drawer to pull out forks, knives, and spoons for four people.

"You all right?" Mom asked.

"Yep."

I set the table, avoiding eye contact with anyone. I felt Neil watching me. Jill set the salad bowl and lasagna on the table, then

BECAUSE I LOVE YOU

Mom called for us to sit. Finally, I looked up. Neil leaned against the opening between the dining room and hallway, frowning.

"Actually, I forgot"—he stepped into the room—"I have an errand I need to run for my mom. So, sorry to bail last minute, but I'm going to need to go." He held his hand out to my mother. "Thanks for the offer, though, Ms. Hamilton. Everything smells great."

Mom shook his hand. "Well, why don't I give you some to go?"

Neil flashed her a smile. "It's no problem. I can take a rain check. Besides, we have so much food in our house, I doubt my mom would appreciate it if I brought more home."

Mom smiled, but I cringed. That was a blatant lie. He was leaving the best meal he'd get all week, and all because of me. I swallowed the lump in my throat.

"Later, Andie," he said with a sad smile. He nodded at Jill then exited through the garage. I flinched when the door closed. Why did I feel the same way as when Dad left for a business trip—afraid I'd never see him again? The bite hit my chest like a sting from a gigantic bee on steroids.

"Okay, girls," Mom said, "shall we pray?"

When she started talking, I closed my eyes and said my own prayer. I didn't thank God for food or friendship or whatever Mom usually asked for. I begged him to help me get through the next few months without giving in and ruining Neil's life. Because I didn't know if I could.

Anxiously, I sat through dinner as Jill flattered my mother to the point of no return, telling stories of her Native American ancestors and the crazies who came into her mother's jewelry store. For how not-hungry I was, I managed to eat two full plates before Jill announced she had to be going. The baby must've really wanted dinner.

"How was your day?" Mom asked as we washed dishes.

If I told her what really happened, she'd go on a rampage through the halls of River Springs Prep, craving blood. Instead, I stuck with, "I don't think I'm going back. Not this year, at least."

Mom frowned. "I'm sorry, honey."

Me, too. But at least I wouldn't have to see Neil's handsome face every day or the way his eyes creased in the corners when his smile was 100 percent natural. Not to mention, I didn't think I could take one more of his sister's pranks. If it hadn't been for Jill—and Neil—I never would've made it out of there in one piece.

After I dried the last dish, I said goodnight to Mom, but she stopped me. "Before you go upstairs, we need to talk."

Nodding, I sat at the table. My stomach put on an acrobatic performance. Mom dried her hands and joined me, pulling an envelope out of her purse and handing it to me. On the front was a watermark from Bethlehem Family Services. My heart smacked against my ribs.

"That's everything I have on your birth parents. It's not much; I know. But it's a start. I don't want you to be in the dark anymore about where you came from. The plan was to share this with you when you turned eighteen. But with everything that happened the other night, I'm thinking this will help give you a little closure. Are you still planning to keep the baby?"

I nodded. My throat felt like sandpaper.

Mom sighed. "Oh, honey." She paused and scratched her forehead. "I still stand by my belief that you'd be better off placing your baby for adoption. You'd be surprised how easily parents fall in love with a child entrusted to their care."

We're seriously having this conversation again? I was about to refuse when she raised a finger.

"But I will do whatever I can to help you. Just don't shut me out."

"Really? I thought . . . Well, I never expected you to be on board."

"I'm not." She stood. "But I love you, Andrea." Mom touched my cheek. "And so you know, not a day has gone by where I haven't loved you like my own. Let me know what you find out about your birth parents, okay?"

A lump caught in my throat. She kissed my forehead then wandered upstairs to take a bath. Alone, I stared at the envelope, terrified by what I might find inside. Would I be disappointed? For years, I'd always thought my *adoptive*-mother was stuck up and nosy, and I would've been overjoyed to learn I wasn't hers. But now, I couldn't imagine being someone else's kid.

Yet, if I didn't know where *I* came from, how could I hope to tell my baby about its family? And finding out more about my biological parents didn't mean I was leaving or betraying the ones who'd raised me.

I needed to know.

Heartbeat thrashing in my ears, I sprinted upstairs, closed my door, and then sat on my bed. I opened the envelope with shaking hands. At least ten pages were stapled together. My breath caught. *I should be doing this with Neil.* I shook my head. *No, you can do this yourself.* I opened the papers.

On top was a copy of my original birth certificate. Born May seventh in Aspen, weighing exactly seven pounds. My parents' names and addresses were missing, but everything else about that day was listed—the hospital, the exact time of my birth, my parents' ages, their occupations. I rubbed a hand against my chest.

Beneath the birth certificate were forms they'd filled out for the adoption agency. Again, their names and addresses were blacked out, but everything else about them—hair color, eye color, interests, ethnicity, medical history—was all there.

I was mostly German and looked like my mother—blonde hair, blue eyes, thin, and not very tall. She was just eighteen when she delivered me. A teenager too. My father was an athlete, and my mother loved science. They were both pretty healthy—skin cancer on my father's side—and they were both from Aspen, Colorado. My birthplace.

Clutching the papers, I smiled, a lump in my throat. I ached to call Neil, not because I felt helpless but because I felt *hopeful*. He'd understand my elation. But I couldn't. Not if I wanted to stick to my decision to stay away.

Not if I wanted to save him from me.

I called Jill instead. Her voice was super perky when she answered, and I couldn't help but grin as I told her about the paperwork. She squealed and promised we would start researching tomorrow.

Although, I wasn't sure I wanted to find them. What do you say to the parents who gave you up? But Jill was so enthusiastic; I couldn't say no. At the very least, maybe we'd uncover more information or family history. And that'd be good, right?

After twenty more minutes of chatting with Jill, I tucked the envelope in the drawer of my nightstand and then crawled into bed. I clutched the polar bear Neil bought me at the zoo and let sleep take me.

CHAPTER 16

The house was empty when I came down the next morning. A note on the counter read: *Take today to relax. I'll stop by your school to figure out what we can do to keep you current. See you later. Love, Mom.*

Smiling, I helped myself to a huge bowl of cereal then wandered to the office at the front of the house. I rarely used the room, but it was the one place with a computer.

Overprotective mother equals monitored computer usage.

Usually, I used my cell phone for the Internet where my mom couldn't track every single click—she refused to buy me a laptop—but for the research I wanted to do, I needed more than access to mobile websites. With no one home and nothing to do until Mom and my guidance counselor figured out how to handle the rest of junior year, I'd get a jump start on the research Jill and I planned to do. Mom knew I'd read what was in the envelope from the adoption agency. She couldn't blame me for seeking out as many details as I could find.

I pulled up my favorite search engine and looked up children born in Aspen on my birthday, hoping there'd be some sort of record as to who the parents were. A few websites were dedicated to people posting "listings" for their birth parents, but none were helpful. Frowning, I tried a few more searches but again got zero results.

Growling through my teeth, I closed the browser and smacked the power button on the monitor. I was going to have to wait for Jill and her rocket-scientist brain.

My phone dinged. A text from Heather. I tapped the notification with my thumb. *Heard ur not coming back. Good. Couldn't have a preggo chick on the cheerleading squad anyway. Beth sez thanks for the co-captain spot.*

I clutched the device tight in my hand and tried not to chuck it against the wall as my lungs forgot how to breathe. Between Carter's denial and Heather's betrayal—

I threw my cell phone onto the carpet, leaned back in the chair, and pressed my fists against my forehead, squeezing my eyes closed and holding my breath. I would not scream. I would not cry.

But I couldn't deny: I wanted my old life back.

I tried counting to ten, attempting to calm myself like I usually could, and failed. I leaned forward, pressed my forehead against the desk, and wrapped my arms around my waist as sob after sob wracked through my body.

This wasn't how my life was supposed to be. Sitting at home, doing God knows what to finish school, scheduling appointments with OB/GYNs.

Doing it all alone.

I shut off my emotions. If I couldn't feel the pain, then I could get through this. No more thinking or feeling—just waking up every morning, doing what I had to, and going back to sleep. Maybe I could just pretend my life was as it used to be.

Sitting up, I wiped the tears from my cheeks, took a deep breath, and stood, grabbing my phone off the floor. I deleted the text from Heather and blocked her number before deleting her from my contacts. So, she had teamed up with Beth against me? Screw her. Screw them both!

After stuffing my face again, I wandered upstairs and grabbed a book off the shelf above my desk. Reading would keep my brain preoccupied. That would be the key—don't let myself think. If I didn't think, I couldn't hurt. I cracked open the novel.

I was about halfway through *The Great Gatsby* when someone

knocked on my door. Mom stood in the entryway, her expression tense.

"Something wrong?" I asked, my stomach slightly flipping. So much for shutting off my emotions.

Mom stepped into my room and crossed her arms. "Why didn't you tell me what happened at school yesterday?"

I frowned. I hoped we wouldn't have to have this conversation. "Because I didn't want to."

Mom plopped on the bed, across from me. "Well, I stopped to visit with your guidance counselor about finishing your classes online, and she told me what happened in chemistry. This Beth Donaghue girl . . . I want to press charges."

A chill ran down my spine. "No. Mom, please, don't do that." As much as I hated Beth, she was Neil's sister, and taking her to court would put another strain on him that he didn't need. Especially when they were scraping by as it was. If we sued, her uncle would never pay for lawyer bills, even though he had more money than most of us could count. Which meant it would be up to Neil to fork over the payment.

I didn't know if I'd ever be able to forgive Beth for what she did, but I couldn't let my mom hurt Neil in the process.

"Andie, that video was harassment."

"Yeah, and she harassed *me*." I grabbed Mom's hand. "Please, let it go."

She and I stared at each other until she sighed. "I'm at least going to talk to her mother. She needs to be aware—okay, what aren't you telling me?"

I popped my lip out from between my teeth. I didn't realize I was squeezing Mom's hand that hard.

I let her go and sat back. "Beth's family is . . . complicated." How else could I explain it without giving away the entire Donaghue sob story?

"Yes, I know about her father's death and her mother's problems. But Beth's mom still needs to know what her daughter did to you."

"Mom, *please*." I tugged on my hair. "If I can let it go, so should you. They already have enough going on without threatening a lawsuit."

Mom's eyes narrowed. "This doesn't have anything to do with Neil Donaghue, does it?"

My stomach fell. *How did she know?* He'd used Owen's last name.

Mom let out a disgusted noise. "I knew when I saw that kid that he wasn't a *Danielson*. Please stay away from that boy."

I leaned away from her, my cheeks hot, and crossed my arms. "He's my friend, and he's been nothing but kind to me since all of this started."

"Andrea, you have to trust me here. That boy is nothing but bad news."

"Oh, yeah? How would you know?"

"Because I've known his mother a long time, and he has quite the reputation amongst the girls at the university."

I ground my teeth and slammed my book on the bed. "Yeah, Mom, he built that reputation *on purpose*. I've been to his house. I've seen the handprints his mother leaves on his face. Did you know he was the one who came after me when my cheerleading squad wrote whore on my locker? He was the one who picked me up from the Mini Mart and took care of me when I was hurt. And he was the one who saved me from his sister when she humiliated me with that stupid video."

"Honey, you're also an easy target right now. This is what he does."

I snarled, jumping off the bed. "You know, I was *just* like you when I met him. Judgmental. Bitchy, even." She gaped at me. "But he is *not* like that. Sure, he's not perfect, but look at me!" I motioned to my growing belly. "Neither am I. You are *not* going to pull me down the rabbit hole and convince me to despise him when he and Jill are the only two friends I have left!"

And with those words, my insides knotted. I rubbed my heavy chest. I needed to talk to him, to see him. Maybe I was strong enough to find my parents and grow fat on my own. Maybe I could just shut down and let the world pass me by. But, God, I didn't want to. I really, really didn't want to.

Mom stood with tears in her eyes. She brushed hair out of her face. She was about to speak when the phone rang. I answered it, not wanting to hear another word.

"Hey, can I still come over?" Jill asked.

"Yes, please."

"Okay, cool. I'll be there soon. Got the car tonight!" She sang the last sentence then hung up.

Good. Because we weren't going to be here long.

As soon as I heard Jill pull into the driveway, I flung open the front door before she could even knock.

"Okay, *that* was creepy," she said. "Do you have ESP?"

"No, just supersonic hearing."

She gave me a look that said *yeah right*, but I could see in her eyes that she was hopeful. What would she do if we were ever attacked by aliens? Or zombies? Probably have a heart attack from nerdy excitement.

I half-smiled and pulled her into the office. "I need you to do me a favor."

Jill tipped her head slightly. "Okay?"

"Can you take me to Neil's?"

"Ooh, he was extra cranky at school today. He'd probably egg my car if I did that."

I bounced a little and pressed my hands together. "Jill, please. I promise we'll do a sleepover tomorrow, and we'll even watch *Star Trek*. But I really, really need to see him."

She brightened at the mention of her favorite show. I'd said the magic words.

"Okay, fine. But you have to give me something to look up tonight because your adoption paper thingy made me feel like a private investigator, and I can't wait to start."

Grabbing a piece of paper and pen from the desk, I scribbled my birth date and the hospital I was born in. "Here."

Jill grinned like I'd given her a Golden Globe. She followed me into the foyer where I called up to Mom—she hadn't left her room since our argument earlier—that I was going to Jill's and would be back by ten or eleven. I didn't wait for Mom to remind me I was grounded, and I barreled out the front door while texting Neil.

Are you home? When I sat in the passenger's seat, my phone chimed.

At Owen's. Y? Neil typed.

I need to talk to you.

Jill sat behind the steering wheel, staring at me with a raised eyebrow. I was about to make a comment about being patient when Neil replied with *Come on over* and sent Owen's address.

Thank you. Be there soon.

O baby. I'll have a cold shower running.

I rolled my eyes. Even through text messaging, he had to throw in a sarcastic comment.

"He's at Owen's," I told Jill. "He lives by—"

"I know where he lives." Jill put the car in reverse. I raised an eyebrow, and she shrugged. "Did some research on him to make sure he wasn't the one helping Beth with her video prank."

"And?"

"He's clean." She smiled.

I sat back in my seat. "You do realize that's kind of CIA creepy."

Her eyes widened. "Really? That's my dream job. Well, the CIA or NASA."

I shook my head. Thank God I was on Jill's good side.

"By the way, are you not allowed to see Neil or something? I thought your mom liked him."

I crossed my arms. "She figured out his last name wasn't really Danielson."

"Oh." Her face lit up. "This is *so* cool. We're, like, on a secret, undercover mission. *Classified.*" The way she said the last word reminded me of Batman.

I laughed. "You are the strangest person I know."

"I'll take that as a compliment."

I smiled and looked out the window, excited and terrified for what would happen when I saw those aquamarine eyes again.

CHAPTER 17

Owen's house was in the nice part of River Springs, the area where all the doctors and lawyers lived. We drove past a gate and down a long driveway lined with beautiful trees every shade of red, orange, and yellow. I pictured myself riding a horse-drawn carriage down the road, dressed in a big gown. How much fun would that have been?

His house was a classical mansion, with three stories, a stone front, and a dark green, perfectly manicured lawn. They probably even had a butler. The driveway curved to the left, and a massive, matching detached garage sat next to the house.

In front of it were four shirtless boys playing basketball, Neil included.

Seeing us pull up, the boys halted their game, and Neil rested the ball on his hip, a cocky grin on his face. My eyes bulged. I'd never seen him half-naked before. His arms, chest, and abs were carved, but not bulky like those guys who spent too many hours in the gym and could crush someone if they squeezed too hard.

Since the day Heather and I had discovered boys were sexy, we'd spent many sleepovers flipping through magazines and ogling the shirtless models. If Neil had been one, his picture would've been taped to my wall. And regularly drooled over.

The two boys I didn't know wandered toward the house, but Owen turned around, stared at me with a goofy grin, then howled like a wolf at the moon. He made a few inappropriate gestures with his hips before a basketball hit him, hard, on his bare back. He laughed and flipped Neil off, grabbed the ball, and then jogged toward his house. My cheeks burned.

Jill laughed at me. "Oh, man. Seeing you right now was so worth the drive."

And now my face was roasting. "Thanks for the ride." I stopped gawking at Neil, who was still smirking. "I'll see you tomorrow?"

"You bet. I'll be anxious to hear all about this little rendezvous." She wiggled her eyebrows.

I rolled my eyes and pushed open the car door when she laughed again.

Neil held a cigarette to his lips as I walked across the asphalt. He flicked the cigarette into the grass and crushed it before the lawn caught fire. "Like what you see, Princess?"

"Shut up." My cheeks burned hotter. The closer I got to him, the more I could see. Each lightly-defined muscle. The tattoo on his left pec—two skulls entwined with twisting vine, a ripped ribbon, and words that, when put together, read: *Don't forget the music.*

You're here to talk to him. That's it. My heart fluttered, and I turned my gaze toward the house. "They didn't have to leave."

"Game was over anyway." He shrugged and crossed his arms over his chest.

I jumped when his muscles flexed. He really needed to find his clothes.

"Can we go somewhere?" I asked, tucking hair behind my ear and fighting the blush in my cheeks.

"Well, that's a little faster than I usually go, but if you want—"

I groaned, and he laughed.

"Come on," he said. "We can talk in the garage."

I followed him, my arms wrapped around my waist. Neil flung open the door to the detached garage. The building was big enough for four cars, but only Neil's truck was parked inside. The other side was filled with lawn equipment, a small cot, and a refrigerator with a crumpled shirt on top of it plugged into an outlet in the back wall.

Neil flipped open the hatch on his truck before reaching inside and pulling a blanket from behind the seats—a blanket that matched those on the cot. I frowned. He slept here often. This routine was too natural.

After spreading out the blanket inside the truck's bed, he jumped down and patted the tailgate. "Hop up."

"Only if you put a shirt on."

He smirked. "Well, all right. If it'll help you concentrate." Neil wandered to the refrigerator, snatched the shirt, and pulled two green bottles from the machine. I climbed onto the truck's bed, and he handed one to me. I eyeballed the bottle like it was a bomb.

"Don't worry; it's not booze. It's a clear, fizzy drink some idiot named Sprite," Neil said.

I took it from him with a glare. Popping the cap, Neil tipped his soda back and chugged the entire thing. Then he tossed the empty container into a yellow trashcan on the other side of the garage. A goofy grin split his face. I half expected him to shout *three pointer*, but he just turned back to me, leaning on a rear corner of his truck.

"So, what's up?" he asked.

I bit my lip.

"Come on, Andie. I know you didn't come all the way out here to stare at my abs and hold an unopened bottle of soda in your hands. Now, spill."

Butterflies threw a party in my stomach. "How many girls have you been with?"

His eyebrows rose. "Seriously? *That's* what you wanted to ask me?"

I flinched. It wasn't what I'd come here to say; it sort of just popped out. But now that it had, I was curious, and I couldn't stop my mouth from continuing, "It's just . . . my mom heard from some of the girls at the university—"

"Here we go again." Neil's face reddened, and he stepped away from the truck, turning his back to me with his hands in his hair.

My fists clenched. "Why can't you just answer me?"

He spun around, flinging his hands out to his sides. "Because I thought we were past this! What do I have to do to get you to trust me?"

"Answer my question."

He growled. "I don't know, all right? I didn't keep track. Happy now?"

I clenched my teeth and turned my head, my cheeks burning. What had I hoped for? Him to fall on his knees and shout *Oh, but none, my love! For I have been waiting for you!*

The real world didn't work like that. I was proof.

"The first," Neil said, his voice calm, "was when I was fifteen, and it was awful. Like, I'm pretty sure that the majority of my slobber went up her nose, and I spent the whole rest of sophomore year terrified the nickname 'One Second Man' would follow me to Hell."

Unable to stop a smirk, I pressed my lips together. I didn't look at him, but I felt him getting closer.

"The second was Owen's sister, Lila. She was two years older than me, and we had a thing for a few months. But it never went anywhere. She was the one who first got my reputation going, though. Never did thank her for that, but I probably should have. And the rest . . . they were stupid, one-time hookups to—I don't know—forget about all the shit at home."

I winced. Any tiny grin that covered my face moments before died. Was Mom right? Was a fling all he wanted from me? I should've stayed blind to his experience. Not that I had any room to talk. Yes, I was inexperienced—Carter was my only, and it lasted, like, two minutes—but I was *pregnant*, for goodness sake. Definitely shouldn't be judging Neil.

"Why are you telling me all this?" I asked.

"Because I'm tired of you thinking I'm trying to hide the truth or manipulate you."

Looking at the ground, I picked at the cap on my Sprite bottle. I hadn't really thought any of those things, not anymore. Why had I let my mother get in my head?

"What's this really about?" Neil asked. By now, he stood in front of me, and he took the bottle from my grasp and then set it on the ground.

I stared at a spot on the wall. "I can't remember."

"Okay, well, let me take a stab at it. I like guessing games. I usually win."

I rolled my eyes.

"Your mom figured out who I was and warned you to stay away from me. But because you're stubborn, you came here to prove her wrong, and now you're concerned that she might be right, and you think that if you let yourself feel, for even a millisecond, that I'll break your heart."

Finally, I looked at him, and the dread in his eyes made me want to wrap my arms around him and tell him he was wrong, that I was 100 percent confident he'd stick by my side through the good and the bad. But that was a lie.

For someone who worked so hard at pretending he didn't give a damn, Neil was one of the most observant, intuitive people I'd ever met.

"The last time I let myself care about anyone, he did break my heart," I said.

"Then screw him. He's a freaking fool."

My eyes burned. "But how do I know I'm not just going to be another one of your flings?"

Neil sighed, blinking slowly. He pinched the bridge of his nose, and the short pause made my pulse sprint. Then he dropped his hand and lifted his gaze to mine. "Because you make me feel something. Because I can't stop thinking about you, wondering if you're okay, aching to spend another minute with you. Because I always notice when you walk into a room. Because being with you doesn't just make me happy—it makes me want to make *you* happy."

I held my breath. My stomach was in my chest, and my heart was in my knees. He was being honest—I saw the truth in his glossy, unblinking eyes.

"I care about you, Andie. I've cared about you since the third grade, since the moment you put that flower in my hand and told me I was worth something. Every day, I've regretted what I did two years ago, when I fucked up everything between us. But I promise you, I will never make that same mistake again."

I gripped my pant legs, every cell in my body shaking. This was what I'd wanted, wasn't it? To hear that I wasn't just another conquest? That he really did care about me? Lord knows I'd come to deeply care about him. And now I had my answer. A sincere, earth-shattering, beautiful one. So why was I still so terrified?

I swallowed tears. "Neil, I . . . I care about you too. More than you know. But . . . I can't. Not when I'm . . ." I bit down on my tongue. Physical pain to keep in the emotional pain.

Neil touched my knees. "I meant what I said before about that not mattering to me. I need you to trust me on this."

I shook my head and turned away. My voice was barely more than a whisper when I spoke. "I can't ask you to be a father figure to a baby that isn't even yours. As soon as it's born, you're going to change your mind about me."

A pause. Then he tucked a loose strand of hair behind my ear. "Would you please stop assuming you know how I think?" His finger-tips lingered along my jaw line, and a chill ran down my spine. "Give me another chance to prove that I want to be here for you."

I looked into his deep-blue eyes. His gaze was intense and unfalter-ing. A vice gripped my heart. Did I dare to let him in? I reached up and held his wrist, unable to breathe.

"Promise me we'll move slow?" I asked.

"Promise." Neil lifted my chin and leaned in, and my palms sweated.

"If you break me, I don't think I'd ever recover," I whispered, his lips inches from mine.

"Then it's a good thing you won't have to."

Neil lightly touched his lips to mine, but the kiss still made the hair on my arms rise. He pulled back just enough to look into my eyes, and the concern I found there for my comfort—for *me*—made me feel like I was floating. This was definitely a different Neil than the one I'd kissed years ago. I gripped his wrists tighter and leaned into him, and his mouth found mine again. He kissed me long and deep, sliding his hand to the nape of my neck. My toes curled.

Everything about Neil felt so right—so perfect. The way he held me, the way he smelled, the way he tasted. When he kissed me, missing pieces of myself fell back into place. Carter said he loved me, but with Neil, it radiated from him with every glance, every touch. I should never have denied this.

Wrapping my arms around his neck, I kissed him harder, my body tingling. His other hand touched my lower back and pulled me closer. Neil's tongue slipped into my mouth. My skin flushed. My legs parted slightly, beckoning him nearer. A soft noise escaped his lips, and Neil's hands moved to hold my face. Soon, our kisses slowed, and he pulled away.

He rested his forehead against mine. "Man, you are not going to make it easy to go slow."

"Sorry," I replied, my pulse still thrashing in my ears. I attempted some humor. "I'm actually kind of surprised you have a go-slow setting."

He lifted his forehead off mine and smirked. "Look at you, being all snarky." He stroked my cheek with his thumb. "With you . . . I want to do it right, this time."

The blue of Neil's eyes seemed to glow, and his cheeks were flushed. Seeing him like this, after such an intimate moment, made my head spin again.

"What do you say I take you home before your mom starts wondering where you are, and we pick this up later?"

"Yeah, I don't think I can walk yet."

He laughed, the corners of his eyes crinkling, and I couldn't help myself. I flung my arms around his neck, and the kissing started all over again.

It was only 7:00 p.m. when Neil and I climbed into his truck, so instead of taking me straight home, we went out for a bite to eat.

"Mom gave me my adoption papers," I said before shoving a piece of chicken in my mouth.

"Well, that's good. At least we know you weren't kidnapped."

"Really?"

He smiled.

I shook my head then told him what the papers said and how Jill was going to try to dig up more information on who my birth parents were.

"You know the court probably sealed that information, right? You can't get it until you're eighteen," Neil said.

I frowned. Eighteen? I had to wait 'til I was *eighteen?* That was two years away. Two years of staring at women in their mid-thirties, wondering if I looked like them, if they could be my mother. Goodbye appetite. I swirled my chicken in the cheese sauce on my plate. I was never going to make it that long.

Neil seemed to understand where my thoughts had gone. "Though, if you want, I can help Jill search for more details. I might not be as skilled as her when it comes to hacking, but I do know how—and Owen's laptop is already equipped for the task."

I glanced up at him and dropped my fork. His eyes were so bright, his smile so genuine. For a second, my thoughts returned to our make-out session in Owen's garage. I stabbed my food, forcing the blush to disappear from my cheeks.

"Wow. I'll have to remember all it takes to get you flustered is talking about breaking the law." Neil rubbed the side of his foot against my calf.

"Shut up." I kicked him in the shin, gently, and he laughed. "Seriously, though, are you sure Owen won't mind you borrowing his laptop?"

"Nah. He'll probably think his cousin took it to download more porn."

I shook my head as he popped the last bite of his burger in his mouth, almost unable to keep myself from bouncing in my seat. Between Neil and Jill, we were bound to find information sooner rather than later, which meant I was one step closer to discovering what my life might've been like had I not been adopted. Thank God I'd decided to let the emotions in, to spend time with the people who cared about me, to not become a zombie.

Soon, I'd have something to tell my own child about where he or she came from, and maybe, just maybe, we wouldn't be part of one family—but two.

CHAPTER 18

Persuading Mom to let me spend the weekend at Jill's was freakishly tough, especially after I ran off yesterday when I was supposed to be grounded. But once I convinced her that I couldn't stay cooped up in the house, waiting to pop like an oversized water balloon, she finally conceded. As long as that was the only place I went, and Jill's parents knew I was going to be there.

Mom dropped me off at Jill's condo in downtown River Springs around noon, waited until Jill dialed her mom to ensure she knew I was staying, then left us alone to have fun. A few seconds longer, and I would've pushed Mom out the door. Literally.

Jill grabbed my bag and barreled up the stairs to the single—albeit, large—room on the top floor. The light-green walls of her bedroom were covered with *Marvel*, *Star Trek*, *Dr. Who*, and *Sherlock* posters, as well as science charts, like the periodic table and a drawing of a DNA strand. It was so totally Jill.

"Sorry it's not quite what you're used to," Jill said. "My room's pretty much an attic."

"I think it's great. It's like a mini-apartment."

She smiled and dropped my duffel near the end of her twin bed.

Which, naturally, was covered by an *Iron Man* comforter. She skipped across her carpet to a desk near her window.

"Okay, so, my mom's closing the store tonight, but my dad'll be off duty around five. And he's a cop. So, if we're going to do this, we should probably get started now." Jill cracked her knuckles before typing a few passphrases on a series of unlock screens.

Somehow, the fact that she had to even hack into her computer didn't surprise me.

I pulled my adoption paperwork from my bag and handed it to her. "This is all I have."

She tied her black hair into a ponytail at the nape of her neck and then took the papers from me. Quickly, she scanned them then laid them on the desk next to a notepad with indecipherable scribbling. Black and green screens popped up on the monitor, and she began typing—what I guessed were—lines of code. I couldn't keep up.

"This is gonna make me dizzy."

Her fingers froze. "Oh, sorry. I forgot you're new to this." She pointed to a set of double doors opposite her bed. "There's a folding chair in there. Grab it while I pull up what I found while you were having sexy time with Neil."

I cringed. "Oh, please don't call it that."

She grinned and started typing again. "Hey, I saw you eye hump him when we drove up to Owen's house."

My face hot, I hurried to the closet and yanked the chair out from behind her clothes. Responding to that comment was bound to dig an even deeper hole, and I wasn't going to admit she was right. I *did* pretty much drool all over myself during my make-out session with Neil.

For the next few hours, Jill broke through firewall after firewall with code after code, but her repetitive swear words told me we were getting no closer to discovering any information. Whatever third party server the adoption agency used had security that was locked "tighter than NASA's."

"Not that I've attempted to break into their systems," Jill said with shifty eyes.

At 5:15, Jill's dad walked through the front door, and the scent of Chinese food wafted up the stairs.

"Jillian, come down and eat!" he shouted. His footsteps followed him past the staircase, deeper into the condo.

Jill hid the thousands of windows she had open on her laptop—okay, that was an exaggeration—and turned to me with a frown. "Sorry I couldn't get more. But at least we know where to start next time. We'll crack it eventually and figure out who was working at the agency the night you were born."

I nodded, unable to keep the frown off my face. "Well, thanks for trying. I didn't realize it was going to be so hard."

"Me either. Kind of weird that the agency's so difficult."

I followed Jill downstairs and into a small dine-in kitchen at the back of the condo. She introduced me to her dad—who apologized for not getting enough food—and the three of us sat at a round, four-person table in a corner where Jill's parents had hung baby pictures on the walls. I shared Jill's cashew chicken as her dad asked me about my interests and family. When I got to the part about my dad dying two years ago, he frowned.

"Yeah, I remember that accident. I was working that night. Took us a long time to catch the drunk driver who forced your dad's car into the tree. I'm sorry we weren't able to save him."

I stopped chewing. I *knew* I'd seen Mr. Anderson before—at my dad's funeral. I hadn't put two and two together, though I should have. He was the only Native American on our police force. Not to mention, his last name was Anderson. I fingered the locket around my neck.

"Dad, seriously, you're bringing the house down," Jill said.

Mr. Anderson's cheeks reddened slightly. I would've laughed had we not been talking about my dad moments before. Being reminded of his funeral, of watching his closed casket lowered into the ground. I really missed him. He always knew how to make me smile through my tears. Lord knew I could've used some of his humor the last few weeks.

Jill squeezed my hand, and I joined the conversation, pushing Dad from my mind. The rest of the evening was absorbed by video games, and after a quick trip to the Mini Mart—where we said hi to Neil and filled two bags full of junk food and caffeine-free sodas—we stayed up until 3:00 a.m. watching *Star Trek* and laughing until our sugar comas took over.

It wasn't until the following Friday that we were able to research again. Between Jill's mom asking her to help out at the store after school and Neil's uncle forcing him to cut grass for customers before the season ended, there was no time for us to play Investigator during the week. So, after five days of tutoring sessions at home and trying to keep up on my schoolwork, I was beyond anxious to do something other than stick my nose in textbooks.

Unlike last time, we had the condo to ourselves the whole night. Jill's dad was on patrol until 5:00 a.m., and Jill's mom was traveling for some jewelry conference. While Jill typed away at her desk, Neil and I cozied on her twin mattress as he logged into Owen's computer. Neil's task: try to dig up information on Denver's hospital employees from sixteen years ago. Like Jill, he typed random letters, numbers, and symbols into black boxes. I wanted to ask if there was something I could do, but my right hip was pressed against his left, and instead of cigarette smoke, he smelled like cologne. I bit my lip and breathed deep. His new scent was intoxicating.

My eyes widened. *I hope he doesn't notice I'm sniffing him.*

"Anything yet?" Neil asked Jill. She was still attempting to break the security walls on Bethlehem Family Service's third party system.

"No. I don't get it. They must've had a professional hacker set this up 'cause it's freaking complex. I think I make progress, and—*bam.* Another wall."

"You know, if you'd show me how to use *your* programs, I might be able to dig up something on my end."

After Neil had commented that Jill's room looked like it belonged to a ten-year-old boy, she'd paid him back by refusing to share her hacking secrets. Owen's laptop did have some of the necessary equipment but nothing like Jill's. I had to admit: Seeing Neil struggle was amusing.

"Yeah, well, next time, don't insult Iron Man," she replied.

"Fine. I'll just fart on his face."

Jill spun in her chair and pointed her finger at him. "You leave your stench on my bed, and I will crotch punch you."

I laughed as Neil smiled. The two of them in the same room was like watching T-rexes slap fight—their heads were too big, and neither wanted to admit the other was the alpha. Or, in this case, smarter.

Not two minutes later, Jill exclaimed, "Yes! I'm in!"

Neil and I leapt off the bed—nearly toppling each other—to peek over Jill's shoulders. She entered keyword after keyword until we narrowed the folders to all the babies born in my birth year. After a few more lines of code, she broke the password on the main folder for May and found all the babies born on the seventh. There were two of us.

"Well, this shouldn't be too hard," Neil said.

"That's what she said," Jill replied. "Wait."

"Yeah, that didn't work. Usually girls like it if—"

"Can we please look through the files?" I interrupted.

Both Jill and Neil smirked, then Jill unlocked the password to the first file. She really was a hacker genius.

"Male, African-American. Unless you've had a sex change and a skin replacement, I doubt that's you," Neil said.

I shook my head as Jill opened the other document. My heart sank. I'd seen it before.

"It's the same one, the same birth certificate. Look"—I lifted the paper—"my parents' names are even missing." My shoulders drooped. We were never going to get any closer than this stupid paper.

Neil wrapped an arm around my shoulders and kissed the side of my forehead.

"If I can just figure out who was working at the time of your birth, I should be able to narrow down who handled your case," Jill said.

Neil took the paper from me, set it on the desk, and led me away from her computer as her fingers started flying over the keys again. Sitting on the edge of the bed, Neil pulled me onto his lap. I rested my hands on his firm chest as he cupped my cheeks in his palms.

"Hey, we're going to keep looking. We've just scratched the surface," he said.

I nodded. There were still so many other avenues we could take to find a key to my past. But I still couldn't help feeling that we were going to fail. That I was going to be no closer to discovering who I was. I had so many questions—who did I take after, personality-wise; did I have any brothers or sisters; why had they given me up; were they even still alive?

Neil kissed me as my bottom lip quivered, sliding one hand to the back of my neck and slipping the other into my hair. I leaned into him and let my sorrows and fears drown in his smell, his touch, his taste.

"Hey, you two. My bedroom is not available for hanky panky." Jill quirked an eyebrow. "Come see what I found."

Neil smiled against my lips as a blush rose in my cheeks, then I hopped off his lap and resumed my position next to Jill. A file was open on her computer.

"A payroll report?" Neil leaned closer to the computer. "That's perfect."

"It only shows me who was working that month, but when you break it down by position, there are only six case workers. One of them has to be Andie's."

Six people; that was it. And we finally had names, a place to start. My pulse drummed in my chest.

"Hopefully some are still living in the area. We'll split the list and run searches on each person. Nice work, Pocahontas," Neil said.

Jill glared at him. "Do you want to be crotch punched?"

He flashed her a grin and plopped back on the bed, pulling Owen's computer onto his lap. With adrenaline forcing my energy level to ultra-awake, I sat next to him with a huge smile, ready to find someone who could tell me about my parents.

CHAPTER 19

We didn't stop until 2:00 a.m. Though we'd narrowed down who'd worked the month I was born, we weren't able to dig up information about what cases they'd handled.

"Because the government's so involved in adoptions," Jill said, "these personnel files are ridiculously secure. It might actually take me a few days to crack these."

I sighed. *Great.*

"I didn't get much, either," Neil said. "Of the six case workers, two are dead. I was able to find current contact information for the other four, but that's about it."

"You sure I can't just hack the court's files?" Jill asked.

"No," Neil and I replied at the same time.

"It's one thing to break into the adoption agency's system. But going anywhere near the court's is bound to set off immediate red flags," Neil continued.

"And I don't want you going to jail for me," I added.

"Fine," Jill mumbled, closing her laptop. "Where do the four live?"

"One's in Seattle now, but the rest are still in Denver." Neil waved three notecards in the air.

I squinted at her. "Why? What are you thinking?"

She shrugged. "Maybe we show up and tell them you're thinking about putting your baby up and have questions about your own adoption." Her hand shot into the air before I could correct her. "I know you're not. But *they* don't have to know that."

Neil nudged my arm. "It's a decent plan, Andie. If they agree to help, they might have access to old records. And if they don't, we can keep doing what we're doing."

I bit my lip. But wasn't it a law that they couldn't share details of my adoption? I didn't want to visit and get my hopes up, just to have them come crashing down. Still, if the person who handled my case *did* agree to talk with me, they'd be able to tell me more than a piece of paper could.

"Okay," I said. "Who do we start with?"

Jill smiled, and the three of us dove into making plans—and didn't stop until 5:00 a.m. After Neil left, Jill and I slept until noon. I groaned when I sat up. Between sharing a twin bed with her and not moving a single muscle the entire seven hours, my body was stiff and exhausted.

I checked in with Mom, then Jill and I proceeded with our agreed-upon plans. One of the four caseworkers happened to be a woman Neil did lawn work for—Regina Miller. She lived the closest, and Neil would be at her house today, ready to jump in if things got out of hand.

"She's a class A bitch," he'd said last night. He wanted to be there when we talked to her, so we decided to stop by her place first.

While I fixed my hair and makeup, Jill packed a duffel bag full of small, high-tech-looking devices from her closet.

"What are those?" I asked.

She jumped. "Oh. Uh, well . . . I just thought if she refuses to tell us anything, she might call someone to let them know we were there, like the person who handled your adoption."

I raised my eyebrows and leaned toward her. "And?"

She cleared her throat then spoke super-fast. "And so I'd bug her house and record all her outgoing phone calls."

My mouth dropped. "Jill, no. That's . . . that's a stupid idea."

"How is that a stupid idea? It's human instinct—you feel threatened, you call the most logical person. In this case, it'd either be her boss or the person who knows your parents. Either way, it's a win-win. We'll know who to talk to next."

I pressed my lips together and clenched my hands into fists. We'd already committed a crime by hacking the agency's files. Did we dare add bugging someone's house to the list? Sweat coated my hairline as I bounced on the balls of my feet. What if we got caught? I didn't want to see her go to jail.

But what if she was right? What if this was my only chance to uncover information about my birth parents? If I didn't want to spend the next two years seeing my face in every blonde woman, I needed to figure out who she was now.

Ugh, this is wrong. This is so wrong.

I bit my lip, crossing and uncrossing my arms while Jill waited for me to make up my mind. I took a deep breath and shook my hands out at my sides. I couldn't wait. I *had* to do this, whether I was comfortable with it or not.

I closed my eyes, exhaled, then opened my lids. "Okay. But eavesdropping on her conversations is *strictly* Plan B."

With a smile, Jill zipped her bag, and I followed her to her car.

A little while later, after we parked across the street from our target's house, I jumped from the car with a smile. Neil's cheeks were flushed from his morning of hard labor, and though the air had a slight fall breeze, he wore just a T-shirt over his jeans. His dark hair was a mess, and he leaned against his rake, grinning. How come when I did yard work I looked like Einstein, but he still managed to look like he stepped out of a magazine?

"It's about time you two showed up," he said. "I was beginning to wonder if maybe you kept partying after I left."

"Dude, the party *began* when you walked out the door," Jill joked.

Neil's grin grew. He wrapped an arm around me and kissed the top of my head. I tried not to notice the small line of skin peeking out from beneath the hem of his shirt as it rose. Or the red waistband of his boxers. My face warmed.

"So what do we need to know about She-Devil?" Jill asked.

Neil shook off the leaves that clung to his rake. "Other than the fact she's screwing my uncle—who's married, by the way? I hear she likes to make fur coats out of kittens and smack Girl Scouts over the head with newspapers."

Jill laughed, and I shook my head.

"Thanks, Neil. That was super helpful." I patted his chest before following Jill to the door.

Jill pressed the doorbell. My heartbeat was in my toes. *Please don't turn us away. Please don't turn us away.* A bead of sweat ran down the back of my neck, and my knees weakened. Jill grabbed my hand.

"Breathe, Andie."

I squeezed her fingers and gripped my pants leg as Jill rang the doorbell again. *Come on, come on.* Someone turned the handle. My knees locked. Then the door flung open, and a woman resembling Cruella DeVille stood on the other side of the screen.

"What is it?" she snapped the moment her glare fell on us.

"Regina Miller, right?" Jill said. "I'm, uh, Jen, and this is Alex. She's pregnant. We know you worked for Bethlehem Family Services, and Alex here had a couple questions about how your past clients are doing. We were hoping—"

"How did you come by that information?" Her dark eyes narrowed as she crossed her bony arms over her chest.

My hand tightened on Jill's, and she flinched.

"Through a family friend," she said.

"Right. Get off my porch." Regina took a step back as Jill took one forward.

"Please, Ms. Miller, if you'd just give us five minutes of your time. See, Alex is—

"No. I'm not allowed to share information about my clients, and even if I was, I don't want to talk to you. Now, leave before I call the police." Regina slammed the door closed and locked the deadbolt.

My grip on Jill's hand slacked as I stared at where Regina had once stood. My throat was on fire. Had we really come all this way for nothing? Jill removed her hand from mine then tugged me from the stoop.

"I'm sorry." Neil coaxed me down the stairs. "I told you she was a bitch."

Once on the grass, I wrapped my arms around his waist and leaned into him as we walked. He tightened his arm around my shoulders, and I swallowed the lump in my throat. What a waste of time.

Jill snatched her car keys from her hoodie's pocket. "Welp, looks like it's Plan B." She skipped toward her car.

Oh, no. She was going to bug the house—and now Neil would be a witness, too. Why hadn't I thought of that before? I couldn't let him get in trouble for our decision.

"Jill, wait," I said. "Maybe we shouldn't do this."

"Do what, exactly?" Neil asked as I let go of him, following me to Jill's car. He peeked over her shoulder as she pulled bug after bug out of her duffel bag. "Whoa, are those what I think they are?"

"Yep," she replied. "We're going to get info out of this chick whether she wants us to or not."

Neil snatched them from Jill's hands.

"Hey!"

"No way. You're not doing this." He dropped the bugs on the ground and crunched them beneath his foot.

Jill screamed, and I covered my mouth.

"You little dick! Do you know how much those cost me?" Jill said.

Neil held up his hands. "I will pay you back, but you are *not* going to get Andie involved in something like this. She could go to jail."

"She said it was fine!"

Neil turned to me, his face red. "Please tell me that's a joke."

I dropped my hand from my mouth, my skin flushing. I opened my mouth to respond, but nothing came out.

Neil let out an exasperated chuckle and put his hands on his head. "Do you have any idea what would happen if Regina found the bugs and called the police?"

"You were perfectly fine with hacking the agency's files," Jill said, her voice tinged with annoyance.

"Yeah, on laptops with IP addresses bouncing off multiple servers across the world. But those things"—he pointed to the broken devices on the ground—"would have both of your prints all over them, and what you were about to do is a *felony*. If you went to jail, you'd be in there for years, and your baby would be taken away by child services. Did you even think about that?"

I faltered backward, wrapping my arms around my waist. I hadn't. He was right; I should've thought this through. The world wavered through my blurry eyes.

The lines in Neil's face softened. He sighed, stepping toward me. "Andie, I—"

"No, I think you've proven your point." Jill moved between him and me.

"Jill, move. Please," he said calmly.

She looked at me, and I nodded before she turned out of the way.

Neil reached me in two big lunges and took my face in his hands. "I'm sorry. I shouldn't have worded it like that."

My tongue felt two sizes too big, and I was afraid if I opened my mouth, the only thing that would come out was a squeak.

He pulled me into his strong embrace and kissed the top of my head. "I'll talk to Regina, okay? I promise I'll get her to tell us what we want to know. Just . . . please forgive me. It's been a long time since I cared this much about anyone but Mom and Beth, and I snapped. I'm sorry."

I nodded, my cheek pressed against his chest, and listened to his heartbeat, trying to calm the shaking in my legs and stop the tears that ached to flow. When Neil let me go, I wasn't ready, and a single droplet rolled down my cheek. He caught it with his thumb.

"We okay?" he asked, brushing hair from my forehead.

"Yeah," I replied, my voice as quiet as a whisper.

He lifted my chin, gently pressing his lips against mine.

"Well, that's all fine and dandy," Jill said, "but you still owe me, like, five hundred bucks."

Neil pulled away, sighed, and turned to her. "I said I'd pay you back, and I will."

She glared at him and crossed her arms. "You better, or your sexy times with Andie are gonna be over."

"'Sexy times?' How old are you, ten?"

"Oh, shut your cake hole." Jill picked up the pieces of ruined equipment off the ground and shoved them in her bag. She slammed the back door of her car closed before hopping into the driver's seat.

After ensuring Neil I wasn't mad at him—which was the truth; I just felt like an absolute fool—I climbed into Jill's Honda as he returned to work.

As she drove away from Regina Miller's house, two realizations sunk in: We might never uncover the details surrounding my adoption; and if Neil hadn't been there to stop me from making the—second—worst mistake of my life, I might've lost the very reason I was so desperate to learn about my family history.

My baby.

That evening, Neil made a point to call me after work to make sure I was okay. At first, it hurt too much to talk, thinking about how close I'd come to ruining everything and how I might never learn anything about my birth parents. But he refused to let me go until he knew I was smiling. So, in typical, Neil Donaghue fashion, he joked until he had me laughing so hard I nearly peed. Since then, we'd spoken every night—or seen each other in person, which often resulted in make-out sessions. And every weekend, I stayed at Jill's house, doing what we could behind the protection of her IP scramblers to uncover Regina's role in my adoption.

Four weeks to the day after we started investigating, I got a text from Jill: *Tell Neil to ask Regina about a Miranda Fuller. I'm about ninety-five percent sure she's your mom.*

I jumped off my bed with a squeal. My textbooks fell to the floor. She'd done it. She'd actually done it. Jill had found my mom. I fought the urge to twirl with my stuffed polar bear like we were starring in Disney on Ice. A glance at the time showed 1:00 p.m. Two hours until school let out. I paced at the end of my bed, trying to decide whether to wait for Neil or start investigating on my own.

Aw, heck—he'll forgive me.

I raced to the computer.

An hour later, the doorbell rang, and I swallowed a shriek. I'd gotten so wrapped up in reading about Miranda that I'd escaped into an alternate universe. Not anticipating anyone, I ignored the visitor. *If it's that important, come back later.*

My phone chimed with a text from Neil. *Just so you know, by not answering the door, you ruined the surprise.*

Pushing aside the curtains on the office window, I spotted Neil's truck in the driveway and smiled. After hurrying to the front door, I yanked it open then leapt into his arms, planting a kiss on his mouth. Neil smiled, his lips against mine, and with hands on my lower back, he guided me into the house and then kicked the door shut.

"You're early," I said between kisses.

"Skipped last period." He kissed me again, sliding his hand behind my neck. "Test tomorrow."

My body vibrated. I held firmer to him, my knees weakening. One more time, Neil's mouth met mine, then he pulled his lips away.

Neil held my lower back. "I hope that's not how you greet all your friends."

"Just the boys."

He smirked. "Well, aren't you chipper today? Did we win the lottery?"

I grinned and led him toward the office. "Even better."

"Please don't tell me this is going to be one of those things where I open a lid and a puppy springs out."

I laughed. "No. There's no puppy."

"Okay, good. I hate those things."

Stopping just inside the room, I stared at him, wide-eyed. "You hate *puppies*?"

He looked at me innocently. "What? They pee and poop and bark and chew things, and they smell all the time."

"They're adorable."

"They're flea bags with rotten egg breath."

"You don't have a heart."

"I know. For Valentine's Day, I'm just going to send you a text that says 'I.U.'" He grinned, and I shook my head before pulling him to the desk.

"Jill sent a text earlier that she's figured out who my mom might be." I pointed at the computer, and Neil sat down. "I guess she won some humanitarian award a few years ago for her involvement in helping to stop sex trafficking."

"So, she's like a modern-day Mother Teresa?"

"I suppose."

"Well, then maybe she'll be up to visiting with you."

I shrugged. "Maybe. But my adoption was closed. She must've done that for a reason, right?"

Scrolling through the webpage, he waved his other hand. "Yeah, but she gave birth to you. I'm sure there's some maternal desire there. I bet I can dazzle her into meeting us for lunch."

"Unless she smacks you with her purse and calls you a confounded hooligan."

Neil tipped his head back and laughed. "Maybe I better call her on the phone." He turned his face toward me, the corners of his eyes creasing as he smiled.

My skin flushed, and if it weren't for the sound of the door closing from the garage, I would've pulled him off the chair and kissed him until we couldn't breathe.

Ugh. What was Mom doing home so early?

"Andie?" she called from the kitchen with a weak voice.

"In the office."

I listened as her heels clicked on the foyer's hardwood floor, then she stepped into the room. "Did you forget about Dr. Brandt?"

Crap. My monthly appointment was today. "Yeah, kind of. Can we reschedule?"

"No. It was hard enough to get her to squeeze you in every month."

"Don't worry about it," Neil said, clicking out of the Internet. "I'll catch up with you tomorrow." He stood and smiled at my mom.

Her glare was hard as her lips barely turned up in a smile. I'd warned Mom a couple days before he started coming over that we weren't just friends anymore, but she still hadn't warmed up to the idea of Neil and me.

Neil kissed my forehead before crossing the room and sticking a piece of paper in his back pocket.

"Have a good evening, Ms. Hamilton," he said before entering the hall. He winked when Mom's head was turned, then opened the front door. I waited until it closed before scolding my mother.

I crossed my arms. "You know, he still thinks you don't trust him."

"I don't." I glared at her. "But I do trust you. So, I'm trying to be accepting. Now, let's go before they cancel your appointment."

After rolling my eyes, I grabbed my purse and followed her to the car.

CHAPTER 20

The soft *whoosh-whoosh* from Dr. Brandt's ultrasound machine calmed every anxious fiber in my body. No more worries of birth parents or hacking databases. It was amazing how much I'd come to care about the little person inside me in such a short amount of time. Almost unbelievable. Impossible. How could any mother have the strength to give up their baby?

I stared at the screen. The baby was still small, but I could make out some of its features. Goosebumps rose on my skin.

"Well, you're looking really healthy, Andie," Dr. Brandt said. "The baby is, too. Whatever you're doing, keep up the good work."

She removed the device from my abdomen, and the screen went black. The sound of the baby's heartbeat disappeared. I swallowed the instantaneous lump in my throat. Stupid emotions.

"I'll let you get cleaned up, and I'll see you again in a few weeks. Make sure you check out before you leave, okay?"

I nodded, then she wheeled the ultrasound machine from the room, shutting the door behind her. I blinked back tears and stood from the bed, reminding myself that, soon, the baby would be in my arms. And I would never have to worry about not seeing it again.

Taking a deep breath, I stepped forward for a wet cloth to wipe the sticky goop from my bloated belly and smiled.

The rest of the week went by without much excitement, and that Friday, I helped Jill and her mom finish inventory for the jewelry store, and on Saturday, Jill got me addicted to *Halo*. With Neil taking over the investigation, the two of us had nothing to do but relax and pick on her dad on his one weekend off work. But where my mom would've been annoyed by our constant pranks, Mr. Anderson turned around and tried to get us back. He reminded me so much of my dad; I couldn't help but smile the entire weekend.

It wasn't until after lunchtime on Sunday that Jill brought me home. Unable to stop laughing, even after I exited her car, I wandered into the house with a huge grin. And then I spotted Mom sitting at the kitchen table with a scowl, holding a hot mug of tea. Her eyes were framed with red, and again, I couldn't help but notice how pale she'd gotten. Before, I thought she was simply nervous about speaking with Carter's mom, but now . . . .

My pulse raced as I took a seat across from her. "Is everything okay?"

"Nothing you need to be concerned about." Mom tried to smile, but the corners of her mouth only twitched.

I frowned. I'd learned Mom's tells enough to know she was lying. Why was she dodging my question?

"How was your weekend at Jill's?" she tried to change the subject.

"Fine. Did something happen?" I pried.

Mom stared at her hands, and my stomach sank. She stood and dumped the rest of her tea down the kitchen sink.

"I guess you might as well know the truth. You're going to find out anyway." She sighed before opening a drawer and pulling out a piece of paper she'd obviously hidden.

I took it from her when she returned to the table.

My body turned to ice. *An eviction notice?* Mom had never given the impression her job at the university wasn't enough to make ends meet. But the letter said it'd been months since she paid our mortgage.

145

"Between all our debt, the bills surrounding your dad's death, and . . . everything else we pay for, there just wasn't enough money. I skipped paying for the house, thinking I could pay off our smaller debts faster, and now . . . . "

I glanced up at my mother, my heart in my throat, hearing the words she hadn't said. *And now we have your medical bills to worry about.* Her expression twisted in pain. Regret. Love. Sympathy. I turned away and pressed my fist to my chest, forcing down the emotions that bubbled in me like a volcano nearing eruption. I was the domino to knock the rest over. Was this why she'd thinned out so much and gotten so pale? Was I literally killing my mother?

Mom put a hand on top of mine. "Andie, listen to me. This has been two years in the making. This is *not* your fault. There is far more going on here than you're even aware of."

My eyes pooled with tears. "So, tell me!"

She pursed her lips and then sighed. "Honey, you don't need to be carrying around more burdens than you need to."

I shook my head, and she squeezed my hand.

"I need you to trust me that this would've happened even if you weren't pregnant. This isn't your fault."

I nodded, but I couldn't keep my thoughts from churning, my ribs from burning, my throat from aching. Here I was, selfish, wanting to keep my baby when we couldn't even afford things for the two of us. My lungs felt ten sizes too small for my body. Maybe Mom was right; maybe I *should* put the baby up for adoption.

My insides clenched. I knew now what it felt like to yearn for answers about my identity, where I came from, why I couldn't be raised by the people who gave me life—whether they even loved me. I didn't want that fate for my child. I wanted my baby to *know* how much I loved it, to not have to question my affection or feel abandoned.

Oh, God, what do I do?

When Mom stood to stick her mug in the dishwasher, I waddled up to my room, tears caught in my throat, and without even bothering to take off my clothes or makeup, I fell onto my bed. Mom didn't try to get me to come downstairs that night or the next morning. After she pried the eviction notice from my shaking hands, I retreated to my room, crawled under my blankets, and refused to move, to think. All I wanted was to stay in bed and pretend, for a few hours, that nothing in my life was out of place.

The door to the garage closed as Mom left for work. I still didn't move, not for a glass of water or a bite to eat. I hadn't cried yet, and I really didn't want to. We had until the end of January, according to the letter. Mom was going to file for bankruptcy. The government would hopefully help us with our bills. We'd both work harder to find part-time jobs, and we'd find a nice, small place to live.

"Maybe even close to Jill, in an apartment over one of the shops downtown," Mom had said, trying to excite me.

But I'd never slept anywhere but this bedroom. I'd taken my first steps on this floor. My first sleepover was on this carpet and my first kiss on the swing set outside. I wanted to share some memories with my child in this house, in this room where I'd had tea parties with my dad and played Barbies with my mom.

I squeezed my watery eyes shut. *Stop thinking, Andie.*

At three o'clock sharp, the doorbell rang. Neil. I'd told him the garage keypad's code in case he left school early again and that he could come in that way. And, as expected, a minute or so later, the door from the garage into the kitchen opened.

"Andie?" Neil shouted from downstairs.

Not in the mood to yell, I texted him: *I'm in my room.* His phone chimed, then I heard footsteps march through the house and up the stairs. A second later, he was in my doorway. Spotting me still in bed, he leaned against the wall.

"Must be nice to sleep 'til the middle of the day." He grinned at me playfully. His dark hair was extra messy, and he'd yet to untuck his white River Springs polo shirt from his black pants. The muscles in his forearms popped as he crossed them, and the affection that glistened in his eyes made my heart stammer.

God had been way too generous with Neil's genes.

But seeing him reminded me why I'd stayed in bed all day, and I dug my face into my pillow as a rubber band snapped in my chest. I bit my tongue to keep my emotions under control. Neil lay next to me and stroked my hair.

"You should be proud," he said. "I really wanted to make a comment about the sight of my handsomeness bringing tears to your eyes, but I withheld."

I lifted my head. "I'm not crying." *Yet.* "And you just did."

Neil was on his side, facing me, one hand holding up his head. His other rested on my arm over the comforter.

"Yeah, I guess I did. But it got you to look at me."

When I glared at him, he smiled so big and bright. The corners of his eyes creased, and I couldn't help myself. Digging out from under the blankets, I attacked him. I wanted him to make me forget, if only for a few minutes, that my life wasn't spiraling out of control. We were losing our house. Mom was filing for bankruptcy. My baby might not have a home. And I was the one who detonated the bomb.

My assault caught him off-guard. He tipped onto his back as I kissed him with ferocity. I gripped the bottom of his shirt and tried to lift it over his head, but Neil grabbed my arms and pushed me onto my back. His lips left mine.

"Slow down a minute," he said. "First, tell me what's gotten into you, then we can return to the current program of Horny Teenagers on a Bed in an Empty House."

Jaw clenched, I smacked his hands off my cheeks and pushed him, hard. He grunted and swayed backward, giving me the room I needed to climb off the bed. His face was full of pain when I spun around to glare at him, and my chest squeezed. But someone had stuck me on the Roulette Wheel of Emotion and spun. My hands shook, and my knees locked. I was stuck on fear, shame, anger. Even the words that came out of my mouth were out of control, and I couldn't stop them. "A joke. Always another damn joke."

Neil held up his hands. "Whoa, calm down."

"Why can't you ever be serious with me?"

"Why do you think I told you to wait a minute? Something obviously happened to make you stay in bed all day, and I'm *not* going to take advantage of your heightened emotions when I know it'll come back to bite me in the ass. Don't you dare use me as your punching bag."

I screamed, tugging on my hair. He was right; I needed to calm down.

Spinning around, I sat on the bed, my back to Neil. "We're losing the house, all right? Our eviction notice came yesterday."

And here came the freaking tears. I wiped them from my cheeks with a vengeance.

Neil tugged on my arm, and I wound up on my back with my head in his lap.

Before I could get my hands over my face, Neil's lips were on mine. He kissed me, not like I'd kissed him moments before but the way he had when I'd sat on the truck. Tender and gentle. The way he had when he promised to take care of me. Just like he was trying to do now. Another tear broke free. I never should've lashed out at him.

He kissed me a few more times, and, soon, all my anger melted away. Neil must've noticed I'd calmed, too, because he pulled back and wiped my cheeks.

At least he figured out how to get me off the crazy emotion train.

"Believe me when I tell you this: You're going to be okay," he said. "It might not feel like it right now, but I've been struggling to make ends meet since I was eight. It's not ideal, but it's doable. You were already planning to finish out high school at home, right?"

I nodded. I was ahead in my schoolwork and would finish junior year early. Once the baby came, I wanted to be around to take care of it while Mom was at work, so I planned to do my senior year as a homeschooled student too. Mom would sign me up for one of those online school things, and I was pretty good at self-teaching, so I wasn't worried about never going back.

"Well, that's already one thing—one expensive thing—you guys won't have to pay for. And if you pick up some work, between that and your mom's two jobs . . . it'll be a different lifestyle, but you'll be fine."

He stroked my cheek with his thumb, and I leaned into his hand. I couldn't help but feel like Mom was still hiding something, but he was right. My life *would* be different, but compared to what he'd dealt with for the last ten years, I shouldn't complain.

I frowned. "I shouldn't have said what I did."

"Even though I tell too many jokes?"

I looked up at him. The corner of his mouth twitched. After hearing me swear at him, I couldn't believe he was attempting to kid again. But his fearless sense of humor was something I'd come to adore.

"Well, I suppose you can't help it. Considering there's something wrong with you."

He smirked. "Oh, really?" Neil grabbed my sides and squeezed.

I shrieked and tried to jump up, but he tickled harder. I smacked at his hands. "Stop! You're going to make me pee. Seriously, stop!"

He let go with a laugh. Kneeling on the bed, I snatched my pillow and hit him with it. His stunned reaction sent me into a fit of giggles, and when I tried to smack him a second time, he grabbed the pillow and tossed it aside. Then he was on his knees, and the next thing I knew, I was on my back again. Except, this time, Neil straddled me and held my hands above my head.

His playful smile made me ache to assault him all over again, but he called "truce" and sat back when I nodded.

Righting myself, I grabbed my hair tie off the nightstand and pulled my blonde strands into a ponytail. When I turned back to him, Neil twirled something in his fingers. It looked like a folded notecard. I touched his back when his shoulders curled forward.

"You okay?" I asked.

He played with the notecard for a few more seconds then held it out to me. "I forced Regina to look up info about Miranda."

I took the folded card from him.

Before I could ask him what he meant by forced, he continued, "Turns out Jill's information was wrong. Miranda Fuller isn't your mom."

I opened the notecard. Regina had scrawled a name inside. *Jodi Greer*. I touched my throat. "So, is this . . . ?"

"Your birth mom. Yeah. The right name, this time." His voice was melancholy. Why wasn't he happy?

I could barely contain my joy. We'd found her. We'd actually found her.

"Andie, I looked into it," he continued. "Your mom's in prison for robbing a bank at gunpoint about five years ago. It'll be another fifteen years before she gets out."

My insides clenched. My mom was a criminal? Before I'd heard of Miranda Fuller, I'd expected the possibility my birth mom was poor or single. Heck, I'd even considered she was a drug addict or an alcoholic. But a gun-wielding bank robber? That one hadn't crossed my mind.

Still, ever since Jill, Neil, and I started looking, my longing for this moment had grown. I couldn't give up on meeting Jodi, not when I was so close.

"Then I'll visit her in jail," I said.

"It's not that simple. There's a process for visiting an inmate—an application you have to fill out. And you're a minor."

"You'll be eighteen in a month. I mean, wouldn't it take them that long to process my application anyway?"

Neil shook his head. "I can't take you. It has to be a parent or legal guardian."

I frowned. How could I ask my mom to accompany me to see the woman who birthed me? I didn't want Mom to think I was telling her she wasn't good enough.

But if I wanted to meet my birth mother, it was the only choice I had. I'd regret it if I didn't.

"I'll . . . ask my mom." My voice sounded as sad as I felt.

Neil touched my cheek. "I know this isn't what you wanted. I wish I had better news, like your birth mom's a millionaire movie star. Not some Bonnie or Clyde."

I sighed. What else could I have expected, though? Parents didn't give up their kid unless they had to. Or, at least, I hoped they didn't. Maybe my mom had a good reason after all. I just hoped the decision wasn't easy for her—that she'd loved me, even a little.

"Where do I get the application?" I asked.

Neil stood and held out his hand, and when I took it, he tugged me to my feet. "Well, see, there were these really smart guys who invented something called the Internet."

I backhanded his abs, and he laughed.

CHAPTER 21

I knocked on Mom's bedroom door a couple hours after dinner. She'd needed a few hours to grade papers and relax after her first day working a second job, and she'd barely made it through dinner—and barely ate her food—without dozing off.

A soft "come in" rang through from inside the room. Pushing the door open, I found Mom on her bed, propped by pillows with a book stuck under her nose. Quickly, she shoved what looked like a pill bottle under the comforter. I narrowed my gaze and nearly accused her on the spot of continuing to hide something from me, but then Mom said something I couldn't discern, and I remembered why I was there.

"Can we talk?" I asked.

Mom dropped her novel, squinted at me, then nodded and laid the book next to her on the bed. Where Dad used to sleep. "Everything okay?"

I sat by her feet and scratched at my wrist. "Yeah. I talked with Neil about everything."

"What did he say?"

"That we'd be okay."

"Well, he would know. Do you believe him?"

I nodded, looking up at her. She knew there was more I wanted to say; I could see it in her eyes. I shot off a quick prayer this wouldn't hurt her. "Also . . . we found my birth mom."

She didn't even flinch. "That's great, honey. Are you going to write to her?"

My heartbeat raced. Here came the big request. I took a deep breath and spoke slowly. "I was kind of hoping you'd maybe go with me to meet her?"

I stiffened, waiting for Mom's piercing cry of betrayal, but she just smiled. A barely-there one, but a smile nonetheless. I pressed my lips together to keep my mouth from gaping.

"I was afraid you wouldn't ask," she said.

I beamed, and, soon, Mom's smile matched mine. Then my face fell. What would she say when I told her *where* we had to meet Jodi? I played with them hem of my shirt. "There's a little problem, though. We sort of have to go visit her at the jail."

Mom sighed, and again I braced for impact. *Please, don't say no.* I held my breath, each second that passed feeling like an hour.

"Then, I guess that's where we need to go," Mom said.

My heart leapt into my throat. I threw my arms around her, despite how frustrated I was with her secrecy. "Thank you."

She patted my back. "I want you to know your birth parents, sweetie. If this is what it takes, then so be it."

I squeezed her. "I love you, Mom."

"I love you, too."

After a quick smile, I wandered back to my room, anxious for the day I'd meet my birth mother.

Luckily, the rest of November went fast. We checked the mail every day for any sign of the prison's response, but it wasn't until the Monday before Thanksgiving that it came—my application had been approved, and Jodi had agreed to meet with me. We scheduled our trip to the prison for December 2. It was a medium-security prison that housed only women. Pulling into the parking lot, I was shocked at the size of the place. It was like a small community college, and if it hadn't been for the barbed wire fence around the outdoor recreation area, I'd never have been able to tell it was a prison. The security was what I expected, though, and after Mom and I were patted down, we entered the waiting room and gave our names. The place smelled old and musty, and a light buzzed in the ceiling.

I sat in one of the green, plastic—and very uncomfortable—chairs. My legs bounced as I waited for my name to be called. Would Jodi cry tears of joy when she saw me? Would she tell me to come see her again? Butterflies threw a dance party in my gut.

At 10:15, a guard entered and shouted, "Visitors for Jodi Greer."

Mom and I followed the man down a long, brightly-lit, white hall and into a visitation room. Prison guards stood at perfect intervals along the walls, and a few inmates, dressed in dark green jumpsuits, sat at small tables. Almost all of them had tattoos on their forearms, and I was shocked by the difference in ages. One appeared in her twenties; the other had to be at least sixty. Every one of them, though, looked like they itched to destroy the universe.

The guard led us to a table and instructed us to sit. My heart sprinted, and I wiped my clammy palms on the legs of my jeans. This was it. I was going to meet my birth mom. If I didn't pass out first.

A woman was led into the room. Instantly, I knew it was her. Jodi's light-blonde hair was pulled into a messy ponytail, and her face was so like mine—small nose and lips, high cheekbones. It was as if I'd jumped ahead in a time machine and saw my thirty-four-year-old self.

I gripped Mom's hand under the table.

Jodi sat across from us and eyeballed me, Mom, then me again. "When the prison told me I had a young girl who wanted to visit, I figured it'd be my niece. Do I know you?"

Her voice sounded like mine, except gruff after years of—what I guessed was—smoking. Small lines ran beneath her blue eyes, and a few grays colored her hairline. Up close, Jodi looked older than thirty-four.

But I hadn't missed what she said: I had a cousin. The list of questions I wanted to ask was forever growing.

"I'm Susan Hamilton, and this is Andie. We were hoping you were the one who placed her for adoption sixteen years ago?" Mom asked.

Jodi narrowed her gaze, then a tentative smile built on her face, and her eyes turned glassy. "Oh, I see it now. I was wondering if you'd ever come find me."

I smiled then tried to speak, but when my mouth opened, nothing came out. Mom caught my gaze and spoke for me when she realized I needed help. "Andie wondered if you could tell her a little bit about yourself."

Jodi looked me up and down before she spoke. "Well, I'm not really sure what you want to know, but I had you when I was eighteen. Your dad was a summer fling who ended up goin' overseas for college. The guy was a tool."

Sounded like Carter and me. I bit my lip.

"I was never much good at the school thing," she continued, "but I tried. Liked books, though. Read a lot. I don't know. You got any questions?"

Too many. But we only had fifteen minutes—the prison made people visit a few instances before they allowed any real time—and I'd spent I don't know how long staring at her like a crazed teenager meeting a celebrity. Mom squeezed my hand, and, again, I tried to talk. But my jaw felt wired shut.

"Ten minutes," the guard near our table said.

Had five minutes really gone by already? *Come on, Andie.* Taking a deep breath, I spit out the first thing that came to mind, "Why did you give me up?"

Jodi's eyebrows squished together. "Well, I didn't want to, if that's what you mean. But I had to."

"But why?" My voice shook.

"'Cause I knew you'd be better off with someone else. Like your mom, here. Seems like you two get along."

Nodding, I bit my tongue, hard, to keep the tears from falling. I used to have the ability to keep them in my head. Where the heck had it gone?

"Then you get it," Jodi said. "I couldn't take care of you. I always

wondered where you got off to, but I never regretted my decision."
She paused, tapping her finger on the table. "I ain't done much good
in my life, but I did good by you. Knowing I gave you a chance. And
seeing you now proves I was right. You're beautiful. And it seems your
mom did all right raising you."

She has, I wanted to say, but a lump the size of a bowling ball was
stuck in my throat. I reached across the table, desperate to gain some
connection with my birth mother other than words and teary glances.
A guard stepped closer but stopped when I held my palm up. Jodi
smiled and put her hand in mine. Grinning through watery eyes, I
squeezed.

"It looks like you're gonna have one of your own," Jodi said, dropping her gaze to my small stomach then back to me. When my face
scrunched—I wasn't *that* far along—she chuckled. "Honey, when you
been pregnant before, it doesn't take much to see it in others. You
planning to keep it?"

I nodded. "I think I'll be able to handle it. I mean, I don't know
why I wouldn't be."

Jodi squeezed my hand. "Do whatever you think is right. Your gut
won't lie. Mine sure didn't, and look how you turned out."

I smiled.

After a few more questions, like did I have any siblings—no—and
where did my cousins live—just over the border into New Mexico—
the guard announced our fifteen minutes were up. I fought the urge to
cling to Jodi's hand as she stood. I hadn't spent nearly enough time
with her.

"You write me. Let me know how you're doing, 'kay?"

I nodded, my mouth drying, and she backed out of the room with a
wave. When the door from the visitation area to the cellblock closed, I
covered my mouth, my chest hitching. Mom put her arm around my
shoulders, and I leaned into her. I'd been so afraid that Jodi would
have considered me a burden, that she would've hate me for ruining
her life, like I originally loathed my baby for messing up mine. But
that was so far from the reason she'd placed me for adoption.

"She *had* loved me, Mom," I said, my voice shaking.

"I know, sweetheart. I could've told you that. The fact that she put you first says it all."

I hugged her as a fugitive tear fell from my eye.

"You ready to do some shopping?" Mom asked.

Sitting up, I wiped my cheek and smiled.

CHAPTER 22

"All right. Well, you're eighteen weeks now. How are you feeling?" Dr. Brandt asked at my obstetrician appointment on Thursday.

Like last time, Mom sat in the waiting room. Why I was still super uncomfortable having her present for these conversations, I didn't know. But she'd pretty much be on her phone the whole time anyway —she'd been talking with a lot of people lately—so I tried not to feel too guilty about visiting the doctor on my own.

"Good," I replied.

"Has the morning sickness eased?"

"Yeah. I'm hungry all the time, though."

"That's good. Just make sure you're drinking a lot of fluids and eating healthy foods." She looked at her chart. "Your vitals are great, your blood work is clean, and you're gaining weight. So, let's see how the baby's doing. Go ahead and lie back."

I followed her instructions and jumped when she squirted a big glob of cold, sticky liquid on my expanding belly. Dr. Brandt pulled the ultrasound machine closer and rolled the probe-thing back and forth across my lower abdomen. At first, I was annoyed she'd pointed the machine away from me, but, within seconds, I heard the heartbeat and didn't care. I closed my eyes and let the rhythm take me to another place.

"Looking good, Andie. Baby looks healthy." She continued to hit buttons on the machine and move the probe around my stomach. "Do you want to know what you're having?"

My eyes snapped open. I turned my head to look at her. "You can tell?"

She nodded. "It's up to you, though. Some women don't want to know until it's born; others do. Whatever you want."

I gripped the bottom of my shirt. Did I want to know? I'd bought just the essentials with Mom at the thrift store, since we weren't sure what I was having. It might be kind of fun to look through baby catalogs with Jill though, jotting down items that I wanted to save up to buy instead of watching *Star Trek*.

"I want to know," I said before I could change my mind.

Smiling, Dr. Brandt turned the machine so I could see the screen. Inside a grayish shape that reminded me of a flattened coffee filter was a black blob. And inside that was the fetus. I touched my throat. That little thing, with a head and torso and arms and legs, was inside me. Was my *baby*.

"You're having a boy," Dr. Brandt said.

I'd told myself I wasn't going to shed any tears today, but they came anyway. A boy. As if by some magic spell, my love for him grew.

Dr. Brandt cleaned off my belly and told me to dress while she printed a picture. When I stepped into the hall, she placed the first photo of my son in my hands. In the waiting room, Mom jumped up, worried by the tears on my cheeks, but as soon as I handed her the photograph and told her the news, her face mirrored mine. Arms around each other, we walked to the car. Again, we stopped for ice cream on the way home, and at Sprinkles Ice Cream Parlor, I picked out a name—Ethan.

Waiting for Neil to come over after school the next day was agonizing. Jill had texted me to let me know her mother needed her help again at the store that evening. Which meant there'd be no rushing my visit with my boyfriend so I could get to the girls' weekend. *And* his uncle had given Neil the day off work in exchange for Black Friday. I filled the day with as much studying and homework as I could to keep busy. The faster I finished junior year, the better; the baby was due in April—barring any complications, of course. But about every hour, I pulled out the picture of Ethan, just to look at him. Each time, I cried like someone turned the garden hose on in my head. Somehow, I needed to figure out how to turn off the crazy emotion switch. My nose was sore from blowing it again and again, and my eyes looked like they'd been tattooed with Christmas-red ink.

When the doorbell rang at three o'clock, I leapt out of my chair and sprinted for the front door and then yanked it open with a grin. *Finally*. Then my heart skipped a beat.

Neil's left eye was black, and a cut above his left brow had been stitched closed.

"What happened?" I asked, grabbing his hand and tugging him inside. I touched his left temple with my fingertips.

He winced and tipped his face away from my hand. "I'm fine. It's nothing, unlike your Rudolph nose."

"Gee, thanks. Seriously, what happened? Please tell me you didn't get into a fight."

"I didn't get into a fight." With a shrug, he left me standing in the foyer to gobble food from our kitchen. It'd become an every-day occurrence. Well, weekday occurrence. I never did see him on the weekends. Last time I'd asked him to skip a Saturday of working for his uncle, Neil had warned me the "consequences would be dire."

As Neil stared into the open refrigerator, I put a hand on his back. "You know I can't let you walk in here, looking like that, and not know why."

He sighed, grabbing a container of leftover mashed potatoes. "Mom had a bad night. That's all you need to know." Shutting the fridge door, he walked away from my touch to pop the bowl into the microwave.

I ground my teeth. "She hit you again?"

"Andie, let it go."

"No! She can't do that to you."

He slammed the microwave shut. "And what would you have me do? Call the cops on her?"

"Maybe."

Neil pressed the start button and spun around, pinching the bridge of his nose. "She's my mom. I'm not going to have her thrown in jail. Besides, I'll be eighteen in a couple weeks, and then I can move out without having to go through all the emancipated shit Beth did. I'll get my part of my Dad's lawsuit money, and I'll only have to swing by and check on her once in a while."

I frowned. The microwave beeped, and Neil grabbed his lunch.

"If anyone asks, though, I got the shiner in a boxing match where I won five hundred bucks." He smirked and sat at the dining table.

Rolling my eyes, I joined him, took the spoon from his hand, and stuffed a bit of potato in my mouth. He glared at me.

I shrugged. "Baby's hungry."

"You know, you can only use that excuse so often before someone starts thinking you get kicks from stealing food."

I grinned and played with the corner of the textbook sitting on the table. What would Neil say when he saw the picture? I hoped he'd say something along the lines of *that's awesome.* But would he be moved, like I was? The baby wasn't his, so would he even care?

"You're staring at me. Do I have something on my face, or am I just that handsome?"

"You do realize you're not as attractive as you think you are?" Blatant lie. Oh well.

He clutched his chest. "Ouch. That was cold, Hamilton. Like Jack Frost." I shook my head. "But seriously," he continued, "what's going on? You looked like you'd been crying before I showed up, and now you're gawking at me. Do I need to be worried?"

Biting my lip, I drew out the ultrasound picture from under my homework and handed it to Neil. "The doctor took this yesterday at my appointment."

He dropped his spoon into the bowl and took the photo. "Man, it has got to cut down on all the booze. It's getting a beer belly."

"Neil!" I should've known the first thing that popped out of his mouth would be a joke. But for one freaking minute, it'd be nice to get some sincerity from him when we weren't arguing or I wasn't crying. I stood and entered the kitchen before he could see the tears welling up. *Great. Here we go again. Stupid eye faucets.*

"Oh, come on. You know I'm kidding," he said.

Without replying, I fumbled in the pantry, pretending to look for something to eat. Right now, the tears weren't falling. I wanted to keep it that way.

His chair scooted out, then hands held my hips. Neil tried to spin me, but I dug my heels into the floor.

"Hey, look at me," he said.

"No." My voice was shaky. *Dang it.* I gripped the counter when he tried to spin me again.

With hands still on my hips, Neil rested his forehead against the back of my skull and sighed. "Andie, I'm sorry. It was a joke."

We stood that way for at least a minute, then I broke the strained silence. "Dr. Brandt told me it was a boy."

This time when he tried to turn me, I let him. He relaxed when I met his gaze. Neil tucked a loose piece of hair behind my ear, his smile soft and his touch gentle. I put my hands on his chest.

"That's great," he said.

"Do you really think so?"

"Why else would I say it?"

"Because you know that's what I want to hear."

"Well, I mean it. You know I'm in this with you 100 percent; I want you to tell me everything. So, it's a boy. That's awesome. I think my aunt still has a few things left from when she had my cousin. I could ask her to—"

I flung my arms around his neck and kissed him. Here he was, genuinely excited and offering to ask his aunt for hand-me-downs, like the baby was his. My heart fluttered. I didn't deserve him. Not even a tiny part of him. Yet, he was mine.

A startled noise popped out of Neil, then his hands were in my hair. His lips moved in sync with mine as he gently tugged on my strands. A shiver ran from my mouth to my toes. Breathing heavier, I kissed him harder, hungry to be closer to him. Neil slipped his tongue into my mouth, and his hands wandered down my back. The hair on my arms rose, and I leaned into him, aching to feel his palms on my bare skin.

I froze. What if he was grossed out by my swelling body? Most guys liked toned girls, and I just felt like a walking balloon. Would he change his mind about me? Would he push me away?

"You okay?" His voice jarred me from my mini-panic attack. Somewhere in all of those thoughts, I must've stopped moving altogether. Neil's blue eyes were so bright, so full of genuine concern. I stuffed down my insecurity and kissed him again. Neil was a better guy than that. And for as much making out as we'd done, we hadn't moved past first base—and, deep down, I was *so* ready for more.

I unwrapped my arms from around his neck and moved my hands up his shirt, caressing his abs with my fingertips. His breathing grew louder, and he pulled me closer. Wanting—needing—to see him the way I had months ago, I lifted his shirt over his head. I traced the tattoo on his chest with my fingertips, outlining each letter of the words "Don't Forget the Music," a small pang of sorrow in my gut. I'd forgotten about it, to be honest, and hadn't yet questioned him about it. But I was positive he'd gotten it for his dad.

Neil grabbed my fingers with one hand, stopping me before I could ask, and lifted my lips back to his with his other. Letting go of my hand, he stuck his fingers in my hair as he parted my lips with his tongue. I kissed him deeper and wandered my hands down his toned back. *Please*, I begged him with my heart, hoping he could hear it. Hoping my brain would recognize I was safe with him. I didn't need to be insecure.

Neil trickled his hands down my sides as we continued to kiss, and with each inch his palms moved, the more my body ached for him. Then he slipped his hands under the back of my shirt and caressed my spine, and I moaned loudly. Neil swore, his voice breathy. He kissed my neck, and my legs trembled. I dug my fingers into his back and arched mine, pressing my chest against his. I drank in the feel of his lips on my skin. Goosebumps rose on every inch.

He kissed up to my earlobe. "Please tell me if I go too far."

I nodded, and his lips found mine again. Gently, he pushed me against the kitchen counter. My fingertips stroked his chest and abs. His muscles flexed under my caress. Neil pulled me closer. Our hips touched. I felt his excitement and moved forward involuntarily, my body yearning for him with a passion that surpassed all words in my brain. Neil groaned and ripped my sweater over my head, his gaze wandering.

Unease pitted in my gut. He was seeing my naked stomach for the first time, my small bump distended over my low-cut jeans. *Please don't be grossed out. Please don't turn away.* My hands shook. Nausea swam in my stomach. My eyes burned. But then he kissed my shoulder, and his hands wandered down my back and around my rib cage, stopping on the sides of my belly.

"You're beautiful," he whispered.

Why those two words unraveled me, I didn't know. I blamed it on pregnancy hormones. But hearing him say them in the midst of such an intimate moment overwhelmed me. I cried—not a sob, like I'd spent the first three months doing, but quiet and happy, where a few tears rolled down my face while I half-wept, half-laughed.

Neil jerked his hands to my face in seconds and took my cheeks in his palms. He wiped away the tears with his thumbs.

"Hey, I'm sorry. Damn it; I told you to warn me if I went too far." He pressed his forehead against mine. "Baby, please don't cry."

I put my hands on his neck. "I'm not upset."

Pulling back just far enough that he could look at my face, Neil seemed to notice, for the first time, I was smiling. His eyebrows furrowed.

Answering his question before he could ask, I placed one of his hands back on my belly and said, "I was so afraid you were going to run away, but you told me I was beautiful."

Neil closed his eyes, sighing, and tightened his arms around me. I rested my cheek on his chest. The left side, where the tattoo was. Right over his heart.

"Andie, I can't begin to tell you what it feels like every time you walk into a room. There aren't enough words. But you've got to know by now: I love you. I have since the third grade, and I always will."

I beamed, hearing the words leave his lips for the first time.

"I love you, too," I replied, meaning them with all my soul. I couldn't say it to Carter the night my life changed, and I was glad to have saved those words for Neil. Because my heart had never hammered so hard, and never before had three little words made me want to run marathons. But with Neil, I felt like I could take on the world.

He snuggled me closer and kissed the top of my head. I listened to his pulse beating fast in his chest.

"So, not to ruin the moment, but your boobs *are* almost naked and touching me, and I'm having a really hard time keeping my hands to myself," he said.

With a roll of my eyes, I stepped out of his hold. I picked up his shirt and tossed it in his face. He smiled a goofy grin, and I put on my own sweater, trying to hide the blush in my cheeks.

CHAPTER 23

Two weeks later, Mom and I had the house pretty well-packed, except for a small Christmas tree in the living room to give us a little holiday happiness. My baby belly had really started to show, and even empire-waist sweaters couldn't hide the fact I was pregnant. Everywhere we went, people stared. Usually with sad or judgmental gazes. At first, all I'd want to do is run and hide in the car. Especially when an older woman said I needed Jesus. But after Mom told the woman off, reminding her Jesus loved even those we scoffed at, I began ignoring people. And after Neil squeezed my hand and told me to mentally flip them off, I'd done so when individuals were over-the-line gawking. It made existing in public a little easier.

The few times Jill spotted people's reactions, she'd used the Force and pretended to make their heads explode. Most people ceased staring, having been called out for being rude. And because Jill usually looked like she was about to crap herself.

She played Obi-Wan Kenobi again as we entered the store to pick up Neil's birthday present. The clerk jolted in surprise and hurried away.

"You know, one of these days, you're going to do that to the wrong person, and we'll get tossed from a store," I said.

"And I'll use my Jedi powers to convince him to let us back in. Bada bing, bada boom."

I shook my head and marched to the musical instruments section in the electronics department.

"What are we getting here again?" Jill asked. "I thought Neil wanted a tobacco pipe."

"He was joking because he doesn't want me to get him anything. He stopped smoking a couple months ago when the smell kept making me sick." I halted when I reached the microphones.

"So, instead, you're getting him a mic?"

Grabbing one that seemed good—though I had no idea what I was looking at—I spun the box in my hands. "His mom broke the last one. She has . . . anger issues." *Crap. I probably shouldn't be telling Jill this.*

"No, she has alcohol issues."

Oh. I forgot Jill had investigative tendencies. And that was putting it nicely.

"Let me see," she said, motioning to the microphone I was holding. "I'm a nerd. I know these things."

I handed it to her with a raised eyebrow.

Flipping it over, she read the specifications. "Don't get this one." She stuffed the box on the shelf and pulled off another, glanced at the back, and then handed it to me. "Here."

I grabbed the box and checked the price. "It's fifty dollars more."

"So, take the tag off."

"Have you met my boyfriend? Price tag or not, he's going to know how much I spent, and then he'll kill me." Especially considering my monetary situation. At least I still had a little money left from my—albeit, measly—savings account. I'd withdrawn all of it so I could afford the few Christmas presents I wanted to buy.

"And you tell him to man up and get over it. Problem solved." Jill headed to the register without waiting for a response.

Rolling my eyes, I followed. We paid for his gift then swung by Jill's house to wrap. As far as Mom knew, I was spending the night with her again and visiting Neil tomorrow for his birthday—the only day his uncle let him request off without penalty. But I had other plans. I smiled, dreaming about waking up with him in his bed and forcing him to play something for me on his guitar.

Present and overnight bag in hand, at 10:30 p.m., I hopped into Jill's Honda, and she drove me to Neil's house. I didn't bother texting. He'd be off work by now, and I wanted to surprise him. I clutched Neil's present to my chest, unable to keep myself from bouncing in my seat.

Neil's truck was in the driveway when we pulled up, and all the lights were on in the house. After saying goodbye to Jill and promising to call if something went wrong, I climbed out of her car. I tossed my bag and Neil's gift into the bed of his truck with what looked like a couple duffel bags and his guitar case. Was he moving out already?

The front door was cracked open when I approached. Before I could knock, glass shattered from inside the house.

"You little shit!" a woman screamed, her words slurred. "You poured it out!"

"I was at work. When would I have had time to touch your bottle?" Neil said.

"Then where'd it go, huh? *Why do you keep ruining my life?*"

A chill ran deep into my bones.

"You drank it, Ma. That's where it went," Neil said, his voice hard and angry. "Down your throat like the rest of the liquor from the Mart. You know, the next time you show up like that, I'm not going to be able to stop Uncle Brad from calling the cops. You're lucky I got there before you did any damage."

Silence. Then crying.

"It's your fault I'm like this. You killed him," Neil's mom said.

I leaned against the siding to keep from falling over.

"I know." Neil's voice was surprisingly calm for how fast my heart pounded.

"Now, come on," he said. "Let's go to bed. You'll feel better in the morning."

More glass broke, and Neil swore. I grabbed my cell phone, ready to call 9-1-1. Then I heard his voice.

"You know what? Fuck you. You can climb your own way up the stairs. Don't break your neck when you come crashing down."

Footsteps neared the door, and I stepped back.

"Don't you leave this house, you hear me?" his mom screamed. "Don't you dare walk away from me! Neil! I hate you, you ungrateful bastard! It should've been you that died!"

Oh my God.

Neil flung the front door open, and I covered my mouth with a gasp. Blood trickled from the right side of his hairline down his face. Seeing me, he jumped.

"Damn it." Neil stormed past me without a second glance and marched to his truck. He flung open the passenger's door and glove box, then slammed both before pressing a cloth to his head.

I hurried toward him, desperate to make sure he was okay.

When I reached for the cloth, he stepped back, snarling. "What have I told you about coming here?"

"I wanted to surprise you." Although I kept my voice quiet, it shook. He didn't seem to notice.

"Yeah, well, you did. I'm fucking shocked that you'd have the goddamn balls to show up here when you know I don't want you to. Especially now, considering tomorrow's the day my dad died. *And* you stuck around to listen to that freak show." His nostrils flared.

I turned away, unable to look at him, my stomach churning.

He continued yelling, "You were never supposed to be around for this shit. Ever. Don't you think I have enough on my mind without having to worry about you getting in the way?"

I stepped away from him and wrapped my arms around my waist. His rage shook me to my core. Ten minutes ago, all I'd wanted to do was curl up next to him. Now, I wanted to get away. Far, far away. We'd had our arguments, yes, but he'd never yelled at me like this.

My chin trembling, I marched toward his truck to grab my bag and leave.

Neil swore and chased after me. "Andie, I'm sorry."

Reaching his truck before he could touch me, I grabbed my bag and slammed the gift into his free arm.

"Happy birthday," I said, spinning on my heel to find the road and call Jill to pick me up.

"No, wait."

I kept walking without looking back. Neil grabbed my arm, and I smacked his hand away, hard. The sound echoed through the trees.

"*Don't touch me.*"

Neil's eyes glassed over, and the pain that rolled through me almost made my knees buckle. Turning my back to him, I continued walking down the driveway.

"Andie, please." A strangled noise came out of him, stopping me in my tracks.

I balled my fists, fighting the urge to turn around. My heart still felt lashed by a whip. How could he talk to me like this when just two weeks ago he'd said he loved me?

My feet betrayed me, and I pivoted slowly.

Neil sat crouched, his back to me. The hand not holding the cloth to his head gripped the back of his neck, pulling his chin to his chest. My resolve to run away snapped. I couldn't leave him. Not the day before his birthday—the tenth anniversary of his father's death—and definitely not after his mother spoke to him the way she had.

I took a deep breath. He'd lashed at me out of fear, not hatred. Neil loved me. I knew he did. He'd not only said it, but, for months, he'd shown it.

I hurried back down the driveway and dropped my bag at his feet. My reappearance startled him. Neil jumped up and spun around. I took his face in my hands, kissing him before he could say anything. His hand dropped from his forehead, and his strong arms clutched me to him.

He dropped his face into the crook of my neck. "I'm sorry. I'm so sorry. I just . . . God, if she ever hurt you—"

I stuck my fingers into the hair at the nape of his neck. "I know."

We stood in silence like that until Neil lifted his head. He kissed my forehead before resting his cheek on my scalp. I breathed in the smell of him and listened to his heartbeat. It still pumped fast.

"Do you want to go somewhere?" I asked.

"Like?"

"Anywhere."

He nodded against my head then kissed my hair before pulling away, pressing the cloth to his forehead again and picking up my bag. I entwined my arm with his, and he led me to his truck.

We drove through the mountains until we reached a little cabin, not far from Butterfly Point.

"Where are we?" I asked.

Neil shut down the engine and hopped out. I followed suit and helped him grab bags from the back.

"Owen's family owns it," he replied. "They said I could stay here until I found a place."

I followed him to the front door. He fished a key out of his back pocket and let us inside. The room smelled like a fireplace. I flipped a light switch.

The cabin was small, but, for one person, it was definitely accommodating. The room we stood in made up the majority of the house and reminded me of my own home where the living and dining areas merged. Straight ahead, glass sliding doors looked out onto a lake. Next to them was another door that led to a bathroom. A fireplace was built into the wall on the far right, and to our left was a small kitchenette with a round dining table that sat four. I guessed the bedroom was through the door next to the fridge.

Neil dropped his bags behind a couch positioned in the center of the room, facing a large, flat-screen TV. I tossed my bags in the pile and waited for him to return from snatching the few remaining things from his truck, including my gift. He set that on the coffee table in front of the couch.

"Want something to drink?" he asked.

"Does this place even have food or drinks?"

Neil opened the fridge, one hand still pressed to his head. "I was here earlier with Owen, so, yeah, I stocked it. The plan was to surprise you tomorrow and bring you here once I'd gotten everything situated. But, hey, now's as good a time as any."

Handing me a can of Sprite, he plopped on the sofa and held his own to his head after tossing the bloodied rag into the trash. Frowning, I set my soda on the coffee table and sat next to him. I touched the hand that held the can.

"Let me see," I said.

"I'm fine."

"Neil, move your hand."

He sighed and did as I asked. His hairline had already begun to bruise, and, though the bleeding had slowed, it still definitely needed attention. It was my turn to do for him what he'd done for me months ago.

"Do you have a first-aid kit here?" I asked.

"Bathroom. Medicine cabinet."

Suppose I could've guessed that. Opening the cupboard, I grabbed rubbing alcohol, butterfly bandages, and antibiotic ointment, then found cotton balls under the sink. I returned to the couch. After drenching a cotton ball in the alcohol, I pressed it to Neil's head. He winced. I cleaned the wound and dressed it, trying to keep my touch soft.

As soon as I finished, Neil took my hand. His irises were vivid when he looked into my eyes. My heart jumped. He slipped his hand behind my neck and pulled my lips to meet his, kissing me like he had that first night in the garage. Tender at first, then his kisses intensified until I was in his lap and his hands were under my shirt, stroking the skin beneath my bra strap.

I was about to rip off his top when he grabbed my hands. *Seriously?*

"Wait," he said, his lips not far from mine, "there's something I want to do first. You're going to have to let me up."

Rolling my eyes and groaning, I fell into him.

"Wrong way, Princess."

It'd been a long time since he called me that. Smiling, I pinched his side—not too hard—and he chuckled. After I fell onto the seat next to him, Neil got up, visited the bedroom, and came back.

"Okay, resume position," he said.

"Oh, *now* you want me in your lap."

"I always want you in my lap." Neil smirked, and I punched him in the arm. But I wanted to continue where we'd left off, too, so I straddled Neil's legs, facing him.

"So, what, you ran into the bedroom for a Viagra?" I joked.

Neil's head tipped back with laughter. "Well, now look who's the cheeky one. I don't need Viagra, babe. My stamina's all natural."

"Then show me." I kissed him hard, and he let out a soft noise.

"Andie—" He tried to stop me again, but I fumbled with the belt around his waist, and, in seconds, whatever he'd gone into the bedroom to get was forgotten.

Neil pulled his shirt off as I finally managed to undo his belt, then my own shirt was tugged over my head. Again, the twinge of insecurity burned through my chest, but he kissed me, hard, and I dug my fingers into his back. He'd been patient with me for so long, and after a night like tonight, I wanted to make sure he knew how much I craved him, how much I needed him. I trusted his feelings for me.

Neil tugged on my hair. I moaned when his lips found the pulse point in my neck. Every nerve on my body tingled from head to toe, and my heartbeat pounded in my ears. His fingers trailed down my back to the clasp of my bra. With one hand, he twisted the strap, and it fell away. Neil's gaze flicked to my breasts then met my stare, hesitation in his eyes. I grabbed his face and kissed him, assuring him I wanted to keep going. There was no stopping now. I could already imagine the way he'd feel, the way he'd look when he was naked in front of me. My hips dug into his. Neil groaned then lifted me just enough so he could tug his pants to his knees.

But they only made it past his butt when the door to the cabin flew open. In one swift motion, Neil spun me around, leapt off the couch, and yanked his jeans to his waist. I slapped my arms over my naked chest, thankful Neil blocked me from view.

A familiar voice let out a half-cough, half-laugh and said, "Well, I'd say I came at a bad time."

"Owen, get out," Neil replied. "Now."

Oh, God. My cheeks burned.

Owen chuckled. "Dude, relax. I didn't see anything. But, really, man, does Andie know you're with some other chick right now?"

Neil sighed. "This *is* Andie."

My head drooped. *Kill me now.*

"Oh. Well, in that case, I'm guessing you don't need my help setting up for—"

"No. Out. Now," Neil said.

"Right. Um . . . later, Andie."

I didn't reply—I didn't think I could, even if I wanted to—and waited for the door to close before lifting my chin off my chest. Neil's face was in his hands. I wrapped my arms around him from behind.

"I'm so sorry," Neil said. "I thought I locked the door."

I don't know what came over me—I burst out laughing. Like the kind of laughing that makes your friends disown you at the movie theater. Neil looked at me over his shoulder. His cheeks were almost purple. I'd never seen him so embarrassed.

"You think that was funny?" he asked, raising an eyebrow.

"Yeah. I don't know why. But that was hilarious," I replied between cackles.

He smirked. "You are not right in the head."

My giggling waned. "I know. I'm sorry. Baby brain."

"You can't blame everything on the baby, you know. That includes stealing food and calling a pee break when you know you're going to lose at a video game. And, my God"—his gaze fell to my naked chest —"you've either got to put your clothes back on, or we need to continue where we left off."

I grinned and snatched my bra from the other side of the couch. After all that, the mood was definitely ruined. He mumbled something that sounded like "freaking Owen" and grabbed his own clothes.

"So, I need to ask"—I said as he slipped his shirt over his head —"why *did* Owen stop by? He mentioned helping you set up for something?"

Neil cleared his throat, avoiding eye contact with me, and took the medical supplies from the coffee table. "Yeah, well, you weren't supposed to come till tomorrow. So, there's some, you know, stuff missing." He hurried to the bathroom as I narrowed my eyes. For a master of manipulation, he was a terrible liar.

But I decided not to pry. Neil wasn't one to keep secrets, unless he had a good reason. In fact, I often thought him incapable of keeping his thoughts to himself. Until he decided to spill, I would just have to not let it bother me. The truth always made itself known, anyway, even when you didn't want it to. I touched my belly. I was proof of that.

CHAPTER 24

We crawled into bed around 3:00 a.m., after hours of unpacking Neil's stuff and watching movies—in between make-out sessions—and I awoke seven hours later with his cheek pressed against my shoulder blades. His arms were wrapped around my ribs, and he snored softly. Grinning, I untangled myself and ran to the bathroom before my bladder exploded. After scarfing down a banana, I returned to the bedroom. Neil was still on his side. *Good to know you'd sleep straight through a tornado.* With a smile, I lay back on the bed, facing him.

He looked so peaceful, so opposite of how I'd found him barreling out of his mom's house last night. Even with the dark stubble growing on his face, he appeared years younger, like he didn't have a care in the world. Seeing him so serene stole my breath, and I skimmed my fingertips along his tattoo.

Soon, Neil's soft snores disappeared, and he smirked without opening his eyes. "Just can't keep your hands off me."

"Oh, shut up."

He kept smiling, like he wasn't sure if he really wanted to wake up or not. I continued to trace the tattoo. Ten years ago, his father died. Did he feel like the murderer his mother screamed he was?

"You got this for him, didn't you?" I asked.

Neil's smile fell. He opened his eyes, removing my fingers from his skin. "Today's my birthday, which means I decide what we talk about. And I'm not in the mood to get all sappy. Now, why don't we continue where we left off?"

He tried to pull me to him, but I pressed my hand on his abdomen, stopping him. Why would he never talk to me about the tough stuff? Well, *his* tough stuff. He knew everything about me and saw me cry a thousand times, but he still wouldn't let me in.

"Neil, don't," I said. "Things got . . . heated last night." My cheeks warmed as I thought about how far we'd almost gone. "But you know I heard what your mom said, and I can't stop thinking about it— worrying about you."

"Oh, for God's sake." He rolled onto his back and covered his face with his arm. "Yes, I got the tattoo last year for my dad. Yes, my mother hates me. And yes, I miss him, but I'm done crying about it."

I frowned. The entire speech felt rehearsed, but at least he didn't sound angry. And he didn't sound like he was going to break down. Yet, why would he keep avoiding the topic? A part of him *had* to still be hurting.

I lay my head on his chest and draped my arm over his stomach. *I really wish you'd open up.* But pushing him wouldn't help, and I didn't want to fight today. "Okay."

He uncovered his eyes. "That's it?"

I shrugged. "If you don't want to talk about it, then okay."

Neil threw his arm around my shoulders and kissed my forehead. "I love you."

"I know," I said in my best Han Solo impression.

He grinned. "I'm proud of you, applying a movie line to an intimate moment."

Star Wars was one of the movies we'd watched last night, and I'd laughed so hard at how much the character reminded me of Neil. I wasn't surprised he'd picked up on my snark.

"I learn from the best."

"Wait, say that again. I'm the . . . ?"

"Egotistical maniac."

He laughed, and I smiled.

Then something in my belly twitched. Not painful, just awkward. It happened again. *No way.* I shot up with a gasp and put my hand on my stomach.

"Whoa, you okay?" He touched my lower back.

My heart danced. "Give me your hand."

Seeing me grinning, Neil relaxed a little and sat up. I placed his palm on my bare belly, right where I felt the twitches before.

"Wait for it," I said.

The room was eerily quiet, and my heart raced. I was terrified I wouldn't feel the baby again, but then another flutter tickled my stomach. I laughed. "Did you feel it?"

"What—is he moving?"

I nodded, beaming.

"Shit, no, I didn't." Neil slid closer until my back was against his torso and a knee was on either side of me. I leaned into him. "Are you sure I'll be able to?" His hand remained exactly where I'd put it.

"I don't know. Maybe not."

Again, we sat silent and unmoving, my hand over Neil's. After a minute or so, Neil said, "Dance, puppet, dance."

"Really?"

He chuckled. "Sorry."

I frowned. "I can't feel him anymore."

Neil kissed the side of my head. "Well, it's not like the kid can do exercises all day. Although, it would be pretty sweet if the guy came out ripped from the start. He'd get all the ladies at daycare."

"Oh my God. You teach him any moves before he's thirty, I'll kill you."

"You didn't mind my moves last night." His voice was mischievous, and his hand wandered down my stomach.

I trembled, remembering again how far we'd gone, how close I'd come to being with him. Oh, I wanted him so bad, but we couldn't lie around in bed much longer. I'd already made plans for his birthday.

Neil nibbled my neck, and I almost lost my willpower. His kisses were like mythological sirens. I sat up straight and removed his palm from the inside of my thigh before I gave in. He chuckled as I jumped off the bed.

"Actually, I know plenty of guys who kiss better," I joked, crossing my arms with a smirk.

He raised an eyebrow. "Well, then I think you need to help me practice."

He leapt from the mattress, and I ran from the room, giggling.

A few hours later, I took Neil to an arcade-restaurant in Denver for his birthday. Jill and Owen met us there, and the four of us filled our stomachs until we thought we would puke. We spent hours—and lots of Owen's money—in the arcade. His birthday present to Neil. The night turned into a boys versus girls event, and seventy percent of the time, Jill and I were victorious. Which was awesome. There was nothing like hearing a boy shout "rematch" after losing to a girl.

Though I'd only met Owen a few—awkward—times, I'd come to enjoy his company and saw why he and Neil had been best friends since childhood. The two of them bickered like an old married couple, and Owen matched Neil's sarcasm in ways that left Jill and me clinging to each other in uncontrollable fits of laughter. I'd never seen Neil smile so big and for so long, and by the end of the night, my sides hurt from laughing so much.

Jill was still laughing at all the inside jokes we'd acquired as she sat with me during my last OB/GYN appointment of the year. Why I didn't mind Jill being in the room with me, I didn't know. Maybe I was finally ready to share some of these moments with someone. I'd have to muster up the courage to let Mom in, next time.

Dr. Brandt wheeled the ultrasound machine into the room. "Hello, ladies. How are you feeling today, Andie?"

"Fat." I smiled. Sort of. I was really not looking forward to ballooning even more than I already had.

Dr. Brandt chuckled. "It's only temporary. A few more months, and you'll be able to see your feet again. Ready to get started?"

Ethan was so much clearer now. I could finally make out some intricate details of his features, the shape of his nose, his fingers, his toes. I swallowed my tears, silently pleading with my ridiculous emotions to stop striking the string in my brain that made me cry. Luckily, Jill began chatting about all the things she was going to teach Ethan as he got older, and soon all I could do was laugh. Then Dr. Brandt announced everything was progressing nicely, and I was free to go.

"I *do* get to be called Aunt Jill, right?" Jill asked as we left the building.

I smiled at the ultrasound photo in my hand. "Of course you do. I never would've gotten through all of this without you and Neil."

My phone buzzed in my purse when we reached the parking lot. I snatched the device from my bag and glanced at the screen. Twenty missed calls from a number I didn't recognize. What the heck?

I tilted the screen for Jill to see. "Do you know this number?"

Jill eyed my phone and squinted. "Yeah. That's my dad. Maybe he was trying to find me. Hang on." She pulled her cell out of her purse and frowned. "That's weird."

I jumped when my phone vibrated again. "It's your dad." I thumbed the 'Answer' button. "Hello?"

"Andie? This is Mr. Anderson, Jill's father. I need to talk to you about something. Do you have a minute?"

Tingles ran down my limbs. Jill tipped her head slightly. I pointed that I was going to stop for a second and stuck a finger in my other ear.

"Um, yeah, Mr. Anderson. What's up?"

My heart vibrated in my throat, my knees, my fingertips. Why was Jill's dad calling me? I'd given him my number in case of emergencies, but I never thought he'd dial. Had the police discovered we'd hacked the adoption agency?

Jill watched me, her face full of worry.

"There's, uh, well, hon, it's your mom," he said.

My legs wavered. I'd heard similar words from the police before, the night they stopped by to tell me my dad was dead.

"Why? What happened? Is she okay?" I blurted, my voice at a borderline scream.

"Hey, just stay calm, all right? Come to the hospital, and I'll explain everything."

The phone nearly fell from my hand. *No.* A wave of nausea rolled through me. This couldn't be happening. Not now.

"Andie, tell me you're going to drive safely."

I tapped the end button without a response and pressed the back of my hand against my forehead to stop the world from spinning.

"Andie, what's wrong?" Jill said, touching my arm.

I shook my head, my pulse thrashing in my ears. "The hospital. We have to go to the hospital."

"What? Why? What happened?"

"My mom. I need to go. I need to go." I pushed off her, bounding into a car's bumper when my knees weakened.

"Whoa, slow down." Jill reached out to help me balance, but I shoved her away.

I needed to get out of here. I needed to find out what happened to Mom.

Trembling, I ran for Jill's car and climbed into the passenger's seat as she hopped behind the wheel, gunning the engine. I took deep breaths, trying to hold myself together, as we sped through the city. When Jill swung her car up to the hospital's main entrance, I flung my door open and raced into the building.

"Can I help you?" the woman at the front desk asked, her eyes worried.

"My mom. Please, I need to see her. Susan Hamilton."

The secretary typed something into her computer. "Are you family?"

Did you not just hear me? "Yes! Now, let me back there, please!"

"I'm sorry. You're going to have to have a seat in the waiting room. I'll let the officers know you're here."

"What?" I shouted. "She's my mom!"

Jill, appearing out of nowhere, tugged me toward the chairs. "Hey—"

"No! I want to see her. You have to let me see her!"

"Andie, stop!" She gripped my shoulders. "They'll let you back there as soon as they can. But she might be in surgery right now, and it could be there's nowhere for us to go yet. We have to wait. There's nothing else we can do."

The woman at the desk shot Jill a look—an apologetic thank you. I nodded and followed her to the waiting area, but I couldn't sit still. Not while Mom might be in surgery. Not while she might be—

Don't, Andie. Don't think it.

Neil and Owen dashed through the door a few minutes later, and the woman at the desk pointed in our direction. I stood to give Neil a hug, but as soon as his eyes found mine, I broke. Quickly, he crossed the waiting room and gathered me into his arms. I clung to him and cried into his chest, unable to form words. I couldn't lose my mom. I couldn't.

Neil eased me into a chair when my sobs slowed. He wiped the tears from my cheek and planted a kiss on my forehead. "Don't give up on her, all right?" he said. "It might not be as bad as you think."

I nodded, another tear falling, and he caught that one, too.

"Neil, come here a minute," Owen said, separating from Jill.

Neil looked me over, silently asking if I'd be okay. When I nodded, he stood and sat in the chair next to his best friend. One hand folded over the other, he leaned on his knees, pressing his fist to his lips. The tension in his face was stronger than I'd ever seen. Out of the corner of my eye, Owen whispered something in his best friend's ear. Neil's head drooped. My heart ricocheted off my ribs.

"They're talking man stuff." Jill plopped down next to me. "No need to worry."

Neil sat back in his chair and put his hands on top of his head. His eyes were glassy. He and Owen spoke in hushed voices, but the rage—no, the fear—on Neil's face reminded me of when I showed up at his house unannounced.

"But—" I started.

"Just sit with me," Jill said. "Hey, tell me how things with Neil went. I got bits and pieces from dinner that Owen walked in on you guys. Did you end up, y'know, doing the touchdown dance?" She wiggled her eyebrows.

My chin trembled, and the room blurred. I didn't want to talk about sex, not now.

"Oh, God. Jill, what if—?" I covered my mouth with shaking fingers and grasped the locket around my neck with my other hand.

She rubbed my back. "Let's not jump to conclusions here. Would Hermione panic until she had all the facts? *No.* Maybe all they're doing is resetting her arm or something."

Neil balanced on the edge of his seat, watching me, his face lined with concern. I shrank into the curve of my chair and rubbed my eyes, determined to keep any tears from falling.

Jill stuck her hand in mine.

"Thank you for calling him," I said.

I lay my head on her shoulder, and we sat like that for at least an hour. Then Neil perked up in his seat. I turned my head. Behind me, Jill's dad approached wearing his cop uniform. I was on my feet in seconds, Jill by my side. My pulse pounded in my ears, my chest, my knees.

"Sit down, Andie," Mr. Anderson said.

Oh, no. It was two years ago all over again. My knees gave out, and Jill guided me into the chair.

Mr. Anderson took a seat in front of me. His dark eyes were kind but full of sorrow and anxiety. He leaned forward, rubbing his chin. "I don't know what to tell you, kiddo. Your mom made me promise to keep this to myself months ago, when you girls first started hanging out."

I held my breath. I couldn't take any more secrets. I thought back to how Mom had acted the last several months. Yes, she'd lost a lot of weight, and yes, she seemed to be sleeping a lot more, but that was just stress. Between work and me—and lately the added weight of our bankruptcy—I understood. What could she possibly have been hiding from me this whole time?

I caught Neil's stare. His face was so white, and the crease between his eyebrows was deeper than I'd ever seen it before. His anxiety only added to the heart-wrenching panic in my gut.

"Andie."

My attention snapped back to Mr. Anderson. His eyes had filled with tears. "Hon, your mom had been battling the late stages of cancer for months, and nothing was working. With all that was going on, she didn't want to worry you and instead chose to enjoy the time she had left with the person she loved most."

My heartbeat raced as Neil leapt out of his seat and stormed from the waiting room with Owen on his heels. Jill took one of my shaking hands in hers. *This isn't happening, this isn't happening.*

Jill's dad put a hand on my right knee and pursed his lips. "When she collapsed at school earlier, they rushed her to the ER, and the doctors did everything they could to save her, but . . . she didn't make it."

At first, my brain shorted. Every atom in my body froze. I couldn't move; I couldn't breathe. But seconds later, I heard myself hyperventilate, as if I were floating above the room. Finally, as Jill's arms flew around me, it sank in:

Mom was dead.

CHAPTER 25

People say during traumatic events, time moves slowly. In reality, time stands still, and, all of a sudden, weeks have gone by and you can't remember how you got there.

I remembered Neil returning to the hospital's waiting room minutes later and holding me in his arms for hours while screams and sobs ripped through me. I remembered falling asleep at the hospital and waking in Neil's bed the next morning. Mom's peaceful face as she slept in her casket. Her soft, cold hand beneath my fingertips. Faces I couldn't place telling me they were sorry. My aunt telling me she'd make sure I was looked after. Neil's futile attempts to get me to eat. Jill stopping by to check on me and bring me clothes. Owen's voice from the cabin's living room. Neil's embrace as we fell asleep at night. Guitar music.

But I don't remember crying again, or talking, or thinking. I don't remember Christmas coming and going. I don't remember how the rest of my belongings got to the cabin. And I don't remember my belly growing as big as it was when I felt the baby move for the second time.

The kick awoke me from my sleep as soft piano music played from the living room. I rested my hand on my stomach, waiting for the baby to strike again. When he did, I felt him in my palm, like someone had nudged me from beneath a pile of blankets.

I raced to the living room of the cabin. After everything, Owen's parents let us stay as long as we needed. Neil sat at his keyboard, surrounded by boxes, a pencil in his mouth. When he caught sight of me, he did a double-take, eyes wide, and jumped up.

"What's wrong?" he asked, his face pale.

"Ethan. I think you can feel him now."

Neil set the pencil on his music stand and took two giant steps toward me. He slid his hand beneath mine. Eyes wide, he looked down at my belly and waited. Then the baby kicked again, and Neil grinned.

"You feel him?" I asked.

"Yeah. I'm thinking we might want to enroll him in Irish high-stepping later. Unless that was a punch. Then maybe karate."

I shook my head, thankful that Neil hadn't lost his sense of humor. Then reality knocked the wind straight from my lungs. There wouldn't be karate lessons or soccer games—because I had no money, no way to support my son.

I was *alone*.

I wept for the first time since leaving the hospital. Even at Mom's funeral, I managed to rein in the tears. Mostly because I was so angry with her for not telling me the truth. But now, a cannonball might as well have blown a hole through my chest.

"Hey, come here." Neil held me in his arms and led me to the couch. Sitting, he pulled me into his lap.

I clung to him, breathing in his scent and listening to his heartbeat.

"I'm all alone," I said, my voice shaking. "They're both gone. Mom and Dad. I can't—oh, God, it hurts."

Neil rubbed my back with his fingertips, slow and soothing. "I know, baby. I know. But you're not alone. I'm here. I'm not going anywhere."

"But what about Ethan? I haven't even finished high school yet. How am I supposed to support him by myself?"

"Who says you have to? Contrary to common belief, I am pretty good at these things called jobs. I can get one with Owen's dad, and I'll make good money. Between your part-time job and my full-time one, we'll be fine."

I shook my head against his chest. "No. Neil, this isn't your problem. You can't give up your life for me."

He lifted my chin, forcing me to look at him. "We've been over this. You are important to me, which means *he* is important to me. Blood doesn't make a family, Andie. I will take care of you—both of you."

Owen's dad owned one of the most successful home building companies in Colorado. And Neil *was* like a son to Owen's father, at least from what I'd gathered. But Neil's dream was to run his own music studio. There was no way I'd take that from him. I shook my head as breath left my lungs again. "But what about your music? No, I can't—"

"Hey," Neil said, putting a finger on my lips. "Who says I'm giving that up? It will always be part of my life."

"What about your studio? What about Harvard and your business degree?"

He put a finger on my lips. "Screw Harvard. I never ended up applying anyway. Promise me you won't worry about this anymore. Say the words."

I took a deep breath. Could we be okay? And after everything, shouldn't I have learned to trust him? When he raised an eyebrow, I nodded. I was *petrified* but not yet ready to give up on Ethan. Not yet. Even if I had to take two part-time jobs to make ends meet.

"Sorry, I must be going deaf. Try again," Neil said.

Rolling my eyes, I whispered, "I promise."

Neil kissed my forehead, and I leaned against him again. He held me close with his strong arms. A few more minutes we sat there, arms around each other. My thoughts turned away from Ethan to my mom, my parents. The hole Dad had left behind had never truly closed, and with Mom gone too, it was miles wide and beyond repair. How had my life ended up this way? Why did I only get such a short time with them?

"I thought I told you to stop worrying," Neil said.

I buried my face in his neck, mumbling about how that was impossible. He let out a half-chuckle and kissed the top of my head.

"How'd you do it?" I asked. "Move on, I mean. You know, when your dad died."

Neil tensed against me, and I swallowed the urge to say never mind. But if there were some trick to how he'd kept himself from falling apart, I needed to know it.

He didn't speak but relaxed and leaned into me. His chest filled with half-breaths. "You don't. Not really. Eventually, the pain gets easier to handle, but there's always a hole. You just have to find the things that make you happy and dwell on those instead." He paused again. "I know that's not the answer you wanted."

I wasn't sure how to respond. He'd finally let me in, spoken with honesty about his dad. And, yes, I would've loved for him to say *after a couple years, the pain goes away and they become a distant memory*, but I knew better. My dad *had* been gone a couple years, and I still missed him like he'd passed away yesterday. I was glad Neil didn't sugarcoat it.

I wiped a few tears from my cheeks and sniffled while he rubbed my back. "Is that why you kept up with the music? 'Cause it reminded you of him?"

He nodded. "Besides the fact that I love it, yeah. It was my way of reaching out to him, letting him know I hadn't forgotten. For a long time, only that and visiting his grave helped."

I looked into his eyes, and he touched my cheek, his emotions flowing into me like a supernatural ability—his love, sympathy, understanding, sadness. I tipped my chin up, and he met my lips.

"Will you take me . . . ?" *To my mom's grave*, I couldn't add. I bit my lip. "Today? I don't really remember saying goodbye to her at the funeral, and I don't want her to think—"

He put a finger on my lips, silencing me. "Whenever you're ready."

With a nod, I kissed him again and then left to shower. If I was going to visit my mom, I wasn't going to do it smelling like a locker room. Even after Dad's death, Mom always looked put together when she went out in public. I wanted to at least look like I was, for her.

I took my time, letting the hot water cascade from head to toe. Every joint in my body ached with weeks of sorrow and immobility. After braiding my wet hair, I left the bathroom. Neil still sat on the couch, but he held his guitar and played a song I didn't know. A beautiful, sorrowful melody, like that *Time to Mend* song by Barcelona. Neil's eyes were closed, and he rocked with each beat. His features downturned, I saw the pain on his face, felt it in each note. This was one of *his* songs.

He played the last note and paused before opening his eyes. They were red, but when he set down his guitar and spoke, I never would've guessed that, moments before, he'd laid his soul on his guitar strings.

"You ready?" he asked.

When I nodded, he grabbed my coat from the closet near the door and helped me into it. The jacket barely fit over my twenty-three-week belly. I followed Neil through snow to the truck. The inside was already warm. He must've started it while I showered. The corner of my mouth twitched as I tried to smile and failed.

I grabbed his hand as he drove away from the cabin. Neither of us let go the entire way to River Springs's cemetery.

And I clung to Neil as soon as we hopped out of the truck. Each step we took across the snowy ground was heavy-footed and slow. My chin trembled, and, soon, each gravestone blurred. I shouldn't be taking this walk. Not again. Neil tugged me closer to him when my steps faltered.

We stopped underneath a large oak tree. The dirt over Mom's casket still hadn't settled. She was buried right next to Dad, like I expected, but I couldn't remember what dress they'd put her in or whether her lips were in a smile or a line. All I could remember was a glimpse of her peaceful face, like a reflection in a rippling lake.

Neil let go, and I knelt in front of the stone. Snow seeped through the knees of my pants. I ran my fingers across Mom's name. The marker was ice cold. Kind of how I imagined she felt right now. How my heart—my body—felt.

I sat back on my feet and crossed my arms, holding my breath, swallowing the ache in my joints, my throat, my stomach—fighting the tears. She was gone. She was really gone. Unable to hold in the pain any longer, I slumped forward and cried.

Who was I going to go to now with baby questions, with mother questions? She was supposed to watch me graduate, to see her grandson, to give me away at my wedding some day.

I bit my trembling lip, the world around me spinning. The winter chill penetrated my bones as I rocked, holding in the scream that wanted to rip free. But I didn't care. I wanted to lie on the ground and be as close to her as I could. Let the ice take me.

Oh, God, why did you take her, too?

I gripped the locket Mom and Dad had given me on my eighth birthday, and my resolve broke. I covered my face, weeping, each cry tearing the hole in my chest wider. I unclasped the chain from around my neck and placed it in front of her grave marker. Then, leaning so I could reach my father's gravestone too, I placed my hands on their names.

I wish you were still here. I wish we were a family again. All you ever did was love me, and I miss you both so, so much. I never should've gotten so wrapped up in my identity. Neil was right: Blood doesn't make a family.

My palms slid down the stones until my hands hit the ground, and I fell forward. I couldn't do this. I couldn't move on without my parents.

My sobs came out in rasps. I clawed at my cheeks, whimpering in pain. *Fill it with happiness.* I let my mind wander to all the moments I'd had with them, the memories I carried of them—the smiles, the laughter, the love. I breathed deep, counted to five, and willed myself to stop crying, though every cell wanted to turn to stone. I had to live, even if I didn't want to. For them. For me. For my baby.

When my blubbering calmed, I pushed out a few shaky breaths and opened my eyes. *Get up, Andie.* I forced myself to my feet and flung my hands out to balance when my legs shook. *Now, turn around.* I spun slowly, like I was stuck in quicksand. I reached out for Neil. But he was gone.

Wiping my wet cheeks, I wandered the small graveyard. Just when I was about to call out to him, I caught a glimpse of his dark hair. He was crouched in front of a grave, his head drooped. I didn't have to look to know whose name would be written on the stone. Still, as I neared Neil, my gaze drifted to the marker.

MARK DONAGHUE. BELOVED HUSBAND, FATHER, AND SON.

My heart pinched.

I ran my fingertips through the hair above his ear and knelt next to him, my knees already frozen. The circles around his eyes were darker than before, and the muscles in his jaw were taut. I slipped my arm through his.

"It *was* my fault, you know," he said finally.

"Neil . . . . "

"I called him to come pick me up in the middle of the night, and all because I was scared. He told me to be brave, to tough it out, but I cried into the phone and told him I needed him. And like the dad he was, he drove across River Springs in a damn blizzard."

Acid burned my throat. "You were eight."

He shook his head. "That's not good enough. If I'd listened to him and grown some balls, he'd still be here. My mom wouldn't be one arrest away from time in prison, and Beth wouldn't be the way she is. He was different. Always had a joke. Would've fought dragons for Beth and me. And, God, he loved my mom." Neil's voice broke, and the icy dagger in my chest dug deeper.

A tear escaped.

I could see now where he got it from—his sense of humor. His unfailing love for me. His devotion to his mother, even though she beat him. I laid my head on his shoulder and squeezed his arm.

"I'm still paying for it. For killing him," Neil said.

I snapped my head up. Though he wasn't crying, the agony he was going through—had been going through for a long time—radiated off him. His eyebrows creased, and his chest rose and fell sporadically, like he held his breath to keep the emotions reined in.

My throat tightened, and I shook my head. "Don't talk like that. It's not your fault."

He closed his eyes and swallowed deep.

Oh, Neil. I took his face in my hands and spoke as sternly as I could. "Your dad's death was *not* your fault. You are *not* cursed, Neil. Not when you make my life better. Not when you're the most genuine person I've ever met. My mom cared for you, and I know your dad would be proud of you." I leaned my forehead against his. "Please stop blaming yourself."

Neil held the sides of my neck and brushed his thumbs along my jawline. "I don't deserve you, Andie."

I almost laughed. Hadn't I thought the same about him months ago? I used his words against him: "Why don't you let me make that decision?"

He tried to smile but failed. Then he kissed me like the world would crumble beneath his feet if he didn't. Though it was freezing outside, my skin flushed. I grasped his arms, a final tear streaking my cheek.

When he pulled away, slow and reluctant, I spoke confidently, without letting him go. "I love you."

He kissed my forehead. "I love you, too. More than I ever thought I could."

My insides fluttered, and I grazed his lips with mine. How could I have, once upon a time, thought the worst of him? If I could have one wish, I'd go back in time and fight for him, refuse to let him push me away with that silly kiss in the high school library.

Neil ran a hand down his face then stood and helped me to my feet. Arms around each other, we returned to the truck, and I sat as close to him as I could on the bench seat. Never wanting to let him go.

CHAPTER 26

My cell phone awoke me the next morning. I lay on my side, with Neil's arms wrapped around me, and considered letting my voicemail answer. But on the second ring, Neil muttered, "Stop the noise," and I grabbed the phone. A one-eyed peek at the screen showed Jill name. At 8:00 a.m.

"Since when do you get up this early?" I asked after thumbing the answer button and pressing the cell phone to my ear.

"Since my dad stuck ice cubes down the back of my shirt."

I almost smiled at the image of Jill swatting at her father and screaming bloody murder.

"It's your boyfriend's fault, really. He texted my dad yesterday to say you were doing better, and now Dad wants me to invite you over. Something about New Year's dinner, four o'clock, and Christmas presents. Seriously, they've been sitting under our tree since your aunt named him temporary guardian. You need to open them."

I bolted upright, startling Neil. "He's *what?*"

She yawned. "Relax. It's no big deal. Your aunt didn't want to make you up and move halfway through your junior year of high school, so my dad offered. I guess they still have two years on their London contract."

My eyes burned. Not only was it hard to believe Aunt Kathy would let me stay, but Mr. Anderson taking on guardian responsibilities? There were no words.

When I spoke, I forced my voice to stay calm. "Okay, tell your dad we'll be there at four." I needed to say thank you to him in person.

"Roger that. Wake me up when you get here, 'kay?"

I shook my head. "Bye, Jill." I set my phone on the nightstand and glanced at Neil. He watched my every movement, his expression full of concern. But instead of tears, a smile broke free.

"Get up," I said. "We need to buy Christmas presents."

At 3:45, we parked in front of Jill's downtown condo. After three quick knocks, Jill yanked open the front door, and, before I could say a word, she crushed me in her arms. Smiling, Neil touched my back and slipped past us, Christmas gifts in hand. I squeezed my best friend, fighting tears. *Already?* Making it through the day was going to be emotionally impossible.

"I missed you, too," I said as Jill let me go.

"Don't do that to me again." She pointed her finger at my face.

I rolled my eyes and smiled.

Neil and Mr. Anderson were already chatting in the small living room by the time Jill and I joined them. It sounded like they'd gotten to know each other pretty well over the last few weeks. Jill had said Neil texted her dad last night. How often had they talked? And why did their conversation look so intense?

Spying me, Jill's dad rose from his chair. "Hey, kiddo," he said, opening his arms.

I walked into his hug. "Thank you for everything."

He chuckled and dropped his arms. "You're very welcome. Besides, it's really that guy over there who's been looking after you." He nodded toward Neil, who half-smiled. "I merely gave Jill a few dollars to buy you a few things." He held up a hand. "Don't say you'll pay me back. Neil already tried."

I shook my head, my gaze blurring. "But you signed guardianship papers to keep me from having to move. I have to repay you somehow."

Mr. Anderson put his hands on my shoulders. His dark eyes were happy. "Just stay out of trouble, and we'll call it even."

I smiled as I sat next to Neil, and he laced his fingers through mine.

For an hour, we listened to Jill tell stories about her extended family visiting over Christmas, and when her mom came home around 5:00, we exchanged gifts and ate dinner. After a few rounds of Super Mario Bros with Jill and Neil, I wandered to the kitchen while they faced off in one final, winner-takes-all round. Their voices carried through the condo as they bickered like ten-year-old siblings. I couldn't help but smile as I popped a potato chip in my mouth.

"So, how are you really doing?" Mr. Anderson asked from where he sat at the dining table, his laptop open in front of him.

"I'm okay, I guess," I replied. Okay was too calm of a word, but it was the best I could come up with, considering.

Jill's dad nodded. "Well, you've gotten through the hardest part. Each day, it'll be a little easier to wake up in the morning."

A loud scream echoed from the living room.

Neil laughed. "Get ready to pay up, Pocahontas."

"You cheated!" Jill shouted. "Verbal contract violated. I am *not* doing your math homework."

I chuckled in response, and almost as if Ethan sensed my happiness, a stick rammed into my ribs. Jumping slightly, I pressed a hand against my stomach and smiled when he kicked again.

"When's the last time you saw your OB?" Mr. Anderson asked.

"Not since before Mom . . ." *Died*, I finished in my head, frowning. The pain of having to do this without her burrowed into my chest again. I leaned against the counter to keep from wobbling.

"I'm sure Jill would be happy to take you. And if you need help paying the bill—"

I shook my head. "No, that's absolutely not necessary. Neil and I have a plan. We'll be okay."

He pressed his lips together then sighed. "All right, kiddo. But you know you can come to me about anything, right? If this gets to be too much—and, trust me, kids are a full-time responsibility—you just tell me what you need. Jill says you plan to keep him, so be sure you're okay with everything both you and Neil are sacrificing."

I swallowed a lump in my throat. Hadn't those same thoughts already crossed my mind? Mr. Anderson was only looking out for me, but Neil assured me he wasn't forfeiting anything. And I'd given up the whole doctor dream months ago. I had to trust we'd be okay; I didn't know how not to.

"Thanks," I replied. "I'll let you know if anything comes up."

"Yo, household," Jill yelled. "The Rockin' New Year's Eve crap's about to start!"

Mr. Anderson shut his laptop. "I guess that means we're supposed to carry the snack bowls into the living room."

Forcing a smile, I snatched the chips and dip and followed him down the short hall.

A week or so later, Neil shook me awake the morning of his last day of winter break. I tucked the comforter over my head and didn't come out until he tugged the covers from my face. He chuckled and pulled them away again. I grabbed his pillow and smooshed it over my face.

"Get up," he said with a laugh, snatching the pillow out of my hands and tossing it across the room. "I'm tired of seeing your sad face, so I planned something fun for the day. Now, get out of bed, or I'm going to tickle you."

I glared at him, and he winked. Rolling my eyes, I sat up and brushed loose pieces of my hair down so I didn't look like Medusa on meth.

"That's better. Now, I'm leaving, but Jill's going to pick you up in an hour. So, do whatever you need to get ready. And dress warm. It's freaking cold out there." He kissed my forehead. "See you in a little bit."

My eyebrows furrowed as I watched him leave the room. What the heck did he have planned? Sighing, I hurried through a shower and then threw on black leggings and a long-sleeved, blue sweater that hung past my butt. Any fatter, and my outfit wouldn't have fit. I *had* to go shopping for bigger clothes soon. After curling my hair and applying makeup to cover my raccoon eyes, I sat on the couch with five minutes to spare.

Exactly one hour after I climbed out of bed, the doorbell rang.

Jill looked me up and down. "Please tell me you're dressing warmer than that."

"I don't even know what we're doing."

"Do you have something warmer than leggings?"

"Not that fit me. I'm hot all the time, anyway. And I have a coat and boots. I won't freeze for . . . whatever crazy event Neil planned."

"Hey, I tried to talk him into a *Star Trek* marathon, but he said no."

I smiled. The two of them planning an outing together had to have been hilarious. Slipping on my snow boots, I wrapped myself in my winter coat—now barely big enough to button over my belly—and grabbed my purse off the end table. After locking the door behind me, I jumped into Jill's car.

She pulled out her cell phone. "Okay. Just in advance, you owe me a big thank you for agreeing to this idea."

"What are we even doing?"

"A scavenger hunt. In the snow. Your boyfriend's crazy, let me tell ya." She punched in an address on her GPS and drove down the mountain toward Denver.

My heart hammered. *A scavenger hunt?* That was so unlike Neil. How long had he been putting this together? And how had I not noticed?

When Jill pulled into the zoo's parking lot, I laughed.

"What?" she asked.

"I can't believe he's doing this. Neil took me here months ago when I wanted to skip school. Sort of a first date, I guess."

Jill turned doe-eyed. "Aw, he didn't tell me that. He just said where to go and where to find our first clue. Okay, I take it back. This is going to be *so* much fun."

Shaking my head at her sudden one-eighty. I opened the Honda's door and followed Jill to the gate. She paid for our tickets, and we walked until we reached the Information Booth.

"Okay. He says"—she scrolled through her text messages—"and I quote, 'Tell her the polka bear will get her started.' What does that mean?"

I grinned and headed toward the polar bear exhibit. "He tried telling me this joke about a white bear in lederhosen. I totally called him out on it. His face was priceless."

Jill laughed. "Awesome. The Hamiltonizer put the Mighty Donaghue in his place."

"'Hamiltonizer?'"

She shrugged. "What? It's your superhero name."

"Well, then I must be a pretty lame superhero to go by *that*."

Jill blushed as we entered the polar bear viewing area. A few children stood around, watching with their parents. Separating, Jill and I wandered, trying to find whatever clue Neil had left behind.

"Over here," Jill said, pulling a notecard from underneath a rock.

How did she see that?

She handed the card to me, and I flipped it over.

Hey, Princess.

My goal today is to make you smile. There's a gift waiting for you in the Kibongi Market. Give the clerk your name. It'll tell you where to go next.

Because I love you, Neil

I bit my lip and smirked. Jill snatched the card from my fingers.

"Okay, new rule," she said. "The woman of my dreams better send me on a scavenger hunt."

I giggled and took the card back, sticking it in my purse. Jill and I raced from the polar bear exhibit and grabbed a map.

"It's the one near the entrance. Not far. Let's go," Jill said, leading me to our destination.

Upon giving the clerk my name, he handed me a picture frame. A simple, metal one with a bit of a bluish tint and painted white snowflakes in a random pattern. It was beautiful. Jill and I opened the back of the frame when we stepped outside the store. Another note card had been stuck behind the stock photo.

Ice cream's on my dime. Take Jill to Sprinkles and ask for Joe. He knows what to do.

Because I love you, Neil

Sprinkles was the parlor Mom and I had visited all the time. Showing Jill the note, I seized her hand and led her out the gate and to her car. I gave her directions to the ice cream shop, then I asked the girl at the register for Joe when we got there. He smiled when I told him Neil sent me and grabbed a notecard from beneath the register.

"Your boyfriend paid for both you and your friend. So, what'll it be, ladies?" Joe asked.

Once Jill and I chose our desserts, we picked a table, and I read my next clue.

Hope you finish every bite because you're not going to eat again for a while! Tell Jill to move on to Phase Two.

Because I love you, Neil

"Neil says to move on to phase two," I said.

Jill grinned, clutching her head. She pointed to her skull with her other hand. "Brain freeze."

I raised an eyebrow. "Jill, what's phase two?"

She dropped her hand. "Well, I can't tell you *that*, now can I? You'll just have to wait and see. Seriously, though, brain freezes suck."

I shook my head, the corner of my mouth twitching, and finished my snack.

Jill drove across the city to an apartment complex a few blocks from the university. "Okay, his text said to go into the main office and say, 'Neil Donaghue sent me.' Well, if that doesn't sound ominous," she said.

My heart fluttered. *No way.* I leapt from the car and raced inside. I said exactly what Jill told me to, and the landlord smiled.

"Neil said you'd be in. Got your keys all ready. Hang on a sec." She left me standing in the waiting area. A minute later, she returned with an envelope marked *431—Donaghue* and handed it to me. "Here we are," she said. Clinking metal rang out from inside. "Four-hundreds are in the building behind this one. You're up on the third floor, first place on the left. Welcome to The Meadows."

"Oh. Thanks." I shook her hand and ran back to the car. I sat in the passenger's seat with a giggle.

"What?" Jill asked.

"Drive around to the building behind this one."

When she did, I used one of the keys to get in, and Jill followed me up two flights of stairs to the first apartment on the left. When we stepped inside, my jaw dropped. The apartment was small but cozy, with tan walls and fresh flooring. The entryway opened into a room that split in half—kitchen/dining on the left, living area on the right. A laundry room was to my right, and a short hallway to my left ended with a white door.

"Oh, wow," I said, walking through the living room. Everything was already furnished. *Neil, you brat.* He'd been planning this for a while. His portion of his dad's lawsuit money became available on his eighteenth birthday, but I had no idea he'd made these kinds of plans already. Then I looked a little closer at the furniture. It was my parents'. *Oh, Neil . . .* I held my chest. This was too much.

"Did you know about the furniture?" I asked Jill, pointing to the couch.

She nodded. "My dad helped him save a few of the pieces before everything went to auction."

I pressed my fist harder into my breastbone, swallowing tears. My parents had picked the couch together. It was silly to be so attached to an object, but how could I not be when it brought back so many memories? I could never repay Neil or Mr. Anderson for saving it.

Running my hand along the top of the familiar sofa, I entered a small hall at the back of the apartment. The bathroom was directly ahead and a decent size, with—what appeared to be—a brand new shower. At both ends of the hall were doors. One had a notecard stuck to it. I grabbed the card and flipped it over.

Good news: Owen's dad gave me a position at his company. A full-time one with benefits. Between it, my dad's lawsuit money, and your part-time job, paying the bills should be a piece of cake. Told you I could take care of you.

Welcome home, Andie.

Because I love you, Neil

P.S. Your next clue is in a box on the bed.

I clutched the notecard and grinned so hard my face hurt.

"Dude, just sayin', this place is cool," Jill announced from the living room.

Still smiling, I pushed open the door. Neil's bed from his mom's house was against the far wall, and on it was a yellow, oversized shoe box. I stuck the notecard in my purse and opened the container. A pair of white ice skates were inside. I covered my lips and giggled. I'd taken ice-skating lessons when I was younger, but then gymnastics and dance became more important, and I dropped out. Knowing that he remembered left me breathless.

Another notecard was stuck inside the box. I pulled the card out and flipped it over. An address lined the back with one sentence: *Bring these with you.* Running from the room, I grabbed Jill's hand and pulled her into the hall, handing her the card and locking the door to Neil's —*our*—apartment behind me.

CHAPTER 27

I almost squealed when I saw where we ended up. Crystal Lake—one of the places on my bucket list. It was a small ski resort whose focal point was a beautiful, twenty-acre body of water kept frozen all season long. Its bank was lined by pine trees and a two-story warming lodge where visitors could grab a cup of hot chocolate or eat dinner, and the ski slopes behind the lodge were as tall as small mountains. The scene was more beautiful than a Thomas Kinkade painting. Especially when the lake was frozen and people skated to music blaring from speakers on the patio.

When we entered the warming lodge, I spun in a slow circle, searching for Neil, while Jill found the desk to rent a pair of skates. He was nowhere in sight. Pouting, I joined Jill in line. After she purchased her shoes, we walked to the edge of the lake.

"Fair warning," she said, "I've never done this before."

"Then hold my hand. I took lessons for years."

"So she can pull you to the ground? You're insane if you think I'm going to let you go out there in your condition with a newbie," Neil said from behind me.

I spun around, beaming.

"I see my plan worked. You're smiling," he said.

I ran into his embrace and flung my arms around him. He chuckled.

"I can't believe you did all this."

"Hey, now. I'm the lord of mischief. Mastermind plots are my specialty." He winked when I looked up at him. "Though, the last few years, I helped the elementary school put together Easter egg hunts for the first graders, and they never turned out well. Lots of crying kids and missing plastic eggs."

I shook my head and kissed him. "Thank you."

"Blech," Jill said. "Are we going to skate, or are you two just going to stand there and make out?"

Neil smiled against my mouth, and I stepped away. Owen came from behind me with the two other guys who'd played basketball the night Jill dropped me off at his house. They both said, "Hey, Andie," as they passed, the blades of their skates sinking into the snow. Owen grabbed Jill's hand and pulled her onto the lake. Her squeal made me laugh.

"Reed's the one with the red hat. Logan's the other. They're Owen's cousins," Neil said.

I nodded. *Good to know.* "Can you help me get my skates on? I think I might actually be too fat."

He chuckled, but instead of helping me to the ground, he pulled me away from the lake, taking my skates in his other hand. "Actually, I was wondering if we could talk."

I squinted at him. He didn't look upset or sad or angry, but his cheeks were slightly pallid, and he couldn't make eye contact. "O . . . kay?"

He sat me on a bench overlooking the lake. I might've been mesmerized by its beauty again if it weren't for the nauseated expression on Neil's face. He set my skates on the ground then twisted as he sat so he half-faced me and tucked a loose strand of hair behind my ear.

"Remember when you asked me why Owen stopped by the night before my birthday?" When I nodded, he continued, "Well, truth was, I'd originally planned to do this when I brought you to the cabin *on my* birthday. But then everything . . . happened, and there was never a right moment, and then Owen accidentally told Jill about my plan, and then she said—"

"Neil, get to the point." My heart was pounding leopard-speed.

He let out a long breath and pulled a small box from his pocket. I froze as he popped the lid open and inside was the engagement band I'd seen every day for fifteen years—on my mother's finger.

"Oh my God," I said, unable to stop my hands from shaking.

"I talked to your mom the weekend before she died. You were at Jill's, but the lights were still on in your house after I got off of work. So, I knocked on the door, and she let me in. I told her everything—how I went out of my way every day since grade school to catch a glimpse of you in the halls, how I screwed everything up between us your freshman year, and how, since that moment, I wondered if I'd ever get a chance to make it up to you. And then, three months ago, you climbed into my truck, and I knew I'd do *anything* to make sure that you were always safe and loved."

A tear rolled down my cheek, leaving a frosty trail behind. I pressed the fingertips of my right hand against my lips as Neil placed the ring box in my other palm. Another tear betrayed me, and he wiped it away with his thumb.

He continued, "And when I flat out asked her if she'd consent to me taking care of you forever, she gave me this. So . . . " Neil slid off the bench to kneel in the snow.

Holy crap. He was on one knee. He was actually on one knee.

"If you'll let me," he continued, "I promise to love you like my dad loved my mom, to fight dragons for Ethan, and to tell you a joke every day, just so I can see you smile. I love you, Andie. I have since that day on the playground, nine years ago, before I even knew what love was. Marry me."

In the distance, Owen and Jill shouted, "Come on!" and "Say, yes!"

Unable to hide my smile, I dropped to my knees in the snow, in front of Neil, and put my hands on his chest. But unease wormed its way into my gut, and the words spewed from my mouth before I could stop them. "Are you sure? I mean, it's just—"

He put a finger on my lips. "Please don't make me say my speech all over again. I actually got it right the first time. And my knee is really cold."

Wrapping my arms around his neck, I planted a kiss on his lips. He pulled me closer, and on the lake beside us, Jill, Owen, and his cousins whistled and hollered. Neil smiled against my mouth before pulling his lips away.

"I take it that's a yes?" he asked.

With tingles fluttering through me from head to toe, I replied with a smile, "Yes."

For the next two hours, the six of us twirled on the ice. Well, three of the six of us did, anyway. Neil wouldn't let me do much besides glide slowly, for fear I might fall. And Jill spent more time crawling on her hands and knees than actually using her feet. Once our legs started to tire—and Reed nearly chopped off Owen's arm with his skate—we returned to the bank, changed into normal shoes, and then wandered into the warming lodge.

We ate dinner in the resort's restaurant then grabbed chairs around a large fire pit on the back patio. Owen and his cousins told stories about camping trips they'd gone on—some with Neil, some without. Each one more hilarious than the last. Once the sun went down and most of the visitors left, we finally agreed it was time to go.

"Thank you so much for today," I said as Neil pulled out of the resort's parking lot. "I don't think I've ever smiled so much."

He grabbed my hand and kissed my fingers, the corners of his eyes crinkling as he grinned. "You're welcome."

No snark. No sarcasm. Pure sincerity. I slid down the truck's bench seat and rested my head on his shoulder, reveling in the woodsy scent of his cologne—a smell now associated with love, safety, security.

Neil rested his hand on my leg and stroked my knee with his thumb. A flutter shot up my leg. A flash of his fingers in my hair, his lips on my neck, and my palms on his strong chest volleyed through my mind. Hot tingles covered my body. I wanted—needed—to feel his touch again.

"How far are we from Butterfly Point?" I asked, my insides already squirming in anticipation.

He looked at me out of the corner of his eye. "Not far. Why?"

My pulse raced. "Well, I just thought maybe we could, you know, stop there on the way to the cabin? We never did visit before Christmas."

He jumped and cleared his throat when I palmed the inside of his thigh. "Uh, yeah. We can definitely take a detour."

I giggled and kissed his neck, rubbing my hand up and down his leg. His eyes never left the road, and I didn't feel the truck jerk even slightly. My inhibitions left me like water separates from oil. We'd been wrapped up in so many things since his birthday that we'd yet to move past brief kisses and falling asleep in each other's arms after long, exhausting days. It was time that changed.

I kissed his neck again, letting my tongue linger on his skin. Neil's breath caught, but his composure was incredible.

"Andie, do you want to make it there in one piece?"

Smirking, my lips left his neck, but I didn't remove my hand from his leg. Five minutes later, he turned the truck through trees down a winding, dirt path spotted with snow, and we reached the plateau that overlooked our city of River Springs.

Within seconds of Neil popping the truck into park and turning off his headlights, I reached up and pulled his lips onto mine. A soft noise escaped him, then his hands were on my cheeks, and his mouth opened and closed mine. I melted under his touch. I'd never be able to understand why he chose to love me, in spite of everything. But, God, I was so glad he did.

Neil nudged me down the truck's bench seat, away from the steering wheel, and pulled me onto his lap. I faced him as best I could, straddling his hips. His hands dropped to my lower back, beneath my coat and sweater. Each place he touched burned with the thrill of what was to come.

I ripped his jacket off and tore his shirt over his head. My palms ran from his neck to his abs, stroking every line of every muscle. Neil moaned, freed me from my coat, and lifted my sweater over my head.

Our lips met again as his fingers worked the clasp on my bra, and then he tossed it aside. I shivered when his hands wandered down my back, around my rib cage, up to my chest. *Yes, more,* my body—my heart —begged.

As if he heard me, his mouth left mine to trail kisses along my shoulder and collarbone. My breathing sped up as his fingertips trickled down my sides and beneath my waistband, around my hips to my butt. I lifted his lips back to mine and wandered my hands to the button of his pants.

Neil pressed his forehead against mine, breaking the kiss as I finished unfastening his jeans. "Are you sure you want to do this?"

"Yes," I replied, my voice breathier than I anticipated.

In what felt like one quick movement, Neil tossed the rest of our clothes to the floor of the truck. Then he drew me close, adjusting our position to the one most comfortable for me. I leaned into him, letting him control the pace, and being with him was even better than I'd imagined. My love for him swelled until I thought it would burst through every pore of my body.

Neil was mine, and I was his. And together, we'd conquer the world.

The next day, Neil's final high school semester began while I hurried to finish my junior year at home. And after school, Owen, Reed, Logan, and Jill helped us move our stuff from the cabin to our new apartment in Denver. With only four months until I gave birth, we didn't want to wait any longer to get situated.

Neil came with me to my next ultrasound, and I almost cried at the way his face lit up when he saw Ethan on the screen. I even laughed at all Neil's alien jokes and finally stopped worrying that he was giving up his dreams for me. My seventeenth birthday was in three-and-a-half months, and one year after that, we'd stand in the courthouse and get married. I'd start studying for my nursing degree—part-time—at our local community college, and Neil would continue to work—full-time—for Owen's dad.

My worry dissolved into hope, and for the first time, I felt like maybe, just maybe, everything would turn out like the end of a fairytale.

CHAPTER 28

The Monday morning of my twenty-sixth week, I finished my junior year of school. After piling my books into my backpack, I made an appointment to sit for my exams at the high school then relaxed in a hot shower. I decided to surprise Neil with a date night in celebration and took my time on my hair and makeup before picking up the apartment and staring into the fridge.

"I really need to get my driver's license." I could've used it to go grocery shopping. It looked like we'd be going out to dinner. Not that I minded.

I closed the refrigerator door and wandered aimlessly to where Neil's guitar sat on its stand. I plucked a string. One of these days, I would figure out how to play the dang thing. There were still two hours to go until Neil got back, and boredom was already seeping into my bones. Being able to play guitar would've come in handy. I blew out a long breath then turned on his keyboard. With one finger, I played the only song I'd ever learned on piano—"Mary Had a Little Lamb"—then leaned on my elbow and tapped the same note over and over.

I shook my head. *What's wrong with me?* One day without something to do, and I was going nuts. *I should probably be enjoying this.* After Ethan came, I'd probably be begging for a minute alone.

As I stood and turned off the keyboard, my gaze caught on a corner of a paper sticking out from behind Neil's piano music. The sheet was a different color, a little yellower than what Neil used to write his songs—like the professional-grade stationery I'd seen Mom use when she sent out resumes to universities around Denver. The edge of a seal poked out, and the line of the stamp curved down to the right, shaped like a shield. The inside of the mark was deep red.

I plucked the page out from behind his music. *No.* A letter from Harvard University. He *had* applied, after all. My stomach fell to my knees.

On wobbly legs, I strayed to the couch, my head swimming. I lifted the paper with sweaty hands and read. It was addressed to Neil and came weeks ago—and he'd been accepted on a scholarship. Why had he lied to me?

Because you're pregnant and orphaned, genius.

My movements sluggish, I set the letter on the coffee table and slumped as far into the couch crease as I could. Neil had been accepted to *Harvard.* And he'd have to pay so little to go. My cheeks burned, and my pulse pounded in my throat. I wrapped my arms around my ribs and closed my eyes, fighting the urge to puke.

My worst fear had come true: Staying with me meant I brought him down. Neil *was* giving up a dream for me.

A sob escaped my mouth before I could tell it no. Neil couldn't do this; he couldn't turn down an education like Harvard. I knew the value of college, of a place like an Ivy League school. And for him to have gotten in after ten years of practically supporting himself? This hadn't been a shot in the dark. I knew him too well. He'd worked for this.

No matter how much I needed him, I couldn't let Neil throw his future away for me. He would do anything to keep me protected, comforted; I knew that like I knew the sky was blue. But I had to show him the same selfless love, or I'd forever regret holding him back. Which meant one thing: I was on my own.

My stomach turned to stone. But what about Ethan? Even if I *did* manage to drop out of high school and find a job that paid a decent wage, I couldn't provide for a baby by myself. I couldn't raise a baby in poverty—I wouldn't. My son deserved so much more. But how the hell was I supposed to let him go?

I lay down, resting my head on the couch's armrest, and tucked myself into the tightest ball I could manage, crying until my stomach hurt. I would have given anything to be able to talk to Mom or Dad, to listen to them tell me what to do. Mom's hugs had always made me feel better, and Dad had always known what to say. I couldn't let go of Ethan, but how would I forgive myself if I didn't let go of Neil, either?

My hand shaking, I dug into my pocket for my cell phone. Through bleary eyes, I tapped the send button. Maybe there was still one person left who could help me work through my fears.

Jill's dad answered on the third ring. "Hey, kiddo. How're you doing?"

"Are you at work? Can I—" I could barely speak—"can we talk?"

Whatever he said on the other side was muffled. Then he returned his attention to me. "You know what? I really needed a break, so your timing's perfect. I'm heading to my car so we can have some privacy, but go ahead and start. What's going on?"

A whimper escaped before I could form words. "It's Neil. He got into Harvard, and now I don't know what to do." I covered my mouth with my free hand as another sob wracked through me.

"Wow. He'd said something about turning down a college application, but Harvard? Man. I knew the kid was smart, but not *that* smart. Tell me, what do you want to do?" A car door closed in the background.

"I don't know. I mean, he told me he wasn't sacrificing anything for me, but he was obviously lying. And I *can't* take this away from him. But without him . . . ." I sucked in a shaky breath.

"Well, it's going to come down to one big question: Do you really love him?"

My eyebrows furrowed. What kind of question was that? "Yes."

"Then you have to decide what you're willing to sacrifice—your happiness or his. For me, it was easy. I love my wife more than anything in this world, and when she told me she wanted to stay here in River Springs, open a store, and have a baby, I was 100 percent okay with giving up my dream of working for the FBI. But I was also never in the situation you're in."

I frowned, another tear falling from my eye. Was that what Neil did for me? Even if he had, that's not what I wanted for him. If I had talents like his and got into an Ivy League school, I'd always wonder what might've happened if I'd gone. One of us needed to make a sacrifice, and it couldn't be him, not after everything he'd done for me.

But then what would I do about Ethan? How could I say goodbye to the son I'd looked forward to holding, taking to Donaldson Park, and cheering on at soccer games?

"Can I speak freely?" Mr. Anderson asked.

I nodded then realized I hadn't said anything. "Yes."

"I knew your parents. Not well, but River Springs is a small town. I'd often catch one of them in the store or at the diner or something. I can promise you that until Jill told me you were adopted, I always just assumed you were theirs. Your parents *loved* you, like you were their own. And there are plenty of couples out there, like your parents, who can't start families and would be thrilled to raise your son. You're too young to have to worry about raising a baby, kiddo."

More tears rolled down my cheeks. "But how am I supposed to just let Ethan go? I mean, I can't just say goodbye."

"You aren't saying goodbye. You're saying, 'I love you enough to make sure you can build dreams of your own. And the day you turn eighteen, I'll be right here waiting to see you again.' This isn't the end, Andie. This is your chance to not only find your dreams again, but to give the two people you love most in this world the chance to seek theirs."

I bawled. He was right—of course he was right. This whole time, I'd been nothing but selfish, relying on everyone else when I should've been thinking about them. I did want Ethan to do and see and be everything. And how much could a sixteen-year-old orphan provide?

Though it shredded my heart, I knew what I had to do.

It was time to let them both go.

After saying goodbye and promising Jill's dad I would be all right, I cried until I couldn't breathe. Until my nose ran and sweat covered my forehead. Until I sprinted to the bathroom and left my lunch in the toilet. I bawled with my cheek pressed against the seat, the chill of the porcelain soothing. It was over. I couldn't be Ethan's parent. And I was not going to anchor Neil to the bottom of the sea.

Exhaustion overtook me before I managed to pull myself up from the floor.

I jumped when a hand touched my forehead then groaned at the pain in my lower back. My legs were numb. That's what I got for falling asleep with my head on a toilet.

"Not to burst your bubble, but toilet seats are really uncomfortable pillows," Neil said. His eyes were tight in concern, and his dark hair sat in messy spikes on his head. Seeing his face, hearing his deep voice . . . I'd rather burn alive, tied to a stake, than feel the pain ripping through my chest.

I pushed on the seat, trying to get up. Neil grabbed my elbows and pulled me to my feet. It hurt to not make eye contact, to step away, but I knew I had to, or I'd break again. I grabbed my toothbrush and toothpaste and took my time ridding my mouth of the old tuna stench. Neil's stare burned into me. I cupped water in my hands, rinsed out my mouth, and wiped my lips on a hand towel before turning my back to him and exiting the bathroom.

"Everything all right?" he asked, following me.

My legs felt like Slinkies. Any minute, I was going to fall over. I opened the fridge, my back still to Neil, and grabbed a bottle of water. I fumbled with the cap, and my jaw shook. How would I tell him the truth? Already, it felt like the world was closing in around me, and I was running out of air to breathe. What would it be like when I saw his face—his sad eyes—when I told him I'd found the letter? That I was giving up the baby and calling off the engagement?

A tear fell from my eye when I tipped the bottle back to take a swig.

Neil had stayed a small distance away, but now he caught up to me in a couple big strides and touched my back.

"Andie, talk to me. Did I do something?"

I set the plastic bottle on the counter and met his gaze. As expected, the concern I found there, the dread for what might be going on in my head, broke me. I closed my eyes as another tear fell and took a deep breath.

Neil flicked the droplet from my cheek with his thumb. "Baby, please. Tell me what's going on."

"Why didn't you tell me you got into Harvard?" I asked, my voice as shaky as a 6.0 earthquake. I opened my eyes when he dropped his hands.

He pinched the bridge of his nose. "How did you find out?"

"That's not the point. Why would you hide that from me?"

"Because I'm not going to go. I didn't think it was important." His voice was calm, but his face was tight.

"Not important? Neil, this is *Harvard*. You can't turn down an offer like that."

"Yeah, I can."

"You told me you weren't giving anything up for me."

He growled. "We're not having this discussion. I'm not going. There are more important things that I should be worrying about."

The lump in my throat nearly cut off my air. I knew what I had to say—what I had to do. Swallowing my tears, I gripped the edge of the counter and spoke as strongly as I could. "Not anymore."

Neil's face paled, and he stiffened. "What?"

"I told you once that being with me would only bring you down. If I don't . . ." I covered my mouth when my voice squeaked. "I would never be able to live, knowing I kept you from a future like Harvard."

He shook his head, and his eyes glassed over. "Don't do this."

I continued, my entire body shaking, "I love you. And it's because I love you that I can't let you give this up. I'm sorry, but I can't be with you. And I'm putting Ethan up for adoption." I was crying now, and I wasn't alone.

Neil's eyes had closed, and a tear rolled down his cheek. I wanted to run to him, to throw my arms around him and apologize and take back everything I said. But I knew I had to do this. To let him go.

I held onto the counter tighter. My bottom lip trembled, and I breathed slowly to keep from bawling. *I have to be strong. I have to be strong.*

Neil ran a hand down his face, sniffling. When he opened his eyes, my heart broke into thousands of tiny pieces. He was in pain. So much pain. And I was doing it to him. *God, help me. Please, help me.*

"So, that's it, then? After everything, this is the line you can't cross?"

"You deserve so much more than me, Neil. I'm not going to be your albatross." And with that, I pulled my engagement ring from my pocket and set it on the counter.

Neil followed the movement of my hand. When I let go of the jewelry, he stepped away from the ring like it was a land mine and clutched his chest.

"I'll ask Jill to come pick me up."

"No," he replied, his voice breaking. He cleared his throat. "Don't put yourself out. I'll stay with Owen."

"It's okay. I like being there."

Neil nodded then shook his head. "No, this is ridiculous." He moved so fast, I had no idea what was happening until my face was in his hands, and his lips were on mine.

A tingle ran down my spine. His kiss was powerful, urgent, and so full of passion; my head spun. But this was wrong. I couldn't let myself give in.

I pushed off him with a squeal and stepped out of his reach. "Neil—"

He growled and dug his hands into his hair. "When I tell you I love you, do you think it's because I believe you want to hear the words, or because I'm trying to start a conversation? *God.*" He flung his arms out to his sides. "I say it to remind you that you are the best damn thing that has ever happened to me. And I will spend every last breath fighting for you."

I whimpered. "Don't you dare say that! Don't you dare make this any harder than it already is!"

"A degree from Harvard, a billion-dollar music contract—nothing would mean anything without you. Every song I write is about you. Every note I play is for you. If you want, we can talk about what to do about Ethan, but I will not let you walk out that door."

He'd stepped closer to me as he spoke, his voice strong and powerful. And now, as my knees weakened and tears blanketed my cheeks, his stare was unwavering. Neil was only an arm's reach away. Could we still have everything we wanted together while giving Ethan an opportunity at a better life?

My heart fluttered. Damn it if we didn't try.

I flung myself at Neil and wrapped my arms around his neck, smashing my lips against his. He held me close, squeezing me tighter than ever before.

"I'm sorry," I cried into his mouth. "I'm so sorry."

Neil's mouth moved in sync, with a hunger I couldn't compare. My body tingled from head to toe, and my heart swelled like my chest wasn't big enough to contain it. Then as fast as the kissing began, it ended. He pressed his forehead against mine, let out a shaky breath, and ran his hands up and down my sides. My pulse had to be over one hundred.

"I love you, Andie," he said.

I put my hands on his chest. "I love you, too."

For a couple minutes, we stood there, arms around each other. I pressed my ear to his chest, and as his heart rate slowed, mine did, too.

"You owe me big time for stealing a couple years of my life with that stunt," he said. "I should make you ad lib a *Muppets* show. Or sing karaoke in the nude."

I shook my head. "How about karaoke in the nude? You play, and I'll show you how terrible my voice is."

He smiled.

CHAPTER 29

After sharing what Jill's dad said about giving Ethan a better life—and admitting that I'd been naïve in thinking I could be a parent—Neil and I agreed to start looking at adoption agencies the following week. In the meantime, Neil would defer his enrollment at Harvard for a year and work for Owen's dad to pad his bank account while I finished up school.

"Until then, the only thing I want you to worry about is what would make you happy," Neil said, running the back of his knuckles along my cheek.

We faced each other on the couch, knees touching. I leaned into his hand and closed my eyes. He lifted my chin and gently pressed his lips against mine. The hairs on the back of my neck rose. Neil kissed me again then pulled away, turning so both feet were on the floor. When he lifted an arm, drawing me close, I curled—as best I could—against his side. He stroked the edge of my shoulder.

"I probably need Carter's approval, don't I?" I asked.

"Dunno. Couldn't hurt, though."

I listened to Neil's steady heartbeat, relaxing beneath his touch and with every smell of his cologne. It was funny how some sounds, feelings, and smells could make me feel safer than anything else in the world.

"You don't happen to know how to find a number you deleted from your phone?" I asked.

"Nah, I'm thinking that sucker's gone. Though I am kind of surprised you don't have it memorized."

"Not all of us have photographic memories, you know."

"Yeah, you're right. It is pretty awesome, being me."

I shook my head and sat up, smoothing down my hair. "Too bad God forgot to give you a big nose with that ego."

He tipped his head back and laughed. I smiled. I loved that sound. Then I realized what I would have to do to get Carter's number, and my shoulders fell. It'd been months since I'd spoken to Heather. What did I say to someone who bailed on her friend?

Neil squeezed my knee. "Hey, you don't have to call him tonight. It can wait."

I shook my head. "No, I want to get it over with. Putting it off will just make me more miserable."

He sighed. "Tell you what—how about I go pick up some food while you call? I don't know about you, but I'm about ready to eat everything in the pantry. Including the shelves."

The corners of my mouth twitched. "Sounds good."

He kissed the side of my forehead. "Okay, then. I'll be back soon."

As soon as the door closed, I dialed a number I never thought I would again.

Heather answered on the fourth ring. "Hello?" Her question was slow, controlled. She never expected me to call her, either.

"Hey. I need Carter's number. Would you be able to help me?" I cringed, ready for her to tell me off.

Instead, the familiar sound of her bed squeaking carried through the phone. "Yeah, sure. How . . . how are you?"

"Good," I lied. "Considering."

"Yeah, I heard about your mom. I'm really sorry, Andie. For . . . everything."

I bit my lip. How was I supposed to respond? I couldn't just say it was okay, because it wasn't. I'd needed her, and she turned her back on me. A best friend wasn't supposed to do that. If roles had been reversed, I definitely wouldn't have.

"All right," she said when I didn't respond. "Well, I'll text you Carter's number. You know he's in California now, right?"

"Yeah." Ironically, I'd been relieved when he'd moved. At least I didn't have to worry about seeing him around town.

"Oh. He said he called you, but—never mind. I'll talk to you later, okay?"

I nodded then an old question popped into mind. "Wait! I have to ask, and I promise I won't be mad if you say yes." At least, I'd try not to be angry. "Was it you who told Beth I was pregnant?"

A long, awkward pause penetrated the silence. "Yes," she said at last, before my phone beeped in my ear.

She'd hung up.

I dropped my hand, my breath hitching. While there was no one else who could've done it, part of me hadn't believed Heather would betray me like that. Now that I knew, I wished I'd never asked.

My cell phone chimed with a text from Heather—Carter's number and the words: *I really am sorry.*

My thumbs shook over the keyboard, my brain unable to form a response. I closed the message. Maybe I would wait to talk to Carter tomorrow after all, yet it wasn't until Friday, while Neil was at school, that I found the courage to call my ex-best friend. Jill had begun her research on adoption agencies earlier in the week, and Mr. Anderson assured me he'd run background checks on all the prospective parents. Like father, like daughter, I supposed.

When Carter's voice came through the phone, I lowered myself to the edge of my bed, unable to speak. His voice brought back so many childhood memories; in the deepest parts of me, it was good to hear him speak again. But with all the happy thoughts came those filled with pain. He'd lied to get out of child support. He'd abandoned me— his son—and never once looked back. What did I say to him?

"Andie, I know it's you. Your name still comes up on my screen."

I swallowed and ran a fingertip along a seam in the comforter. "Yeah. I, uh, I've decided to put the baby up for adoption."

He sighed. "I'm sorry. Look, it's kind of late to be saying this, but I really regret not helping you through this. I'll do whatever you need."

Kind of late? He could say that again. My teeth ground. "Just write a letter or something and sign it, saying you agree to giving him up, then scan it to me. If I need anything else, I'll let you know." My voice came out as annoyed as I felt. Good.

"Right, yeah. I can do that."

Of course he could, now that he was getting his way. I grasped the comforter and resisted telling him all the nasty things running through my head.

After answering a few of his questions—like, it's a boy, and yes, I'd tell him which agency I picked—I hung up and threw my phone into the mattress with a scream.

The following Monday afternoon, Neil and I began our visits with the agencies, and after a week of listening to the lists of couples looking for babies, my emotional exhaustion level hit an all-time high. I spent that entire Saturday in bed, and only the promise of getting to see Owen make a fool of himself in the Senior Class Play on Sunday drove me to leave the apartment. He joined the Drama Club to convince Monica White—my cheerleading co-captain—to go out with him, apparently. Afterward, the three of us spent hours playing video games at Jill's, and by the time we left, my mood had elevated enough to sit down and pick four couples I wouldn't mind meeting.

After my OB appointment the Thursday of my twenty-ninth week, Neil and I joined the first couple for dinner at a nice restaurant in downtown Denver. Alyssa and Tom Sullivan had driven all the way from Cheyenne, Wyoming to meet me. Hand-in-hand, Neil and I entered the little Italian bistro and spotted them near the back.

The paperwork said they were only in their late twenties. In person, they looked much younger, well-dressed, and in good shape. But it wasn't their appearances that drew me to them—it was the way they smiled when they caught me gawking. It was like I was their best friend returning from war or a long-lost sibling about to be reunited. Genuine. Loving. Kind.

"You ready?" Neil whispered in my ear.

I couldn't speak but found it easy to step forward.

The couple stood as we approached, their eyes bright and judgment free. Tom shook hands with Neil as Alyssa hugged me in a warm embrace.

"It's so wonderful to meet you," she said, her voice pleasant and happy. "Please, sit. Both of you. Dinner's on us."

"No," Neil said, pushing in my chair. "There's no need for you guys to do that."

"Of course there's no *need*. But we want to," Tom replied, smiling. "Please, have whatever you want."

Neil met my gaze, and I shrugged as he took his seat with a grin. "Then, thank you."

For the next half-hour, I chatted with Alyssa and Tom about my hobbies, my likes and dislikes, and what I hoped to do after high school. When they asked about my family, I admitted to being adopted myself then shared what I did know from my paperwork and about the parents who raised me. Alyssa and Tom hung on my every word, reacting to every story with sincere enthusiasm. And with each passing minute, I found myself relaxing more and more, unafraid to open up to them about all that had happened and my fears for Ethan.

Alyssa took my hand in hers. "I can promise you that we would love him unconditionally and do everything in our power to make sure he has all the things a boy could want." Her eyes glistened. "To be able to do what you're doing takes so much love, and we would always make sure he knew that. You're his angel, Andie."

The second my tears broke free, Alyssa was out of her chair and wrapping her arms around me. Tom crouched next to us, one hand on his wife's back while his other rubbed mine. This was it, the moment I needed to know Ethan would be okay. I pictured my parents in Tom and Alyssa's shoes, Jodi in my chair—and a weight lifted off my chest. Memories scrolled through my head: dancing in a princess dress on Dad's feet; baking cookies with Mom for Santa; Dad's contagious laugh; Mom's ice-melting smile; Dad telling jokes as he carried me off the football field when I broke my ankle in seventh grade; Mom curling my hair before my first homecoming.

I hadn't been biologically theirs either, but I could've gone my whole life and never known. With Alyssa and Tom, I knew Ethan would be loved the same way.

After I managed to compose myself, and Alyssa and Tom returned to their chairs, wiping tears from their own cheeks, I turned to Neil, beaming. He smiled, taking my hand in his, and even he couldn't keep the emotion from his eyes. It wasn't nearly as hard to choose them as I'd thought it would be, and the first Monday of March, the four of us sat in one of Bethlehem Family Services' conference rooms, listening to a lawyer drone on about my rights to Ethan once I signed the papers. I'd only receive updates once a year on his birthday until he turned eighteen. At that time, it was up to Ethan to seek me out. I could never search for him.

But I wasn't afraid anymore. By now, Alyssa had emailed me pictures of their house, I'd met my son's grandparents via Skype, and she'd taken me on a virtual shopping trip—she texted pictures of clothes and toys, and I vetoed the ones I didn't like. I knew she'd take good care of my son.

And, if what Neil said was true, and my son *was* like me, Ethan would have no problem finding friends to hack government databases to find me.

Once I agreed that I understood all he was saying, the lawyer had me sign a few documents then slid the final paper across the table— the one where I officially signed over my son to Alyssa and Tom.

Neil held my hand under the table, and with my heart in my throat, I squeezed his fingers like I'd fall to my death if I let go. I stared blankly at the paper for at least a solid minute.

"Can I write a letter?" I asked. "You know, for him to read when he's old enough?"

The lawyer looked at Alyssa and Tom, the people who would raise Ethan, who would hear him call them Mom and Dad. Take him to football games and music lessons. Put a bandage on his knee when he skinned it falling off his bike. Straighten his tie on his way to his first homecoming.

"Of course, sweetheart," Alyssa said.

Nodding, I looked at the form that signed over my baby to his new parents. I grabbed the pen, my hand shaking, closed my eyes, and took a deep breath.

Neil leaned over. "Everything will be okay." He caressed the inside of my wrist with his thumb.

I squeezed his hand harder. Then, opening my eyes, I touched ink to the page and signed my name.

CHAPTER 30

The morning Ethan came was no different than any other. The Monday of my thirty-seventh week—April eighth. I made breakfast. We watched TV. Neil wrote music while I read a book. The same routine we'd practiced for days. He'd taken his final exams a week before and officially graduated with a 4.2 GPA—thanks to honors classes and a photographic brain.

About halfway through my novel, exhaustion slammed into me, like a linebacker picked me up and threw me into the ground. Setting the book on the couch, I leaned my head back.

Stupid pregnancy symptoms. The doctor had said the last few weeks were going to be awkward. Wished she would've been wrong.

Then my skin flushed, like someone popped me into an oven, and nausea rolled through my gut, into my chest. I threw an arm over my eyes and breathed through my nose. Was this normal? Oh, no—was I going into labor?

No, I couldn't be. I didn't feel any pain. It would pass, just like every other time my stomach decided to fondle the reject button.

"You okay over there?" Neil asked from where he sat at his keyboard.

"Yeah. Just a little queasy." I pushed myself off the couch. Well, more like I rocked back and forth until I gained enough momentum to get up. I waddled through the living room, hoping that, by allowing myself to throw up, the sickness would go away.

But as soon as I stepped into the bathroom, my insides constricted. Like a menstrual cramp on steroids. Gasping, I tipped sideways and leaned against the sink, placing a hand on my belly. A boa constrictor might as well have been circling my midsection, squeezing me until I popped. *Oh, crap.*

I stepped out of the hall. Neil's eyes were closed. He leaned back in his chair with his hands clasped over his abs. His pencil was in his mouth, and his foot tapped to whatever beat he heard in his head. When I said his name, my voice shook. Neil's eyelids popped open, and he did a double-take. Then seeing me holding my stomach, he jumped from his chair.

"Hospital?" he said. When I nodded, he grabbed the bag I'd packed weeks ago. Hand-in-hand, we raced to the truck and to the hospital where I was in labor for fourteen hours. Alyssa and Tom arrived about halfway through, though I refused to let anyone into the room with me except Neil. When I wasn't walking around, I made him sit close to my head, facing me at all times. Last thing I needed was him scarred for life.

The first eleven hours were easy. Well, eas*ier*. A contraction here. A contraction there. All of them like the ones I'd had in the bathroom. Pain till the point I thought I would faint, then they subsided. Neil left a couple times to use the restroom or grab a candy bar or a cup of coffee, but he was never gone long. And every chance he got, he'd make me laugh. Typical Neil Donaghue fashion.

But the last three hours were excruciating. For an hour and a half, the contractions worsened to the point I clung to the bed's handlebars, mentally cursing out every nurse who walked in without an epidural. Neil rubbed my back with each contraction, telling me to hang in there, that I was strong, that I could do this. Finally, they gave me the shot, and the pain lessened.

By the time the nurse informed the doctor that I was delivering, I'd been pushing for an hour. My back and neck ached, sweat coated my forehead, and the blood vessels in my face felt seconds from bursting. I wanted to scream to just knock me out and cut me open, but after a few moments to catch my breath, the doctor sat down.

"You're doing great, Andie. You're almost there," she said. "Give me ten more seconds, okay?"

Neil lifted my fingers to his lips the moment I squeezed his hand. I reined in the tears and screamed through my teeth. A few more rounds of exhaustive struggling, then the pressure released, and I fell back, gasping for air.

A second later, Ethan cried.

I couldn't stop the emotion flowing through me. The love for my son. The terror at never seeing him again. The ache to hold him in my arms. The absolute agony that, starting now, he was no longer mine.

I closed my eyes, wanting to see him but afraid of what it'd do to me, and the howl that broke through me gave me whiplash. Why had I thought I could do this? Why had I thought I could give him away?

Oh, God, help me. What have I done?

Neil squeezed my hand in both of his and kissed my fingertips. "Hey, you're all right. It's over."

I shook my head and winced, covering my face with my other hand. The one Neil held shook. "That's the problem!" Another wail flew out of me, and I sobbed, my entire body convulsing. My stomach burned. Every joint in my body ached. I wanted to scream or grab a scalpel and stab my leg.

Why did I sign the papers?

God, just let me die.

"We're going to take him to get cleaned up," a delivery nurse said. "As soon as you're ready, Andie, let us know, and we'll move you to postpartum."

The moment the door to my room closed, Neil spoke. "Hey, you need to breathe. We've talked about this. You're doing the right thing. Think about Jodi and what she did for you. It's hard; I know. He's not even mine, and I'm hurting, too."

Another sob.

"But Alyssa and Tom are going to love him, like your parents loved you. Think about their faces when you signed that paper, how happy they were. Remember what Alyssa said at the restaurant? Focus on that. You're not only giving Ethan a chance at a better life, but you're doing the same for them. You're his hero, Andie."

I cried until my throat burned, then his words sunk in. *I'm saving my son.* I thought about what Jill's dad said. *This isn't the end.* I pictured Alyssa's face, smiling and tearful, and imagined what she'd look like when the doctors placed Ethan in her arms. *You're his angel, Andie.*

I wiped my hair off my forehead and looked up at Neil. His eyebrows were drawn together, but his gaze was unfaltering, affectionate. He touched my cheek and put my palm over his heart. I'd told him once how much it relaxed me to hear his pulse. It beat beneath my hand, and I closed my eyes, breathing deep and letting his love, his peace, soothe me.

He'll be all right. It's time to let go.

When I opened my eyes again, my tears were gone. Neil wiped my cheeks with his thumb.

"Will you tell them I changed my mind? That I want to hold him, at least once?"

He nodded and pressed the call button, asking the nurses if they'd bring back my son.

I squeezed his hand. "Thank you. For everything."

"I'm Sir Donaghue, remember? Slayer of dragons—"

"Yeah, I know. Kiss me?"

He smiled, the corners of his eyes creasing, then he leaned over, lifted my chin, and kissed me as tenderly and passionately as the night I sat on the bed of his truck and let him into my life—my heart.

Best decision I ever made.

A knock on my door brought a nurse holding Ethan a moment later, and I held my son for an hour, memorizing his face, his smell, the feel of his soft skin. His eyes were a vivid, deep blue, and the few fine hairs on his head were the color of sand. He fit so perfectly in my arms. I couldn't stop staring, touching his cheek, rubbing his tiny fingers between mine. Neil wiped away every tear and whispered jokes in my ear to make sure I never stopped smiling. It wasn't until my eyes began to droop that I knew it was time to say goodbye.

Neil kissed my forehead then left the room to find Alyssa and Tom. Minutes later, the door creaked open. Neil was the first to step inside. He mouthed, "You ready?"

When I nodded, he led my son's parents into the room.

Alyssa clung to her husband's arm, and the moment she spotted Ethan, Tom practically carried her to my bedside.

"Oh, Andie, he's beautiful," she said, her face wet as she stroked the fine hairs on Ethan's head.

"You can hold him, if you want," I replied, my body too drained to cry anymore.

Alyssa nodded and wiped her cheeks before sliding her arms beneath Ethan's tiny body and lifting him out of my hold. My throat tightened the moment cool air hit the skin where my son had once been. But as Alyssa and Tom's faces flushed with bliss and happy cries left their lips, my heart filled with the same joy.

"Thank you," Tom said as my eyes fluttered closed. "I don't know how we'll ever repay you."

I smiled softly. "Just love him."

Alyssa cry-laughed. "Oh, honey, we already do."

One final tear fled the outside corner of my eye, and lips I knew so well found my forehead.

"I'm so proud of you," Neil whispered, tucking hair behind my ear.

When his fingers slipped between mine, I gave them a soft squeeze, then, finally, the exhaustion won.

My seventeenth birthday, May seventh, fell almost an exact month later. Neil had started working for Owen's dad two weeks before— after helping me through some really awkward postpartum issues and psychotic emotions—and my post-baby body was finally returning to normal.

Neil planned to take me somewhere for dinner, so I climbed out of bed around lunchtime. I still hadn't been cleared for anything more than long walks, but I had to figure out a way to get back in shape if Jill still expected me to join her on a beach vacation in a few months. Besides, I had to do *something* to kill the time until my first night out of the apartment.

I forced myself into workout clothes. It was strange, wearing normal outfits again. I placed a hand on my flattening stomach and fought the tightness in my throat. How was Ethan doing? For months, I'd imagined comforting him when he cried and feeding him when he was hungry. Alyssa and Tom would take good care of him, but I'd give anything to see him one more time.

I took a deep breath and tied my hair back, swallowing my tears. At least I remembered again how to turn off my eye faucets. One of these days, I'd figure out how to better move on. *Each morning, it'll be a little easier to wake up,* Jill's dad had said after Mom died. It was one of the only things that had kept me going these weeks—knowing that, some day, the ache in my heart wouldn't hurt so much.

At 6:00 p.m., seated on the couch and dressed in jeans and a baby-blue sweater, I checked my cell phone for any texts from Neil. He was usually off work by five, and Owen's dad seldom kept them late on Fridays. We were supposed to be leaving at 6:15. Should I call him?

A knock on the front door made me jolt. I tucked my phone in my pocket and answered. A life-size, cardboard cutout of Chris Pine—as Captain Kirk—was in the doorway. Jill's dark eyes peeked from around the side.

"Happy birthday!" she shouted.

I raised an eyebrow. "Seriously?" I'd made the mistake of telling her I thought Chris was hot in the new *Star Trek* movies. After that, every email from her had Captain Kirk's smiling face below the message. And now, this.

"What?" she said. "It's for the nights when Neil's out of town." Jill wiggled her eyebrows.

"Oh, good grief." I snatched Chris Pine from her hands. Leave it to Jill to go *there* over a piece of cardboard. I set the cutout in the living room and eyed it sideways. *He* is *pretty fun to look at.* Besides, Neil's reaction the next time he sat on the sofa and caught Captain Kirk staring at him would be hilarious. I smirked.

"Grab your stuff," Jill said. "Neil didn't have enough time after work to come get you, so he sent me. He's helping Owen set up for your party."

My eyes widened. "My what?" I'd asked him *not* to go overboard.

Jill held up her hands. "Don't worry. It's just the four of us, Logan, and Reed. It'll be fun."

I rolled my eyes, slipped on my white ballet flats, and then grabbed my purse. Figured Neil didn't listen.

Fifteen minutes later, we parked on a side street in Denver. The city was extra busy tonight. I followed Jill as she rambled about some *Doctor Who* episode, and I nearly tripped over my feet when she stopped outside an Irish pub. Their sidewalk sign read live music started at 8:00—some band named Blue Jaguar. *This was where we were meeting?*

"Come on," Jill said. "They have *amazing* food—the super greasy kind that gives you a stomach ache." Her eyes were bright as she yanked on the door.

I shook my head, smiling softly, and followed her inside. Neil and the boys had a table right next to a small stage at the front of the restaurant. Band equipment was already set up, and behind the drum set, a large window gave a great view of the city. I'd expected more of a shady, hole-in-the-wall kind of place, but the inside was lively and cozy, decorated with Irish décor. Stairs to the left led to a balcony, where the bar was located, and the deceivingly-large dining area was filled with tables draped in black tablecloths. With the live music, Neil *had* picked a great place.

Neil stood as the two of us approached and wrapped his arm around my waist. He kissed my temple. "You look beautiful," he whispered in my ear, sending a wave of hot tingles down my spine. "That shirt matches your eyes."

I caught his happy gaze and smiled, squeezing his hand as I sat in my chair.

For about an hour, we ate and laughed—and convinced Owen *not* to try to trick the waiter into serving him alcohol. Then around 7:45, the manager stepped in front of the microphone on stage.

"Okay, so, you all know we have live music tonight. I've been told it isn't a long set—maybe three or four songs. But the band's going to come up here in about fifteen minutes, so if live music isn't your thing, please let your waiters know so we can bring your checks."

The boys squirmed in their seats, eyeing each other. When Jill smirked and pulled a camcorder out of a bag from under Owen's chair, it clicked.

This was what Jill meant when she said Neil was helping Owen set up.

I stared at Neil. "You didn't."

His lips turned up in a playful grin, and he nodded toward the stage, signaling to the others to get up. "Well, today *is* your birthday. What kind of guy would I be if I didn't go all out on the one day people get to throw gems and kittens at your feet?" He stood as the boys grabbed their instruments, whispering in my ear, "Though, I can't say that my gift will be anywhere near as cool as a diamond necklace or a laser-pointer-chasing furball."

I shook my head, unable to stop a tiny smile. Neil always had a way with words. And I loved it.

At 8:00 p.m. sharp, the manager returned and welcomed the boys. Jill took Neil's chair. A red light shone from her camcorder. The two of us sat center stage, only feet from Neil. He hooked his guitar over his shoulder and whispered with Owen and Reed. As soon as the mic was turned over to Neil, he spoke.

"Hey, everyone. So, in case you didn't see the sign outside, we're Blue Jaguar. Apologies in advance if this really sucks. We haven't played together for, what, two years?" Neil turned to Owen.

"Yeah, that's about right," Owen replied into his mic.

"Maybe our lead singer shouldn't have broken up the band," Reed said, plucking a string on his bass.

"Hey, you shitheads fought so much, it was either that or blow my brains out," Neil replied.

"And we would *never* want you to do that," Owen joked.

My grin grew to my ears as murmurs and light chuckles filled the bar. The boys were so comfortable on stage, still themselves and goofing around. This was so awesome to watch.

"Ha, ha. You're funny, Danielson." Neil smirked then looked me straight in the eye. "So, our first song of the night is one I wrote for my beautiful fiancée. Twice, you made a difference in my life. It didn't take me long to know what I wanted to say. I love you, Andie."

My throat tightened the second the music started. It was a slow, rock tune that began acoustic, with just Neil singing and strumming his guitar. His gaze never fell from mine. Then the other three joined in, and the pace picked up. Neil strummed harder and moved with the beat, his expression glowing with the love that poured through his words: *Your voice calls me from the dark. I'll never be the same, not after loving you.*

God, I was floating.

I held my breath, my heartbeat in my ears. Watching Neil perform, front and center, catching my gaze every now and then, my love for him grew with each chord, each lyric. I gripped the edges of my chair. He'd said the song would be terrible and suggested the four of them wouldn't play well together, but it was so far from the truth. I closed my eyes and let the melody seep into my soul.

This was the Neil I'd fallen in love with—the guy who sang what his heart was thinking and left his blood on guitar strings and piano keys. I couldn't wait to see his dreams come true, to have front row tickets to all he would become. Yes, I missed Ethan with every breath and beat of my heart . . . but maybe we all were exactly where we needed to be.

By the time the last note played, I was blissful and tingling. I opened my eyes to find Neil watching me, his eyes glowing. A soft smile lit his face.

Clapping and cheers took over the restaurant as Neil stepped off the stage and pulled me from my chair.

"You're right. That was terrible," I said, smirking as tears caught in my eyes.

He chuckled and brushed the back of his knuckles along my cheek. "Ha, ha. You're hilarious, Hamilton."

The corners of his eyes creased as he grinned, and my heart fluttered, mesmerized by my favorite smile.

Neil lifted my chin and lowered his face until I could feel his words on my lips. "Happy birthday, Princess."

I pulled his mouth to mine, kissing him with every ounce of my soul, and the happiness followed me through the week and beyond.

EPILOGUE

Dear Ethan,

I can feel you in my belly right now. Your kicks are powerful. Bet you'll become a star soccer player some day. It's surreal, loving you so much when I haven't even seen you yet.

I hope you know it's because I love you that I trusted Alyssa and Tom to take care of you when I couldn't. I never wanted to say goodbye. In fact, it was the hardest thing I ever had to do. But you're my baby boy, and you deserve so much more than I can give you.

I think about you every day. I'm sure that will never change. Even when I'm old and gray, a piece of my heart will always belong to you. I hope, some day, we'll meet again.

Remember: One small act of kindness can change a person's life. Your gut will never steer you wrong. And it's the people around you, those who would do anything for you, who make your true family.

Love you, always,
Mom

ACKNOWLEDGMENTS

To my editor, Krystal: Thank you for all your hard work and ripping the manuscript apart. You were right! It never would've become the book it is today if it weren't for you. Thanks for falling in love with BECAUSE I LOVE YOU and giving it life!

To my marvelous critique partners—Ava, Laura, Vikki, Caitlin, and Jessica: I am so blessed to have all of you in my corner! Thank you all for your wonderful advice and for sticking with me through revision after revision. You girls are the best!

To all who beta read: Your input was so valuable! Thank you so much for taking the time to read BECAUSE I LOVE YOU and offer your opinions. I never would've written this book without you!

And to my friends and family: Thank you for your continued love and support. I am so blessed each of you is in my life!

ABOUT THE AUTHOR

Tori Rigby grew up in a small suburb of Akron, Ohio, considered being sent to her room for punishment as an opportunity to dive into another book. By the sixth grade, Tori had penned her first, full-length screenplay.

If she couldn't be a writer, Tori would be a Jedi. Her favorite place on earth is Hogwarts (she refuses to believe it doesn't exist), her favorite dreams include solving cases alongside Sherlock Holmes, and if she could fall in love anywhere in the world, during any time period, she would pick Renaissance England. You can find her at www.trigbybooks.com, or on Facebook, Twitter, and Instagram @trigbybooks.

Made in the USA
Columbia, SC
20 September 2018